R.D. BRADY

RETURN THE FEAR

VINCI

BOOKS

Vinci Books

vinci-books.com

Published by Vinci Books Ltd in 2026

1

The publisher and the author have made every effort to obtain permissions for any third party material used in this book and to comply with copyright law. Any queries in this respect should be brought to the attention of the publisher and any omissions will be corrected in future editions.

A CIP catalogue record for this book is available from the British Library.

Paperback ISBN: 9781036700904

The EU GPSR authorised representative is Logos Europe, 9 rue Nicolas Poussion, 17000 La Rochelle, France contact@logoseurope.eu

By R.D. Brady

The A.L.I.V.E. Series

A.L.I.V.E.

D.E.A.D.

R.I.S.E.

S.A.V.E.

Into the Cage

Into the Dark

Chapter One

NOLA

The yellow Corvette roared into the parking lot of Hudson's Hideaway. The family-owned seafood chain was located a few blocks down from the beach on First Street and saw a lot of pedestrian traffic from the sun-worshiping crowd.

It was too early for the beachgoers, though, as the restaurant didn't open for lunch until twelve. At ten a.m., the parking lot was empty save for the "look at me!" sports car and the rented jeep in the back of the lot.

The driver of the Corvette was Tyler Hudson, the owner of the Hudson's Hideaway chain. At forty-eight years old, Tyler looked like he was no older than forty-five, and that small achievement was only accomplished through regular visits to a not-so-reputable plastic surgeon. Deeply tanned with bright white-blond hair and pale brown eyes, Tyler was a fan of hard living, and his body, despite all the advances of the medical community, was unable to stave off the effects of his hard drinking and late nights.

But the drugs that he dabbled in recreationally seemed to, at the very least, keep the weight off. He wasn't quite meth-head skinny, but he was getting there.

Nola sat in the jeep watching as Tyler Hudson tried to hoist himself from the driver's seat. It took two attempts. The first time, he didn't use enough muscle as he pushed off the steering wheel. The second time, he braced his legs against the door frame to give himself leverage. The Corvette was so low to the ground, it was impossible to get out any other way. Once Tyler had extricated himself from the car, his face now red from the exertion, or maybe anger, he ran for the front doors of the restaurant.

Nola shook her head at the spectacle. She never understood why people got cars that they had trouble getting in and out of. You might look good driving down the highway, but the illusion was ruined when you had to contort yourself or get a push to get out of the thing once you'd stopped.

Linus Redfield sat next to her in the passenger seat, fidgeting, his agitation growing as he watched Tyler reach the door. Tyler pulled on the handle, but it stayed closed. He knocked loudly on the glass, but no one appeared from inside to allow him entrance.

"I need to go to work," Linus said.

Nola reached out a hand and placed it on Linus's forearm. "It's all right, Linus. He can't see you."

Linus shook his head, starting to rock from side to side. "That's Mr. Tyler. He's going to be mad. I need to go back to my room. The restaurant should be open now."

"The restaurant's not going to open today, Linus. Remember I told you about that? Today's a holiday. The restaurant is going to be closed."

Across the lot, Tyler was fumbling with his keys, looking

for the ones that opened the lock. Linus rocked faster in the passenger seat. The anger inside Nola burned even brighter.

Linus was fifty years old, but he had the mental capacity of an eight-year-old. He and Tyler had actually gone to school together. Linus was supposed to be two years ahead of him, but due to his cognitive deficits, he'd ended up in the same grade as Tyler. From what Nola and Bishop had been able to cobble together, Tyler had been none too kind about the boy who'd been mainstreamed into the public school.

Tyler's father, Tristan, however, had been a different story. He'd taken a shine to Linus and had hired him to work in the first Hudson's Hideaway in Venice, Florida. It had been a good relationship by all accounts. In fact, it had been one of the most stable and positive ones in young Linus's life. He'd worked for Tristan for thirty-one years until Tristan passed away unexpectedly from a heart attack three years ago.

Tyler had inherited the family business and kept Linus on, but with one major difference: he no longer paid him.

After his father's death, Tyler had expanded the restaurant business. Tristan had begun the expansion, but Tyler had taken it to a whole new level, adding two new restaurants in the same year: one in Key West and this one in Miami.

It was too much too soon, and his bank accounts were showing serious strain. Plus, Tyler had picked up the property at a low price, thinking he had gotten an incredible deal.

Apparently, he forgot about the impact of climate change on Miami. Because when the rains came in, the restaurant was more likely than not to flood. So the Miami

Hudson's Hideaway was underwater in more ways than one.

Across the lot, Tyler finally managed to get the front door open. He yanked it open and stormed inside. The front door slammed back, and Tyler disappeared from view.

"I need to go to work," Linus repeated.

"It's okay, Linus. You won't be working today. You've got the day off."

He shook his head at her. "I don't get a day off."

It wasn't a lie. Tyler had taken Linus from Venice to the Miami location and set him up in the small, cramped space above the restaurant. It couldn't really be considered an apartment. It was one room with no window. The only bathroom access was a bucket in the corner and a wash sink. Tyler locked Linus in each night.

His employees didn't say anything because most of them were illegal or had family members who were illegal, and Tyler threatened to call the authorities on anyone who stepped out of line.

Nola reached into the back seat and pulled over an iPad. She quickly brought up the first episode of *Gilligan's Island* and handed it to Linus. "Your grandmother said that you like this show."

Linus's eyes widened, and a smile slipped across his face. "Gilligan."

Automatically, Linus looked about twenty years younger, if not more. And it made Nola wonder if Tyler had ever tried smiling as a way to retain his youth.

"Now, Linus, I have to go into the restaurant for just a minute. I'll be back. Don't get out of the car, okay?" she asked.

Linus nodded but kept his eyes glued to the screen as he laughed. "It's not going to be a three-hour tour."

"No, it's not," Nola said, thinking the same had been true for Linus. Tyler had told him that he was bringing him to check out the new restaurant, and then he never let him leave.

It was modern-day slavery.

At the time of Linus's abduction, his grandmother had been in the hospital and had been unable to follow up on Linus's disappearance for two weeks. By that time, the uninterested police had faced a cold trail for the disappearance of a mentally challenged adult. They put out calls for information in the Venice area, but there had been no responses.

Tyler had even spoken with police and sworn that he had no idea where Linus had disappeared to. And that was essentially the end of the official search for Linus Redfield. But the grandmother kept trying. And recently, one of her granddaughters created a website asking for any information. Bishop had come across it, and that brought Nola into Tyler Hudson's life.

From the background report Bishop compiled, it was clear that Tyler Hudson had been a bully in high school who'd made Linus a common target of his cruelty. When his father passed, he'd taken the chance to take that cruelty up to a truly despicable level. The workers Nola had spoken with described horrific physical abuse that Tyler subjected Linus to.

It was so bad that Nola was a little worried that when she got her hands on Tyler, she wouldn't be able to pull herself back from the edge she always tiptoed up to in these cases.

But she'd come up with a plan to deal with that.

A search of social media photos taken at the restaurant had shown a few with Linus in the background. If the police in Venice had done a more thorough job, they should have been able to track down Linus. But apparently, he hadn't been much of a concern for them.

With one last look at Linus, who was still staring fixatedly at the screen, her anger burning hotter with each step, Nola headed across the parking lot to have a little chat with the Hudson's Hideaway owner.

Chapter Two

The air inside Hudson's Hideaway was cool as Nola pulled open the glass door and stepped inside. So cool, in fact, that a chill broke out along her skin. The restaurant had a nautical theme with boats, sharks, and other seafaring accoutrements lining the walls.

A hostess station stood straight ahead with a red-and-white life preserver attached to its face. The floors were a dark polished wood, and the booths were a combination of bright white and blue.

Nola had to admit it was actually a nice-looking restaurant.

And that was part of the problem. Apparently, Tyler figured if he was going to Miami, he might as well go big and had splurged, hiring a ridiculously expensive interior designer to update the look. The result was incredibly attractive but also came with a hefty price tag that Tyler was still paying off.

"Linus! Linus, where are you?" Tyler's angry voice called from the back of the restaurant.

Nola wended her way through the tables and the booths and slipped through the swinging doors into the kitchen. She wrinkled her nose as she stepped inside.

How this place had ever passed inspection was beyond her. While the exterior of the restaurant looked beautiful, the kitchen left a great deal to be desired. Fruit sat rotting in a corner, stacked up in gray bins. A few pans were in the sink, which was loaded with dirty dishes.

Nola knew it wasn't the staff that had left the place looking like this. Tyler had decided to have a few friends over last night and had had Linus serve them.

The plan had originally been for Nola to show up this morning and set up some cameras inside to catch him in the act. But Bishop realized they didn't have to: Tyler had his own camera system set up that stored the files on an off-site server. It hadn't taken Bishop all that long to tap into the feed and start recording. And it had taken only a few hours to get everything they needed from the live feed. Bishop had also downloaded older recordings, which no doubt had just as much on them as the few hours they had already seen.

Once Nola had seen the footage, it had taken everything in her not to bust in and pull Linus right then. But she'd been a few hours away at the time, setting up the special surprise guests for this morning. She'd had to wait so that they had enough to charge Tyler with when they brought everything to the cops.

And last night, he had implicated a couple of other business leaders by having them take part in the illegal poker game in the back of the restaurant.

Tyler came stomping down the stairs that led to Linus's apartment and stopped still when he caught sight of Nola. "We're not open yet."

"It doesn't look like you're going to be open at all," Nola said, looking around the empty kitchen.

"Just a small staffing issue. But I'll be happy to give you a free appetizer if you come back again later. Let me show you to the door."

Nola planted her feet. "I'm afraid I'm not going anywhere. You, however, are going somewhere rather unpleasant."

Tyler stopped, narrowing his already small eyes. "What are you talking about? Who are you?"

Nola smiled. "I'm a friend of Linus's."

Fear flashed across Tyler's face before he took on a neutral expression. "Linus? Who's Linus?"

Nola scoffed. "If that's going to be your legal defense, I strongly encourage you to come up with a better one. You know exactly who he is. You went to school with him since kindergarten. And what, were you mad that Daddy dearest was better to Linus than he was to you? Or was it just the fact that he was decent to Linus that bothered you so much?"

"I don't know what you're talking about, lady, but you need to get out of here. You're trespassing."

"Oh, yes, and you're such a stickler for the law, aren't you? Tell me: How much do you pay your employees? And how often do you threaten to turn them in to the authorities if they complain?"

His face red, Tyler grabbed a ladle from the rack to his right and slammed it onto the silver counter. "You don't know what you're talking about. Now, I said you need to get out of here."

Nola raised an eyebrow at the kitchen utensil. "What do you think you're going to do with that?"

Tyler smiled. "Show you that you can't just come in here and make threats."

Nola shook her head. She'd seen a few of the recordings that showed Tyler using just such a kitchen tool on more than a few of his employees, and definitely on Linus more than a few times.

Her vision turned red as she pictured Linus crying in the corner as Tyler beat him. And the reason? Linus had been found making himself a sandwich in the back of the kitchen.

Nola took a step forward. "You're going to pay for what you did to Linus."

"I didn't do anything to Linus."

"Really? Because five minutes ago, you didn't even know who I was talking about. You really need to be a little more consistent with your lies. That's where people get tripped up."

His face screwed up in anger. Tyler glared. "You need to get out of here."

"Actually, that's probably a good idea."

The kitchen door behind her swung open. Two big and muscular men stepped inside. Tyler paled considerably when he saw them. "Vinnie. Jose. What are you guys doing here?"

Her arms crossed over her chest, Nola stepped to the side to give Tyler a better view of his visitors. "Oh, they came because I told them that you don't have the money you need to pay them back for the bet you placed on last week's game."

Tyler's eyes widened as he stared at Nola, and then he looked over at the two men. "She's lying. I've got the money. I was . . . I was just on my way to go pay you guys. You can tell Randall that I'll have the money to him in an hour, tops."

Nola shook her head again. "Oh, Tyler. They know that you don't have the money. I showed them your books. They didn't realize how underwater the restaurant was. Using it as collateral doesn't actually help when it owes more than it's worth. So yeah, Randall's not real happy with you."

Backing away, Tyler held up his hands. "You don't know what they'll do to me."

"Actually, I know exactly what they'll do to you. That's why I called them." *And better them than me this time*, she thought.

The two men strode forward. Jose stopped and looked at Nola. "You probably should get going."

As much as Nola wanted to see Tyler get his comeuppance, she didn't want to leave Linus in the car on his own for too long. She smiled over at Tyler. "Well, Tyler, I hope you enjoy the rest of your afternoon. Gentlemen," she said, nodding to the two enforcers.

She slipped through the kitchen doors as the first cry of pain came from the kitchen. And she smiled at the sound of Tyler finally getting a small sliver of what he deserved as she crossed the dining room and let herself out of the restaurant.

Chapter Three

The entire time Nola had been in the restaurant, Linus had stayed glued to his program. He hadn't even looked up as she positioned herself back behind the steering wheel and pulled out of the parking lot. It wasn't until the closing credits had finished that he looked up and smiled. "I love Gilligan."

"Me too," Nola said.

Linus looked around with a frown as if finally realizing that they weren't at the restaurant anymore. "Where are we going?"

"We're going to go talk to a friend of mine. I want you to tell her about how you've been living for these last couple of years."

"I don't want to talk about that." Linus's smile faded from his face.

That wasn't surprising. "I understand," Nola said softly. "But it's important that you do. Because Mr. Tyler shouldn't have treated you that way."

Rocking once again in his seat, Linus wrapped his arms around himself. "Mr. Tyler's not a nice man."

"No, he's not," she agreed.

"But Mr. Tristan was. I miss him." Linus stared out the window, a small tremble in his chin.

Nola wasn't sure what to say to that. "Your grandmother's been looking for you."

Linus's head shot up. "Nana? But Nana's dead."

"Did Mr. Tyler tell you that?"

Linus nodded.

It took everything in Nola not to turn the car around and join Vinnie and Jose in beating the living snot out of that useless human being. She took a deep breath, trying to cool the rage rolling through her. "Your nana's not dead. And she's been missing you. She's been looking for you. She was in the hospital, and she was sick, but she's okay. And she wants you to come home."

"I want to go home," Linus said softly.

"Then that's exactly where we're going to take you. But we have to make one stop first."

That stop took hours. Linus needed to swear out a full statement about his experience at Tyler's hands. There were lots of stops and starts but Chandra Wilson, an attorney Nola had known for years, had been really good with him. She'd flown down to help with his case and took down the statements from all of Tyler's employees. She also managed to convince them that they would not have to worry about deportation if they swore out statements against him.

Now Linus sat eating a bowl of ice cream and watching yet another episode of *Gilligan's Island*.

Chandra stepped outside of the office, stretching her back and looking over at Nola. Nola nodded toward the spot at the table next to her. Chandra strode over, looking like she was on the catwalk.

Nola had never had a walk like that. Very few women had walks like that, but for Chandra, it just came to her naturally.

As Chandra slipped into the chair, Nola pushed over the takeout container. "Thought you could use a little something."

Raising an eyebrow, Chandra flipped open the lid and then nearly swooned at the sight of the pulled pork sandwich and cheese fries inside. "Oh, you know me so well."

Nola laughed. "At least I know your love of barbecue. There's a place that gets really good reviews around here, so I thought you deserved a little treat. How's it going?"

Chandra had already taken a bite, so she held up a finger while she chewed and then wiped the barbecue sauce from the edge of her lips. "Good. With the CCTV camera footage and the statements, we should have more than enough to put the entitled, arrogant jerk away for a long time."

"It's the least he deserves."

Nibbling on a fry, Chandra shook her head. "I don't get why he recorded everything."

That was not a mystery to Nola. Picturing the room Linus had lived in, Nola said, "Because he wanted to watch his little slave. Probably got off on seeing how he completely controlled Linus."

Cameras had been placed in the restaurant and also in Linus's room. The man had been watched twenty-four hours a day, seven days a week. He'd had no privacy. He had no independence, no freedom. He was in every possible way a modern-day slave.

And Nola knew he wasn't the only one. In the United

States alone, over 400,000 people were entrapped in a form of modern slavery, taking the form of both forced labor and sex trafficking. Of those trafficked in the US, 98 percent were American citizens, and the remaining were foreign nationals. Globally, the number of slaves reached over forty million.

"What's going to happen to him now?" Chandra asked, watching as Linus giggled at something Gilligan had done on the screen.

"Now Linus gets to go home," Nola said.

Chapter Four

Planes terrified Linus, so flying back to Venice was out of the question. Which meant Nola was in for a long car ride.

But she didn't mind it. Linus was quiet company, which is exactly what she liked in a travel companion. He managed to sleep in the back seat for some of the ride, and the rest of the time, he contentedly watched a Gilligan marathon. Once he'd seen all three seasons, he just started back at the beginning.

The fact that someone as sweet and kind as Linus had been so cruelly treated was an absolute disgrace. As far as Nola was concerned, it was clear proof that some humans simply didn't deserve to be called by that name. Anyone with a beating heart would be able to see the kindness and innocence in Linus. Taking advantage of him was like taking advantage of a child.

But Tyler Hudson didn't care about any of that. Spoiled since he was a child, he thought the world owed him. And he thought Linus was his personal property.

From what the employees reported, over the years, he'd

had Linus do demeaning tasks for him over and over again. His father had apparently tried to keep some of that in check but hadn't caught all of it. But he had to have known what kind of kid he was raising.

Nola shook her head. What was it with parents turning a blind eye to their own kids' destructive tendencies? The behaviors you ignored, you set loose on the world.

Not that she thought that the father was to blame for who Tyler was. Tyler was an adult. He was responsible for his own messes.

She smiled as she pictured the hospital report she'd gotten on him. He had a broken jaw, two dislocated kneecaps, a ruptured spleen, and a cracked eye bone, along with a number of scrapes and contusions.

He deserved much worse.

The DA was already working up the charges against him, and he was being held in the jail wing of the hospital.

Prison time was a given. He didn't have the resources to hire a fancy lawyer to help him out of his current legal situation. And with the evidence stacked against him he was going to go away for a long, long time.

Nola put on her indicator and pulled off the highway. She turned right at the stop sign, and after two more turns, was on Sycamore Lane. Glancing at the mailboxes, she found number 216 and pulled up to the curb.

The house was a small one-story blue ranch. Sunflowers grew underneath both of the windows, and the door was painted a bright yellow.

Nola tapped Linus's arm. "Linus. Do you see where we are?"

Linus looked up from his screen for a moment and flicked a gaze outside the window. His mouth dropped open. "Nana's house."

"That's right."

The door opened, and a small African American woman stepped outside. She looked at the car questioningly.

Nola quickly got out of the driver's door and gave her a small wave. A hand flew to Haddie Redfield's mouth as she hurried down the path.

Sixty-six years old, Haddie had helped raised Linus. She'd been in a car accident that had left her hospitalized for two months— which was when Linus had gone missing. But now she looked to be completely healed and full of life as she hurried over to the jeep. "Linus. Linus baby."

Linus flung open the door and nearly lost his balance as he got out of the car.

His nana wrapped her arms around him, holding him tight. He sobbed into her shoulder, even though he towered over her.

"It's all right, baby. I've got you," Haddie assured him as she rubbed his back.

Nola felt her chest grow tight as she watched the two of them.

Haddie met her gaze over the hood of the car. Appreciation shone in her eyes along with tears. Nola nodded at her before climbing back into the car. Haddie ushered Linus down the path, her arm wrapped around her grandson.

As Nola drove away from the reunion of grandmother and grandson, she felt good. Two streets over, she pulled over to the side of the road. Grabbing her phone from the cup holder between the seats, she sent a quick text to Bishop. *We're good. Linus has been delivered back home.*

She waited for Bishop's reply, but none came. Neither did the telltale three dots indicating Bishop was replying to the text. Nola found herself staring at the phone, waiting.

She frowned. Bishop always got right back to her. That was weird. But maybe she was caught up with something at work.

Nola sent another quick message. *I think I'll come home for a little bit.* She sent the message, but once again there was no reply.

Frowning again, Nola headed toward the airport, trying to shove away the stirrings of concern.

Chapter Five

The private jet was waiting for Nola at the Peter O. Knight Airport. She'd dropped the car off at the rental agency and now stepped out of the courtesy van that had driven her to the airfield.

She'd sent Darius Tahirovic a text, letting him know she was on the way once she'd dropped off the car. Now the plane was idling on the tarmac.

She quickly climbed the few plane steps and pulled the stairs closed behind her, locking it in place before making her way to the cockpit. A man in his late forties with blonde hair and bright blue eyes looked up from behind the control panel. Darius was Avad's younger brother. Avad was Ileana Hamilton's bodyguard, but he was also family.

Darius was Ileana's on-call pilot as well as a bit of a jack-of-all-trades guy for her. He was also the estate manager. Whatever issues arose on the estate, Darius could do it. He was also the small brother, standing at only six foot four compared to Avad's six foot six. "All good?" he asked.

"All good," she replied, picturing Linus with his grandmother.

"We'll have you home quick," Darius assured her.

Nola nodded and headed back to one of the leather chairs. She strapped herself in and pulled out her phone again. Bishop still hadn't gotten back to her.

Once again, she frowned as she stared at the phone. Something was wrong. Bishop always got back to her. She dialed Bishop's number, and the phone rang out. Nola was about to disconnect the call when a male voice answered. "Nola?"

Nola frowned, recognizing the voice. Her concern rose even higher. "Avad? What are you doing with Bishop's phone?"

"Are you heading home?" Avad asked, ignoring Nola's question.

The hair on the back of Nola's neck rose. "Yes. Why? What's wrong?"

"Bishop's missing."

Chapter Six

BISHOP

ONE HOUR AGO

Pushing away from the desk in her apartment, Bishop stretched out her back. Nola would be dropping off Linus any minute now. Images from the CCTV she'd gone through over the last few days rolled through her mind.

Tyler Hudson had kept Linus Redfield as a modern-day slave. The people Nola and Bishop went after generally had someone in their pocket who kept them from being held accountable. But that wasn't the case with Hudson, or more specifically, Linus. Linus had simply slipped off the grid when no one was looking.

But Tyler didn't just choose Linus simply because he was available. His old man had liked Linus, he'd liked him a great deal. There were pictures of the two of them at various events: ball games, dinners. Tristan Hudson had treated Linus like a son, and apparently Tyler hadn't been a fan. And after his father's death, he'd played out that jealousy in the most dehumanizing way.

Stepping out of the Faraday cage, Bishop cut across the thick wooden floors and headed toward her kitchen. She had to admit, she loved this space. The building was an old warehouse, dating back to the 1950s. It had formerly been a shoe factory. The remnants of the old conveyor belts were still hanging up above. She had created a sleeping loft and office out of half the building. She owned the other half, but the whole space was too large for just her. Maybe one day she'd do something with the rest of the building.

As she walked, she glanced up at the remnants of the old factory. People had worked here for years, eking out a living. It had been good honest work and no doubt taxing. She liked to think they had been decent people.

Then there were spoiled rich kids like Tyler. He'd been born on third base with money and privilege and yet still felt the world owed him.

What a waste of a life he was. He'd gone to a good school, had cars and money at his disposal. His dad wasn't one of the super wealthy, but the kid definitely didn't want for anything. But it hadn't been enough.

That was always how it went with these cases. At their core was someone who always felt like they had been treated unfairly by life. And that they deserved more, no that they were entitled to more.

Bishop scoffed as she pulled a soda from her mini-fridge. She could definitely have a chat with them about the unfairness of life.

She shied away from those thoughts, and not just because it was a part of her life she didn't like to focus on, but also because she knew that with these types of people, it wouldn't do any good. They were a victim in their own minds, and nothing anyone could say would change that.

Her phone beeped, and she flicked a glance at it. *Meeting on the Oakland case in thirty. You around?*

Bishop winced. She'd decided to work from her home office today because of the case with Nola and because she didn't have any meetings scheduled. She'd have to hustle to get back to Langley in time. She quickly typed a reply to her co-worker and friend, Stan Mahoney. *I'm at home. Leaving now.*

Better boogie. You know Latham doesn't like if we're late.

Bishop smiled. That was an understatement. Her boss had snide down to an art, especially when someone was skirting the rules he'd laid down. And he really did not like it when Bishop was late. Somewhere along the way, he'd learned that she was close with Ileana, who was a legend in intelligence circles. And in Latham's mind, that meant that Bishop had gotten her job through her connections and not her abilities.

Nothing could be further from the truth. Bishop and computers understood one another. They always had. In the chaos that had been her life, computers had been a predictable constant. Once you understood what they wanted, you could make them do what you wanted.

The humans in her life had not been nearly so easy to understand. And definitely not so easy to appease.

Her phone beeped again. She grabbed it as she slipped on her jacket and reached for her bag. She smiled at the image on the screen. It was a picture from Sofia and Enzo with Cora. All three had giant grins on their faces.

Cora was the gray-and-white pittie that Nola had brought home. After that case three months ago, Nola had not only brought the dog home but she'd stayed for two weeks. She'd only been away for a few days at a time in the last few months.

And Bishop couldn't be happier. Nola was changing. She was joining the world more. A lot of people thought of Nola as a cold, unemotional automaton. She'd heard some of the comments at the CIA. Nola was another legend amongst them.

But they didn't know Nola. When Nola loved, it was with her whole heart and being, so when that love was killed, it was like a body part had been cleaved off. The cases Nola took were the only way she could stem the rage that boiled inside of her at the unfairness of it all.

Bishop got that. Nola, like computers, was pretty predictable. Her motives were straightforward and simple: She wanted the world to be fair. And when it wasn't, she did everything in her power to even the scales.

No matter the cost.

Nola was, in many ways, a throwback to ancient, honorable warriors who would stop at nothing to see justice done. The modern world wasn't equipped to deal with her, so she operated in the shadows.

For Bishop, helping her was like helping Batman. Together, they made a great team, targeting those the system let slide.

And like Nola, it gave Bishop's life meaning too.

Although Bishop did worry about some of the cases Nola took on. But hopefully they were turning a corner, and she'd be around more. Even though she understood why Nola was driven to do what she did, Bishop missed her. Nola was her sister, her best friend, and her mom all rolled into one. And having her disappear into her cases had been really tough. But Nola had seen Bishop through her toughest times. In fact, she had saved her from them. And so Bishop figured it was her turn to stand by Nola.

So that's what she did, sometimes with her heart in her throat at the obstacles Nola faced. But she always came through the other side, usually a little banged up but still moving forward.

Yeah, Bishop had some serious hero worship going on with Nola, and she was totally okay with that. Other girls could have their Kardashians or influencers. Bishop would take Nola James any day.

Smiling, she shut off the alarm by the front entrance and yanked the door open.

A man stood on her doorstep.

Chapter Seven

Covered in black from head to toe, the man barged through the door and grabbed the lapels of Bishop's jacket as he shoved her back. She stumbled, grabbing his shirt. Dropping to the ground, she brought her right leg up, and kicked the man over her.

He let out a yell as he crashed into the ground behind her.

Heart pounding, Bishop rolled over to her stomach and started to get up. *Oh my god. Oh my god. Oh my god.*

Her knee got caught in her messenger bag, and she took a precious few seconds to untangle herself before she was able to stand. She sprinted for the door.

The man, however, was faster. He crashed into her back. Bishop hit the ground with a thud. She reared back, slamming her head into the man's face.

"Bitch!" he yelled as he grabbed her by the hair and yanked her up. Bishop reached behind her, slipping her hands under the mask and scratching his neck hard enough to draw blood. He flung her away from him.

Her hand still on the mask, she ripped it off as she crashed into one of the kitchen chairs. It fell to the floor as her side jammed into the edge of the table. She grunted as pain shot through her.

The man across from her stared at her, his nostrils flaring. He was in his early thirties, with light brown hair, dark eyes, and a muscular build. And Bishop had never seen him before in her life.

Move, Nola's voice in her head ordered.

Bishop dashed around the table, grabbing a napkin from the top as she did. She wiped the blood from her fingers and flung the napkin at the counter as she pulled a glass from the sink. As her attacker grabbed her, she broke it over his head. With a growl, he punched her under the chin.

Stars burst across Bishop's vision as pain lanced along her jaw line.

The man grabbed her, fumbling in his pocket. He pulled out a cloth and shoved it over Bishop's face.

Noxious fumes swam up her nose. She could even taste them at the back of her throat. Terror roared through her. No. She kneed her attacker in the groin.

He grunted, loosening his grip. She ripped herself away from him and grabbed onto the counter, her fingers slipping under the lip. *Where is it?* Her vision was wavering as her fingers frantically searched. Finally, she felt the small plastic nub. She pressed the panic button just as the man grabbed her by the shoulders and shoved the cloth over her mouth and nose once again.

Spots crept in at the edge of her vision before everything went black.

Chapter Eight

NOLA

It had taken just over two hours to travel from Florida back to Maryland. Nola was crawling the cabin the entire time. When Avad had arrived at Bishop's apartment, the door was wide open, and there was no Bishop. But her phone lay on the ground next to an overturned chair.

Fear stabbed right through the core of Nola of the thought of Bishop in danger. It couldn't be true. Bishop was supposed to be safe. She worked for the CIA, but she was an analyst. She wasn't an agent. Eye strain and sleep deprivation from sitting at her computer for too long were the only dangers she should face. And she knew how to protect herself. Avad had to be wrong.

Dear God, please let him be wrong.

As soon as the plane came to a stop, Nola yanked open the cabin door, lowered the stairs, and sprinted across the runway to the hangar, where she'd parked her car.

Throwing herself behind the wheel, she fumbled getting

herself strapped in, picturing the worst. Her heart pounded as visions of what could have happened to Bishop flooded her mind. Foot firmly on the gas, Nola tore out of the airfield parking lot.

Heading straight for Bishop's apartment, Nola wended her way through traffic, not so silently cursing every red light and slow driver. Bishop had gotten an apartment years ago in her streak of independence. But the reality was she spent most nights at Ileana's estate. Her apartment was for when she had a late work night more often than not.

In fact, she'd set up the apartment as a combination work/sleep area. She even had a Faraday cage that she'd set up with all of her equipment.

And she also had a ton of security precautions, so the idea that something had happened to her there suggested that whatever it was had been planned.

Nola pulled to a screeching halt in the parking lot outside the old, converted warehouse. She vaulted out of the driver's seat and strode for the door, taking note of Avad's car and the white van parked next to it.

Cold fingers trailed along her skin as Avad's words rolled through her mind again. *Bishop's missing.*

She'd met Bishop years ago when she had learned about a human trafficking ring. Even back then, something about Bishop had pulled at Nola, and she couldn't quite get her out of her mind. As a result, she'd ended up fostering Bishop with the intent on just giving her a place to live for a little while.

A little while had turned into years.

Bishop was a strange combination of daughter and sister. And the idea that something had happened to her, well, Nola couldn't even process that right now.

Before Nola reached the door to the warehouse, Avad

opened it. His normally serious face looked even more so. He stood at six foot six with broad shoulders and thick blond hair. Nola always thought he looked like Dolph Lundgren from his *Rocky IV* days.

Avad had met Ileana back when she was working in Bosnia. He'd already been an operative for five years when she saved his life. Nola had never been able to get all the details, but the story involved a sniper that Ileana had been tracking who targeted Avad's family. She'd saved Avad but had been too late for some of the other members of his family.

As Nola stepped inside, she noted the technicians in their white bunny suits going over the kitchen area. Trying to calm her racing fear, Nola looked around, letting the calm of professionalism roll over her. A kitchen chair had been knocked over. The salt and pepper shakers were on the floor along with a shattered glass.

"What happened?" Nola said by way of greeting.

Avad waited until she was clear of the door and closed it behind her. "There's signs of a struggle. It looks like someone surprised her."

"Blood?" she asked, tensing for the answer.

"Maybe."

"What do you mean?"

"There was a napkin. It looks fresh, but generally you don't find a napkin of blood at a crime scene."

"Is it being tested?"

"As we speak."

Nola let out a breath, feeling slightly lightheaded. "Okay, that's good. What about her security protocols? How come none of the tripwires were activated?"

"I think she was grabbed just as she was coming in or

going out. She either just turned them off or didn't have time to turn them on."

Closing her eyes, Nola pictured it. Had she been distracted? Security precautions tended to grow a little stale over time. People became complacent. Had she been focused on something else and not watching her surroundings? It was entirely possible, especially if she wasn't worried about a threat.

"How did you know something was wrong?" Nola asked.

"She activated her silent alarm."

Nola looked around the space.

It really wasn't very homey. It was all duct work and shelving. Upstairs in the loft, a bed was pushed into a corner with a large window that overlooked the parking lot.

But Bishop had been so proud of this space. It was the first thing that she had owned. She'd fixed it up, though Nola had only been here a handful of times over the years. Guilt tore through her. She should have been here more.

"The video was scrambled," Avad said. "We have no footage of her being taken."

"There has to be something. Get an electronics team in here. I don't care how much it costs."

"Ileana already has one on the way. They got stuck in traffic," he replied.

Nola growled. "How long for the blood results?"

"An hour at least to compare to Bishop's, but then matching it to someone else could take all night, and that's only if the person's blood is in the system. If not . . ."

"Then the blood won't tell us anything," Nola finished for him as she looked around. "Do we have anything to go on?"

Avad shook his head. "No, nothing."

Nola took a shaky breath. *Where are you, Bishop?*

Chapter Nine

BISHOP

The thumping woke Bishop. She slowly opened her eyes, wincing at the pain at the back of her head. What was that thumping?

Her heart started to race at the unfamiliar surroundings. It was dark, really dark. She reached up and felt metal up above her. Below her was a thin layer of industrial carpet.

For a moment, she thought she was in a coffin. But then she realized it was the trunk of a car. The thumps were the car going over some sort of bridge. The sound stopped as the wheels returned to asphalt.

Bishop took a deep breath, even as her pulse raced. What had happened? How was she here? Her thoughts were fuzzy. And so she put that question on hold for a minute while she took stock.

She stretched out her legs and arms, checking to see if there were any injuries. They felt cramped due to the fact that she was curled up but otherwise all right. Her head however was a different story. She had a raging headache and her mouth was so dry.

She struggled to remember what had happened. She'd been in the apartment closing out the case with Nola. But she'd had to get back to the office. She remembered shutting down the security system as she got ready to leave, or at least she thought she did. It was such a common occurrence that she wasn't sure if she was remembering what she did today or if she was just assuming that was what she'd done.

But she couldn't remember anything after that. Had someone forced their way in?

She had vague memories of a fight. Slowly, the cobwebs in her mind slipped away. Someone had tried to grab her. He'd rushed in as she'd opened the door.

They'd fought and then finally he'd placed a drugged rag over her mouth and everything had gone dark.

Fear took root in her chest as the memory of the fight fully returned. He'd worn a ski mask when he'd entered but she'd ripped it off him. She'd seen his face. She swallowed hard. That was not good. It meant she could describe him to the cops. Which made her extra worried. Maybe there was a chance before that he would let her go. But now? No, now it would be stupid for him to take that chance.

She was praying for stupidity.

A tremor started in her hands and worked its way through her whole body. Why was this happening? Was it related to her work at the CIA? That was always possible. After all, she worked on some pretty scary cases.

But why target her? She was just an analyst, a nameless no one, a cog in the machinery of the CIA. But what else could she be targeted for?

For a moment, she thought of all the cases she had worked with Nola.

But no one even knew she was involved in those. And it would take someone with supreme computer skills to somehow link her to them.

And even if they did, why bother? All of the individuals that Nola had targeted definitely deserved what they got. And most of them didn't have anyone in their life that would bother with revenge. They weren't exactly the type of people who inspired loyalty in others. They tended to be more the type that repelled people.

But someone had to have targeted her specifically for some reason. She just needed to figure it out.

She spent the next hour going over every case in her mind both for the CIA and for Nola, but by the time the car stopped, she still didn't have any idea who could possibly have targeted her or why.

I guess I'm about to find out, she thought as the car shifted with someone getting out from behind the driver's seat. She tensed as the trunk opened up.

Two men stood there, one holding a gun on her. One was the guy who'd grabbed her. He leered at her. The other one held the gun, and she didn't recognize him either. He also didn't bother trying to hide his face.

Oh, this is not good.

"Get up," the one with the gun ordered.

Squinting against the sun, Bishop sat up and winced as her back protested. Slowly, she climbed out of the trunk, feeling like she had aged during the car ride.

She looked at the two men and then at the house beyond them. It was a massive pale beige home with a terracotta roof. Wooden beams had been added along the front path, and more wooden accents around the windows gave it a bit of an Asian flare.

It was a beautiful home, and Bishop didn't recognize it at all.

Chapter Ten

NOLA

Nola and Avad stayed at the apartment for an hour, going through all of Bishop's computer feeds. But there'd been nothing. They needed to get some feeds from the neighboring businesses to try and track down who could have possibly taken her.

The problem was that normally they would call on Bishop to do that kind of work. Nola and Avad would be able to start the process, but it certainly wouldn't be done as quickly as if Bishop had handled it.

Finally, Nola shook her head, looking around. This work was better left to the professionals. "This isn't getting us anywhere. We need a plan. Let's head back to the estate. See if Ileana's come up with anything or if she has any ideas."

Grunting Avad, headed for the door. Nola watched him carefully. She'd seen the concern in his eyes. Both of them were struggling with the idea of Bishop being in danger and both of them were compromised in their assessments because of it. That would only make it harder to figure out what had happened. But Nola didn't know how to shut her emotions off this time.

The two of them had just stepped outside when Avad's phone beeped. He stopped walking, staring down at the screen.

"What is it?" Nola asked.

"It's Bishop's cell phone record. I'm sending it to you."

Leaning against her car, Nola scanned the phone records, seeing the numbers she recognized—her, Ileana, Rafe, and Avad. But there was another number on there that had called her a few times this morning but hadn't called her even once since then.

"Who's this 816 number?" she asked.

Avad flipped through the records on his phone before answering. "His name is Stan Mahoney. He works with Bishop at the CIA."

"What do we know about him?" She asked.

"Ileana ran a background check on him once Bishop started mentioning him. He came up clean."

Nola gripped the door handle. Stan Mahoney worked for the CIA, which meant he could be very good at hiding things. "Well, Mr. Mahoney hasn't called her since she went missing. So I say we go see what he has to say for himself."

Chapter Eleven

The drab brown apartment complex where Stan Mahoney lived was, in a word, functional. There were six buildings, each two stories and containing four townhouses in each building. Stan's was the second building on the right.

Dark was setting in as Nola and Avad pulled up to Stan's apartment. Nola had never met him. No one from the estate had. But he'd been working with Bishop for the last few years.

As Avad pulled to a stop, he nodded at a small Volkswagen beetle in yellow that was pulling to a stop across from them. "That's Stanley's car."

Nola was out the door before Avad had the car in park. A man with glasses, prematurely balding with a slim build, stepped out of the car. Putting on a burst of speed, Nola grabbed the car door and shoved it back at him, trapping him against the frame.

The man let out a frightened yell.

"Stanley Mahoney?" Nola asked, keeping the door pressed against him.

"Yes? I'm Stan," he said, his voice trembling, his eyes widening as Avad crossed the parking lot to join them.

"Where's Bishop?" Nola demanded.

The man's mouth fell open. He darted a gaze at Avad and then closed his mouth. "I don't know who you are, but I'm not telling—"

Nola pushed the door tighter against him.

He winced, sucking in a breath. "Stop. Stop."

"What have you done with Bishop?" Nola demanded.

Stan did a double take. "What? You think *I* have Bishop?"

Avad placed a hand on Nola's arm. "Nola," he said softly.

Stan's gaze returned to Nola. "Wait, you're Nola? Bishop's Nola?"

She nodded.

Stan winced. "Why are you asking me about Bishop?"

"Because she's missing. And you called her earlier today but haven't since then, which makes me think that's because you knew she wouldn't pick up her phone."

Shaking his head, his trembling only increasing, he said, "What? No, I was in a meeting. Our phones weren't allowed. I forgot to grab mine when I left."

Nola nodded at Avad, who walked around to the other side of the car and opened the passenger door. Nola pulled Stan from the car over to the sidewalk. She stared into his eyes. "You move, I hurt you."

"Uh, um, yes, ma'am."

Avad searched Stan's messenger bag, in between the seats, the glove compartment, and the rest of the car before standing up and shaking his head. "There's no phone."

His eyes pleading, Stan took a small step forward before

a look from Nola made him jump back quickly. "I told you, I left it at work."

Nola stared at the empty parking lot, wishing an answer would appear.

Stan kept his hands up as he spoke. "Look I wouldn't hurt Bishop. What happened? Are you sure she's missing?"

"Yes. When you spoke with her, was she nervous, anxious?" Nola asked.

It took Stan a moment to answer. She could almost see him going through a few stages of shock: confusion, denial, and acceptance. "No, and I didn't speak with her. It was texts. We had an important meeting. She didn't show up. I thought maybe she got put on a different project. How . . . how long has she been gone?"

"At least three hours."

Stan paled, and then he straightened his shoulders. "How can I help?"

Chapter Twelve

BISHOP

Bishop's back ached something fierce. She rubbed it as she walked behind one of the men who'd pulled her from the trunk.

The guy who had grabbed her—she'd heard someone call him Chuck—took a step closer. "You want me to rub that for you, sweetheart?"

The leer in his voice made chills break out over her skin. She almost preferred being locked in the trunk. At least then she didn't have to worry about anything else, except maybe a car accident.

"No, I'm fine," she said.

He chuckled as he stepped back.

Up ahead, the door was opened by a man in a white shirt and black pants. He gave a small bow, then stood back to let them all in before he led them down the hall.

The home had a lot of Asian-inspired designs. She was hoping maybe there would even be some rice paper walls, which would allow her to break out of here, but unfortunately, the interior designer did not take it to that level.

The small butler—because Bishop couldn't think of any other name for the individual who'd opened the door—led them to a room at the end of the hall on the first floor. After opening the door, he stepped back retreating down the hall.

The guy who seemed like he was in charge looked above Bishop's head, talking to Chuck, who stood a little too close for comfort. "Keep an eye on her. I'll go let the boss know she's here."

Chuck glanced over at her and smiled. "I'd be happy to."

The hair on her body once again shot to attention at the smile of ownership on the man's face.

The guy who had led them here gave him a sharp look. "Don't do anything. The boss won't like it."

Chuck smiled. "Sure thing, Brett. I won't do a thing."

Bishop stepped into the room as the man waved her forward, and Chuck stepped in behind her.

She was surprised to find she was in a bedroom with a large four-poster bed on the right. A door next to the bed led to a bathroom. The windows on the other side overlooked a large lawn.

The door closed behind her, and Bishop whirled around.

Chuck leaned against it, crossing his feet at the ankles. "Why don't you make yourself comfortable?"

Bishop stepped away from him, eyeing the room, looking for weapons like Nola had taught her. There weren't a lot of options. There was a lamp, a couple of books over on the bookshelves, and next to the bed there were some candlestick holders. Those would probably be her best bet.

She inched toward them, not taking her eyes off of

Chuck. He smiled, noticing the direction she was heading as he pushed himself up off the door. "Heading toward the bed so soon? My kind of girl."

"You heard him. He said not to touch me."

Chuck shrugged. "As long as I don't leave any marks, it shouldn't be a problem."

"Yeah, well, that's not going to happen."

"Oh, honey, I know your type. I know where you come from. You live for this kind of stuff. You want me as bad as I want you."

Bishop continued moving backward. "No. I most definitely do *not* want you."

"You girls are all the same. You just need someone to get you to loosen up a little bit. Why don't we start by you taking off that shirt of yours?"

"I'm warning you, don't touch me." Still backing up, Bishop wished her voice sounded stronger.

Chuck grinned at her. Then he bolted forward.

Bishop stumbled backward as he reached for her shirt. Grabbing behind her, her hand wrapped around one of the candlestick holders. Pulling it off the table, she slammed him in the back with it.

Back arching, he let out a yell.

She scrambled away from him, still gripping the candlestick holder.

He glared at her. "You're going to pay for that."

Swinging the candlestick in front of her, her heart raced. "Stay away from me."

He dodged toward her. Bishop swung the candlestick holder toward him, but he shifted at the last second, and she found herself swinging wide, leaving her side wide open.

Wrapping his arms around her, Chuck tackled her onto the bed.

Bishop let out a scream and brought her knee up between his legs. But he shifted, and she only got him in the thigh. He grabbed the wrist that held the candlestick holder and slammed it against the side of the bed. She held on to it, not that it was doing her any good.

"You know, I like it when they fight," he huffed out.

"Get off me!" Bishop yelled. She leaned forward and slammed her forehead into his nose. Blood sprayed across her face.

He released the grip on her wrist enough for her to yank her hand out. "You bitch! You broke my nose."

Bishop slammed the candlestick into the side of his head and then scrambled out from underneath him, her back to the door. He reared up again, and she slammed the candlestick into the other side of his jaw.

The door burst open behind her. Someone grabbed her around the waist and yanked her back. Bishop screamed and yelled, trying to break free.

"Hey, hey, calm down. Calm down. Don't make me tase you."

The professionalism in the man's voice finally got through to her, and she stilled. He wasn't interested in her like Chuck was. She wasn't safe, but she was safer.

Brett walked in and stomped over to the bed and hauled Chuck off of it. "What did you do?" he demanded.

Wiping at his nose, Chuck stammered. "N-nothing, nothing. She was coming on to me. It wasn't a big deal."

"I told you not to *touch* her. The boss is going to want to talk to you." Brett glanced over at Bishop and blanched. "Let her get cleaned up. The boss isn't going to want to see her like this." He dragged Chuck out of the room.

The man holding Bishop released her. He took a step back. Bishop stepped back as well, until her legs hit the bed.

The man held up his hands. "Hey, hey, it's okay. You got nothing to fear from me. There's some clothes and stuff in the bathroom for you to get changed and for you to get cleaned up."

Bishop flicked a glance over her shoulder at the door and then shook her head. "Yeah, I don't think I'm going to go pretty myself up."

A hard glint entered the man's eye. "Either you do it or I do it. And I think we'd both prefer if it were you."

Bishop glared over at him but read the determination on his face.

Taking a trembling breath, she nodded. "Fine."

She walked around the bed and into the bathroom. Closing the door behind her, she quickly locked it. She sank against the door and then slid down it to the ground, wrapping her arms around her knees. The tears she'd been holding back rolled from her eyes, and she looked around, feeling completely and utterly helpless.

Chapter Thirteen

NOLA

After the "meeting" in the parking lot, Avad and Nola joined Stan in his apartment. Nola laid out what had happened, and the fear on Stan's face was clear. He promised to look at all cell phone feeds and surveillance in the area. He warned that it would be a while, but he would find something.

Nola believed him. There was something in his voice when he said Bishop's name. He cared about her.

Being Nola and Avad would only be in his way, the two of them drove back to the estate together, neither of them speaking. Nola was lost in thoughts of Bishop, remembering when she had first met her. It hadn't been a heartwarming moment.

By the time she reached the estate, she had to shove the old memories away. They weren't the happiest of her memories with Bishop, and she didn't want to go down that dark road.

Avad stepped out of the car and blew out a breath. "I'm going in through the back. I need to get some air."

Nola watched him with a concerned eye. "You all right?"

Avad shook his head. "No. You, Ileana, and I, we all understand the darkness of this world. We have each lived in the dark. We can breathe there."

"Bishop's lived in the dark," Nola reminded him.

Avad nodded. "Yes. Because she was forced to. The rest of us have chosen that darkness. She blooms in the light. And I do not like to think of her being forced into the dark. She is too good for that."

Nola knew exactly what he meant. Bishop was the spot of good in all their lives. And the idea of that good being harmed, or worse, being snuffed out, well, Nola knew that that act would unleash the darkness not just in her, but in the others who loved Bishop.

Without another word, Avad headed around the side of the house. Nola watched him until he slipped into the shadows.

He was right. The shadows, that was where they thrived. But Bishop was never meant for the dark.

With a heavy heart, Nola made her way up the stairs and stepped into the front foyer. Dark wood lined the floors along with thick Persian rugs. Light-gray walls with crisp white trim lined the space. Somehow, Ileana had made a home that was both stylish and welcoming.

A man with a muscular build, dark hair, and dark eyes walked down the hall toward her. "Nola."

Feeling the weight from the need to find Bishop, Nola's voice was small as she greeted him. "Hey, Rafe."

He pulled her in for a tight hug. "I'm so sorry. Whatever you need, I'm here."

Nola gave herself just a moment to enjoy the embrace before she stepped back. "I need to find her."

"We all do," Ileana said from the doorway of the kitchen. Traces of Afghanistan were still in her voice. She was a striking woman, with dark hair and large dark eyes. She often wore scarves to hide the scar from an acid attack when she was twenty that reached from her chin and went down her neck.

Nola followed Ileana into the kitchen. "What have you found out?"

The kitchen looked like it had been plucked from a magazine. It was all white with stainless steel appliances. A large island with a waterfall counter of white and gray dominated the space. Next to it, a three-tiered display of fruit sat on a long heavy wooden table with thick framed upholstered chairs. A row of floor-to-ceiling windows and a large set of full glass patio doors lined the back wall, offering a view of the patio and the grounds beyond it.

Ileana nodded toward the table. A laptop had been set up there. "I've got one of my contacts running all of the cars that were in the area at the time Bishop was grabbed. We've managed to rule out most of them, but there are two that were rentals that were only in the area for a short time."

Nola glanced at the screen. "Who rented them?"

"I've got the names and contact information. I'm having my people run them down to see where they came from."

"What about the blood from the apartment?" Nola asked.

"That should be coming in at any moment," Ileana said.

Rafe, who'd slipped into the kitchen behind Nola before making his way over to the counter, walked back over with

50

two plates loaded with lettuce wraps. "You two need to eat."

Nola was already shaking her head before he finished speaking. "No, I—"

"Nola, these types of cases are marathons, not sprints. You know that. Eat," Rafe said, his dark-brown eyes staring into hers.

With a sigh, she took a seat and swallowed down the food that was put in front of her, not even tasting it. Her mind simply wasn't present right now. From the corner of her eye, she noted Rafe disappear down the hall with another plate of food, no doubt to make sure Avad ate as well.

She grabbed another wrap from her plate, forcing herself to eat a little more. Because Rafe was right. Starving herself would only make things more difficult down the road. And although she didn't want to eat, she had to admit she felt better, a little more energized, after getting a little food in her stomach. She was just wiping the edges of her mouth when the screen beeped.

Shoving her plate aside, Nola grabbed the laptop and pulled it in front of her. She clicked on the message and immediately opened the attached file. "It's from the lab."

Ileana's head popped up from where she had been checking her phone. She pulled her chair closer to look as the image of a man appeared on the monitor.

With wavy brown hair in need of a cut and style, and small hazel eyes, he was not a looker. The crooked bend to his nose suggested that he'd been in more than a few fights over his life, as did the jagged scar along his jawline. Nola quickly brought up the accompanying criminal file.

The man's name was Charles Fitzpatrick, age thirty-two, and he went by Chuck. According to his record, he'd been in and out of jail on more than a dozen occasions. Reading between the lines, it was obvious he was muscle for hire.

Carrying his empty plate and coffee mug, Avad stepped back into the kitchen.

"We've got a hit. The blood belongs to a Charles Fitzpatrick," Ileana said to Avad as Nola sent him the file.

After placing his plate in the sink, Avad quickly poured himself some coffee. "I'll see what I can find." He slipped back out of the room.

Nola stood up. "I'll go help him."

Ileana grabbed her hand before she could disappear. "Avad's got it. Take a seat."

Nola shook her head. She didn't have time to take a seat. "No, I should—"

"You should sit," Ileana repeated.

Wanting to go do *something*, Nola stared at her mother-in-law, . She felt this burning urge to move. But she couldn't bring herself to deny Ileana something at this moment, even though it went against everything in her nature. So, she sat.

Ileana fixed her gaze on Nola's face. "How are you?"

Nola fidgeted under the inspection of a woman who'd broken more than a few people in small, cramped rooms around the globe. "I'm fine. I just need to find Bishop."

"You're not fine."

Gritting her teeth, Nola narrowed her eyes. "Of course I'm not fine. Bishop's missing. Why would you even ask that?"

Ileana shook her head. "Nola, this is not your fault."

Focusing on the tabletop, Nola grabbed a fork and twirled it in her hand. "I know that."

"Do you?" Ileana asked.

A flippant response was on the tip of Nola's tongue, but she bit it back at the look on the older woman's face..

Did she know that?

She felt the ache in her shoulders and the hole in her chest. A small part of her brain recognized that what she was feeling was guilt. She'd pulled Bishop into her world. She could have given her another home, a safer home.

Ileana, ever the perceptive one, seemed to once again be in mind-reading mode. "You gave Bishop a wonderful life. She wouldn't have had half the joy she's had without the life you gave her. She was never meant to be in a 'normal' family," Ileana said, using air quotes.

Nola let out a breath. "But should I have given it another try? Insisted she go live with someone else? Maybe if I had encouraged her to be more . . ." The words drifted off, and Nola couldn't really finish that sentence.

"Encouraged her to what? Deny who she was? You're not responsible for what happened to Bishop before you met her. And you're not responsible for what's happening to her now."

"You don't know that," Nola said quickly.

"Yes, I do. Whoever took her, they are responsible for what happens to her. And we will do everything to make sure that what happens to her is not very much at all. But you need to lock that anger away, and that guilt, so that you can just focus on getting Bishop back."

Nola stared at her mother-in-law and knew she was right. Emotions would only get in the way. And she didn't have time for emotions, not with Bishop missing. "You're right. I'll lock them all away."

Concern flitted across Ileana's face. "No, that's not what I—"

Avad stepped back into the kitchen. "I've got a lead. Chuck's last job was for the O'Connor family."

"Who are they?" Nola asked.

"Up-and-comers in the drug scene around Baltimore," Ileana said. "They've been making moves against the Iacono family and the Ortecas."

"How do you know that?" Nola asked.

"I like to keep an eye on what's happening in my part of the world."

And Nola was once again reminded at the extensive nature of Ileana's network of information.

"Do you know where the O'Connor family does business?" Nola asked.

"In a little bar that has been in their family for generations, almost since Patrick O'Connor stepped off a boat four generations ago," Ileana replied.

Nola stood. "Then let's go have a chat with the O'Connor family."

Chapter Fourteen

JONAS

The sword blade sliced through the air with practiced ease. Jonas Wagner concentrated on the movement, trying to lose himself in the familiar ritual, blocking out all other thoughts and noises.

He was one with the sword. The sword and he were joined. He finished the exercise and then stopped, studying himself in the full-length mirrors that lined one side of the dojo. He'd had a room like this created in the center of all his homes because martial arts was the center of his life.

In a former life, he knew he had been a Japanese warrior, and he had committed himself to making sure that his skill in this life was just as formidable as they had no doubt been in his previous ones.

As he stared at his reflection, pride rolled through him. He'd been a small chubby boy, constantly picked on at school. But then one day, it seemed as if he had grown four inches overnight and hadn't stopped.

Now he stood at six foot three with a strong build, his dark hair pulled back into a low ponytail, the hair cascading halfway down his back. His eyes were blue and his skin pockmarked. With his bouts of acne as a teenager, the permanent damage had been impossible to avoid. He'd been to a number of dermatologists who'd reduced the appearance of the scars, but they hadn't been able to remove them entirely.

His muscular chest heaved from the exertion of the movement. A true kata, even without an opponent, should tax every muscle in an individual's body. He smiled approvingly at his reflection. *Well done.*

A throat cleared across the room.

Looking over his shoulder, Jonas's eyes narrowed at the sight of Brett. Gerald and Felix held another man that Jonas didn't know between them.

Brett took a step forward. "Hey, boss, I'm sorry to interrupt. That looks really good."

Jonas inclined his head. "Speak."

"Yeah, the, uh, the girl's here."

Jonas's heart began to pound even more. She was here. Finally. But then his gaze shifted to the man held by his security. Blood was dried along the man's face. Tissues had been shoved up his nose. "What's with him?"

"Uh, this is Chuck Fitzpatrick. He's the guy that we hired to get Bishop."

The man flicked a glance up at him, and he noticed the swelling on the side of the man's head. Jonas narrowed his eyes. "And I take it there was a problem?"

"Yeah. He, uh, well, he kind of assaulted Bishop."

Gripping the sword tightly, Jonas went still as rage began to pool beneath his skin. "During the abduction?"

"No, um, in the guest room here, just now."

Jonas went still, his eyes narrowing to slits. "How far did he get?"

Brett spoke quickly. "Not far, not far at all. In fact, she still had all her clothes on. She fought him off. She's strong."

"Yes, she is." He waved the man forward.

His two men pulled him onto the dojo mat and then pushed him toward Jonas.

Chuck fell to his knees and looked around. "Hey, I didn't do nothing to her. It wasn't . . . it wasn't like that."

"You touched her?" Jonas demand, his skin felt like it was on fire. Sweat broke out along his spine as he pictured this groveling animal in front of him touching his Bishop. His own men had backed up to give him room.

"Yeah, but only what I needed to, you know, do the job that you hired me for."

"And in the bedroom? You touched her there?"

Chuck darted a glance at him and then looked away. "Well, you know, she asked me to. You know how these girls are, you know what they—"

His words cut off as Jonas's blade whirled through the air, entering Chuck's neck on the right and exiting on the left. For a split second, his head stayed immobilized, and then it tumbled to the mat.

Hurrying over, Brett handed Jonas a towel. He wiped down the blade, staring at the headless corpse in front of him. Gripping his sword, he only wished he could kill him again. "Get that filth out of my sight!" he screamed, the lid on his control slipping off.

Brett snapped his fingers. Gerald and Felix hustled over and started to drag the body from the room. Brett grunted and nodded his chin toward the head. Blanching, Felix reached down and grabbed it by the hair. Holding it aloft, the two men pulled the body out into the hall and out of view. A blood trail followed behind them.

Brett cleared his throat. "And the girl?"

The world had gone red as Jonas stared after the man who had dared to touch what was his. This was supposed to be perfect. He curled his hands into fists before flinging the sword across the room. "It's ruined! Everything's ruined! I can't meet her now. We're leaving. We're heading to Chicago."

He took a deep breath, his anger still white hot. Bishop had been assaulted. He didn't want her thinking about that when he finally got to see her again. He stomped across the mat and wiped his face with a towel, wishing he could do more damage to the bastard. Maybe he should have his men bring him back, and he could slice his body into little pieces.

"Um, how do you want me to bring her if you don't want her to see you?" Brett asked.

Jonas let out a shaky breath. He needed to think. He couldn't let her out of his sight. His sword lay on the ground. Guilt ran through him. That had been no way to treat his weapon. He crossed the room and picked it up. Wiping it down, he walked over to the back wall and placed it carefully on its holder. *I'm sorry*, he said silently, bowing to the sword.

"Uh, boss?" Brett asked.

Feeling calmer, Jonas turned to him. The reunion had been spoiled by that barbarian's actions. He couldn't see her now. But he didn't want her too far from him either. "Drug her. Just enough for the flight. I need her to sleep the whole way."

Turning his back on Brett, who was already hurrying off to see his order done, he nodded. Yes, this was better. It would give Bishop some time. And he had already waited years. He could wait a little longer for them to be together.

Chapter Fifteen

BISHOP

Bishop paced along the confines of the room. She had gotten changed and cleaned up. Her guard had waited in the room for her. When she stepped out of the bathroom, he looked her over once and then stepped out of the room.

She spent the next thirty minutes looking for anything that could be used as a weapon, opening drawers, rifling through the closet. There wasn't a lot. She found a pen that she slipped into her pocket, but that was about the sharpest thing in the room. She'd taken the cord off of one of the blinds that she could use as some sort of garrote, but overall, she didn't really have much that she could make use of.

Nola's voice drifted through her mind. *Remember: you are the weapon.*

She didn't know how many times Nola had said that to her when they were training. And maybe that was true for Nola. She seemed to have a sixth sense of where her opponents were and what their weaknesses were.

Bishop wasn't quite that highly attuned to the world of fighting. She did well enough when she had a plan laid out: Go in, throw a cross, followed by a jab, then an uppercut. With a plan in mind, she could usually land all of her hits.

When she had to make up a combination on the spot or figure something out on the fly, though, it always took her an extra second or two. And in a fight, a second or two was a very long time.

But she forced herself to breathe easy. She could already feel her heart racing as the tension and stress crawled over her skin. If she started to panic, her reactions were going to be even worse than when she knew what she was doing.

She needed to breathe. She needed to calm down, and she needed to, well, she needed to pretend she was Nola.

Nola and the others were no doubt looking for her. And she hoped that the blood sample she'd left in her apartment helped them figure out who was after her and why.

However, that was also information that Bishop would like at this particular moment. She didn't know why she'd been grabbed. She'd never seen this place before. And whoever had grabbed her had a lot of money.

Her mind raced, wondering if it was one of the cases from the CIA.

At the same time, she was a rather low-level individual to grab. But maybe that was the point. Maybe somebody wanted to use her passcodes to get into the CIA system.

Bishop hoped that was the case.

Because she created some trap doors in the system so that if she used certain passwords, people would automatically be able to trace where they were sent from and would know that she needed help.

So she really hoped that somebody came soon, and they could get this show started.

For a moment, she considered again whether or not this might be unrelated to the CIA. Maybe it was related to one of Nola's cases.

She supposed that was possible too, although that still didn't seem likely. The individuals who they had rolled up weren't the type that would be able to orchestrate something like this.

Nola was no doubt focused entirely on finding her. There wasn't an ounce of concern that Nola didn't realize she was gone. She knew she was gone. She would undeniably be scorching the earth trying to find her.

That actually worried Bishop a little bit.

Something had changed in Nola in the last couple of months. She'd made these huge strides coming back to the real world, and Bishop really hoped that her disappearance didn't throw her off that progress. Which meant she couldn't just sit here and wait for Nola and the others to come help her. She needed to do something to help them.

Which meant she needed information.

All she knew so far was that whoever grabbed her had money and didn't shy away from hiring out. That spoke of someone familiar with the criminal world, which lent itself to the CIA argument.

Although most of their cases tended to be overseas. Maybe it was the Chinese government, and she'd been brought to a diplomatic site. The Asian decor she'd seen throughout the building on her way to this room would seem to support that possibility. Technically that would mean she was on Chinese soil, even though she was on the US mainland.

That gave her pause.

She knew Nola wouldn't think twice about busting into a sovereign nation to free her. But Bishop also knew that

that would cause a huge problem. But she supposed they'd deal with that when they came to it.

The door to the room opened behind her. Bishop whirled around as the man named Brett stepped inside. "Take her. But don't hurt her." He waved the two men who'd walked in with him forward.

Bishop backed up a step, narrowing her eyes. *Okay. Here we go.* As the first one reached her, she slammed her foot into his groin. He dropped with a cry, grabbing his crotch. The second man darted toward her, reaching out with his hand. Bishop slipped to the side and grabbed his wrist, twisting it toward the ground. He dropped to his knees, his arm still held in Bishop's grasp as he contorted himself trying to relieve the pressure.

This is working, Bishop thought in disbelief. *I can't believe this is—*

A quick pinch of pain bloomed in her neck. Bishop glanced over her shoulder at Brett, who held a needle in his hand. In the fight with the other two, she'd left her back exposed.

Her vision began to darken around the edges. Her grip loosened on the man she held. She stumbled back, sitting down hard on the bench. Both men she'd defended herself against watched her warily.

Get up. You need to get up. But her limbs wouldn't listen. It was a struggle to even keep her eyelids open.

And then she lost that struggle and slipped into unconsciousness.

Chapter Sixteen

NOLA

Before heading out to the outskirts of Baltimore, Nola sent the name Charles Fitzpatrick to Stan for him to dig up everything he could find. Then she read over the file that Ileana had sent her on the O'Connor family. The family had been in the enforcement business for a while before shifting over to the drug business in the last five years.

They were a small player, but they were consistent in their supply.

A few blocks from the bar where the O'Connor's did business, Stan came through with a file. Chuck apparently had been an enforcer for them on and off for five years. There wasn't much more in the file than what they had already found through the blood match so she turned back to the file on the O'Connors.

The O'Connor family worked out of an Irish bar, just like the stereotype would suggest. In fact, the bar was even named O'Connor's. It dated back to 1922 when the first

O'Connor had reached the American shores from County Down in Ireland.

Patrick O'Connor had run an under-the-counter bootleg bar during the time of prohibition. So it seemed the O'Connors had been on the wrong side of the law from the jump.

Now, the great-great-grandson of Patrick O'Connor, James, who went by Jimmy, was expanding the business. He'd been making some moves in the last couple of years, pushing back on some of the attempts by a rival drug dealer to move into the area. As a result, assaults and homicides had increased in the neighborhood by a significant amount.

And after that, the criminal justice system had started to pay a little more attention, though not enough that the cops were actually able to do anything. In fact, it seemed all they had done was create a paper trail by taking down statements after the violent incidents occurred. Arrests were few and far between.

Nola wasn't sure if that was because they had no evidence or someone was being paid off. It was probably a little bit of both.

Revlon Street was quiet as Avad pulled up to the curb three storefronts down from the bar. The street had gone through some gentrification, at least on the far end, where there were some high-end clothing boutiques, a yoga studio, a florist, a juice bar, and a vegan restaurant. This side of Revlon, though, was still in need of some help. An old food mart sat on the corner across the street from O'Connor's. A few brownstones that had definitely seen better days sat between the two businesses and the more well-to-do businesses down the block.

As a bar, O'Connor's had the look of a place that had been there for eons and was barely hanging on. The sign, complete with a shamrock and green lettering, looked circa 1970s. Brightly lit beer signs hung in the windows along the front of the bar.

In fact, the front of the bar was made completely of glass, giving a clear view of the street. Two men in leather jackets sat outside on stools talking while also keeping an eye on the neighborhood.

Nola put her hand on the door handle, but Avad grabbed her arm before she could open it. "How are we playing this?" he asked.

Nola eyed the two guys at the front door. Both were in their late forties, maybe early fifties, with heavy jowls and puffy faces that suggested they regularly enjoyed the beers of the establishment they were protecting. And although Nola couldn't see from here, she was pretty sure both men were packing under their jackets. "We're going to get answers."

Avad sighed. "Yes, but you say 'answers,' and I hear 'fight.' Perhaps we should try talking first."

"I'm all for talking, but I'm pretty sure that there is no variation of 'Hey, we need to speak with your boss' that's going to get us a good response. So if you want to stay out here . . ."

"I'm as worried about her as you are," Avad said, his eyes boring into her.

Nola looked into those eyes and knew that he was telling the truth. Avad had a fatherly affection for Bishop. They had spent a great deal of time together over the years.

Some of the bluster worked itself out of her. "Sorry. I know you are. We just need to get some information from them, and I really don't know of any other way to do it other than to demand it. We've got no leverage here. But we do just need to ask them questions."

"Perhaps we can try just *asking* questions and see how that goes?" he suggested.

Nola shrugged. "Okay. We can give it a shot." She stepped out of the car.

Together, the two of them crossed the street. The guys at the door only gave her a quick glance, their attention focused on the Viking next to her.

It was a common response. After all, of the two of them, it definitely looked like Avad was the greater threat.

As they reached the two men, one of them reached out a hand, blocking the entrance. "Can we help you?"

Nola smiled. "Just coming in for a drink."

The man looked her up and down and then shook his head. "I'm afraid we're closed today."

"Oh, that's too bad. Because we wanted to have a conversation with Jimmy," Nola said.

"He's not here."

Nola shook her head, feigning confusion. "Well, that's funny because according to his cell phone, he's right inside."

The first guy narrowed his eyes. "You guys cops?"

Nola laughed. "We are definitely not cops."

"Then I think you two need to leave," the other guy said, pulling back his coat to reveal the Beretta tucked into the waistband of his pants.

With a sigh, Nola looked over at Avad. "I told you talking wasn't going to work."

Avad shrugged. "You were right. But it was worth a shot." He punched the guy closest to him straight in the face.

The man's head snapped back, and his eyes rolled back into his head as he dropped to the ground.

Nola slammed her knee into the guy closest to her,

followed by an uppercut and then an elbow across his jaw. Her guy dropped as well.

She stepped through the doorway with Avad right behind her. The building held a full-length wooden bar along one side with three rows of liquor spanning the entire length of it. Behind the bottles was a bar-to-ceiling mirror. A tin ceiling was up above, and the tables were round thick wooden tables with upholstered barrel chairs. A few booths lined the back wall as well. There was also a door there, shut tight.

There were six individuals sitting at chairs, enjoying an afternoon drink.

But those weren't the patrons Nola was focused on. No, she was more interested in the hired help, because apparently their actions outside hadn't exactly been hidden from the rest of the patrons of the bar.

Four men lined up in front of them, two held knives and one had a gun. The other guy held a bat, which he kept hitting into his palm.

Nola held up her hands. "Hey, we were just coming to talk."

The man with the gun stepped forward. "Yeah, well, talking time's over."

He stepped closer to Nola, now only a few feet away. "We're going to take a ride." He gestured toward the back of the bar and no doubt an alternate exit.

"Get the big guy," the man with the gun ordered. His gaze flicked to Avad.

And that was exactly the lack of attention that Nola was looking for.

Grabbing the man's wrist, she pushed it to the side and slammed a front kick into his groin. He let out a cry as she followed her kick with an elbow into his chin. Stripping the gun from his hand, she slammed the butt of it into his jaw.

He crashed to the ground with another cry of pain. The guy with the bat swung at her head, and she ducked the bat. As she stood back up, she dropped the gun, needing both hands to grip the guy's arm as he swung back. She could have shot him, but a few broken bones could be overlooked at a hospital. A gunshot wound would not be.

Grabbing his elbow and wrist, she swept his arm back, adding to his momentum. Redirecting the bat, she slammed it into his knee and then brought it back around onto the back of his thigh. With a scream, he dropped to the ground. "My knee!"

Twirling the bat in her hand, she turned for the next guy, who raced toward her, his knife extended.

She slammed the bat down on the wrist of his extended hand and then brought it back up underneath his chin. He went flying, sliding along the bar floor a few feet.

Twirling the bat again, she turned to where Avad had one guy by the throat before he slammed him into the ground.

"Enough, enough." A man with gray hair stepped out of the back room, clapping his hands as he looked around with a grimace. Two men flanked him, their hands on the guns at their waists, but wisely, they didn't pull them.

"What's happening in here?" Jimmy demanded.

Nola nodded to the men on the ground. "We told them we just wanted to talk. But apparently they had something else in mind."

"What do you want to talk about?" Jimmy asked.

"Chuck Fitzpatrick," Nola said.

The head of the O'Connor family curled his lip. "That asshole? Why do you want to talk about him?"

"Because he took a job he shouldn't have. And I need to find him."

As he looked around at his men on the floor, Jimmy grunted. "You plan on doing this to old Chuck?"

"I'm planning on doing worse," Nola said.

Jimmy grinned. "Well, then come on back, little lady, and let's have us a little conversation."

Chapter Seventeen

The back of O'Connor's Pub was broken up into three
different areas. The first was a small kitchen that was
surprisingly clean. Beyond that was a private dining area
located across from an office. There was also an exit leading
to a parking area behind the pub. Jimmy led them into the
private dining area.

Nola knew that the reason for that was the office was too
small to accommodate Nola, Avad, and Jimmy's two goons
comfortably. She didn't think it was done for her and Avad's
comfort. She was pretty sure Jimmy wanted to give his guys
a little more space in case they needed to defend their boss.

Not an unwise choice.

As Jimmy took a seat behind the table, he gestured for
them to do the same across from him. One of his guys took
up position behind him.

Nola took a seat, but Avad stood over by the door, near
one of Jimmy's guys. Jimmy's guy gave him a nervous look
and swallowed hard.

Looking between the two of them, Jimmy grunted.

"You two work well together. If you're ever looking for a little extra work—"

"We're good. Now, what can you tell me about Chuck?" Nola asked.

Jimmy sat back in his chair, flicking a glance once again between Nola and Avad. It was easy to see the calculation in his gaze. "Why are you looking for Chuck?"

"As I said, he did a job he shouldn't have. And I need to get some information from him," Nola replied.

Settling back in his chair, Jimmy smiled. "What's it worth to you?"

Nola gritted her teeth. "Quite a lot. And being you only have two guys in here, I would suggest you quit playing around and tell me what I need to know."

Jimmy held up his hands. "Hey, hey. I didn't say I wasn't going to help you. I was just curious as to what he's gotten himself into."

"He took someone," Nola said.

Meeting her unflinching gaze, Jimmy nodded. "Yeah, that's what he's known for. He's kind of good at collecting people. He'll grab them, bring them to wherever you need them to be. He does a blitz attack, grabs them before they even know what's happening."

"Do you know where I can find him?" Nola asked.

"He's got an apartment over on Fourth. But he doesn't go there very much."

Jimmy pulled over a notepad and scribbled out an address. He slid it across the table toward her. "The second address on there, that's the bar he likes to hang out in. You'll probably have better luck finding him there. He's there most nights trying to score with one of the waitresses."

Nola flicked a glance at the paper before slipping it into her pocket. "Does he have any luck?"

"When there's a new one, yeah. But the girls who've been there for a while know exactly who he is."

"And who is he?"

"Someone who doesn't like being told no. And so if your friend's with him, then she's in for a world of trouble."

Nola went still, staring at him with a narrowed gaze. "I didn't say it was a 'she' he grabbed."

Reading the threat correctly, Jimmy put up his hands. "No, but I had a feeling it was. That's Chuck specialty. He generally only takes the cases where it involves a female."

"What else can you tell me about him?"

"He's not a good guy. We had to let him go because we had some trouble with him."

"What kind of trouble?" Nola asked.

Pursing his lips, Jimmy was quiet for a moment. "He got a little too handsy with one of my client's daughters."

Nola narrowed her eyes. "How handsy?"

"We got to her in time. She was shook up, but he didn't get to finish. And after the beating he took, he made sure to stay as far from us as possible. There's a lot I do in this line of work, but there are certain lines that I won't ever let be crossed. And he crossed it that day. He's dead to me now." Jimmy paused. "And I'd be perfectly fine if he was dead permanently. So you need any help finding him, you let me know. I have no love lost for that guy."

Nola nodded, standing up. "If we don't find him, we'll be coming back for a little more information."

A hard glare entered Jimmy's eyes as he stood. "If you come back, we'll be ready for you."

Nola smiled. "No, you won't."

Chapter Eighteen

The address that Jimmy gave them was of a strip joint over on the east end. Avad punched the directions into the GPS while Nola called and relayed what they'd found to Ileana.

Ileana was already in a car heading into the city. She was going to pressure some of her local contacts for help. Nola wasn't sure if it would help. Ileana's contacts had been out of the game for a while, but she would take anything she could get.

The car was quiet as Avad drove. He wasn't a talker on a good day, and today was not a good day.

Her phone rang, breaking the silence when they were ten minutes out from the bar. Her heart rate ticked up a notch when she saw Stan's number on the screen. She answered it quickly. "Stan, what have you got?"

"I haven't been able to nail down which car held Bishop. I'm still going through the footage."

Nola tried to bite back her growl. "You called to tell me what you don't have?"

"No, no," Stan said quickly. "I'm calling about that Fitzpatrick guy."

"You got a hit?" She asked.

"Yeah, a big one. I know exactly where he is."

"Where?"

"The morgue."

Chapter Nineteen

The medical examiner's office was situated in downtown Baltimore on the corner of West Baltimore Street and Warren Street. The building was a mix of pale brick and lots of blue windows.

Most people would go in the large doors at the front, not around to the back where the bodies were brought into the building. No one wanted to see stretchers being carted down the middle of a busy street.

But Avad drove right by the well-signed parking area and headed around the back of the building with Ileana and Nola. Ileana had linked up with them a few blocks away. Darius had taken her car back home.

Avad cut the engine, and they sat quietly as they waited for the back door to open. It didn't take long. As the large garage door slowly opened, a young man in his late twenties in pale green scrubs and a long white lab coat appeared, looking around nervously.

He spied their car and waved them over. The three of them exited the car. Nola glanced around, noting the camera above the door. The back of the building was quiet, with the sounds of afternoon traffic in the distance. She wasn't expecting trouble, but Bishop hadn't been expecting trouble either. Waiting until Avad and Ileana disappeared into the building, she took one last glance around before following them inside.

The young technician glanced over his shoulder as he led them through a narrow hallway. The smell of formaldehyde was thick in the air, along with the scent of rotting meat. He looked at them licking his lips, his eye twitching. Nola could practically see his heart pounding, the guy was so jumpy. "Dr. Templeton told me to bring you to the examination suite. She wasn't really clear on why you guys were coming in through the back door."

"I suppose that's because she didn't want you to know," Ileana said firmly.

The man's cheeks reddened. "Oh yeah, I suppose so. This way."

He led them through a series of three hallways before they finally stopped at two swinging doors. He paused for a second. "I'm not sure if you've been in an autopsy suite before, but the smell gets to some people." He extended his hand. A small jar lay on his palm. "Does anybody want to put some of this below your nose? It'll help."

Ileana reached out and took the small silver container. Opening it, she placed a dab of the mentholated substance on her face.

Avad and Nola both declined. Nola had been around enough dead bodies that the scents no longer bothered her. And Avad, after his years in Bosnia during the war, was well aware of what a dead body smelled like as well.

The assistant nodded, turning back to the doors and pushing them open.

77

A woman in her fifties stood over a table, a notepad in her hand. Her hair was short and curly, and she wore a white doctor's coat over her scrubs. She looked up over the rim of her thick glasses with a slight narrowing of her eyebrows.

From that single glance, Nola got the impression that Dr. Margaret Templeton was not someone who suffered fools lightly. She scanned Nola and Avad before her gaze fell on Ileana. "Ileana."

Ileana nodded back at her. "Margaret. Thank you for this."

Margaret placed the notepad down on a table next to the stretcher in front of her. "There's nothing to thank me for."

In the car, Ileana had explained that she and Margaret had known each other for years. They had crossed paths more than once in a professional capacity when Ileana was working in the intelligence field.

Over time, they had become friendly because back then, there weren't a lot of women in the field. And from the way Ileana spoke about her, Nola knew that she respected her a great deal.

During the drive over, Nola had done a background search on her. The doctor had done her undergrad at Harvard before going to John Hopkins for medical school. And then she had been a resident at the Mayo Clinic in Cleveland. She had been working for a medical examiner's office in Manhattan for years before she was tapped to run the medical examiner's office in Maryland.

The picture of her had been from ten years ago but showed the exact same woman standing in front of them now: a woman of only medium height with the same short cropped curly hair and large glasses, a serious expression on her face.

She was divorced with two kids, both boys. After college, both had gone into the military: one into the Army and one into the Navy.

Templeton had little to no social media representation. In fact, Nola couldn't find anything other than a professional email. It was possible she had accounts under different names, but Nola got the impression she was a rather straightforward woman who didn't want to be bothered with the ins and outs of social media.

Ileana was the same way. She had no interest in exchanging memes about how tough the week was or commenting on the latest political change with a bunch of random strangers on the internet.

Nola herself didn't have any social media accounts either, at least none that she used. She had a few fake profiles for when she did research for different cases. But it wasn't something that she ever spent hours scrolling like people seemed to do.

Templeton raised her eyebrows at Ileana. "I'm not quite clear on how you knew he was here so quickly."

"I've been keeping an eye out for him. We're lucky a cop had a fingerprint scanner at the scene," Ileana said smoothly.

A cop at the scene had taken prints on the John Doe and had immediately gotten a hit on Fitzpatrick. Stan had set up an alert for any news involving Fitzpatrick and he'd been notified almost as soon as Stan's body had been ID'd.

The doctor turned to her assistant. "Sean, why don't you go and make sure that the daily logs have been taken care of?"

"Sure. But I was hoping I could . . ." His gaze started to the drawers on the left-hand side of the autopsy suite.

"Sean, please go take care of the logs," Templeton said firmly.

Sean's shoulders fell. "Yes, Dr. Templeton." He turned and pushed back through the swinging doors.

Templeton shook her head. "He's new. He still gets excited when there's an unusual case."

"And you don't?" Nola asked.

"I've worked in the medical examiner's office for over thirty years. There's never an unusual case." She moved toward the wall of drawers and pulled one out. "We don't have a lot of time."

"Why is that?" Ileana asked.

"Because you're not the only ones interested in this body," the doctor said.

Chapter Twenty

Avad stayed over by the door, casting a glance through the windows, keeping an eye out for anyone who might interrupt them.

Nola moved forward with Ileana toward the wall of refrigerated drawers that held bodies prior to their autopsy. "Who else is interested?" Nola asked.

"The feds. My office got a call about twenty minutes ago saying we weren't to touch the body, that federal officers would be here to collect it and take it from our custody."

"Which branch?" Ileana asked.

Templeton shrugged. "Sean got the call. He didn't note the branch."

Nola wondered if that was because the caller didn't provide it.

The call though meant that somebody else was interested in what good ol' Chuck had been up to, or more accurately, had been interested in the person who had killed good ol' Chuck. Nola doubted they were interested in Bishop's disappearance. They would have contacted Ileana by now if that were the case. No, they were interested in Chuck for a different reason.

Templeton pulled open a long drawer halfway down the wall. The appearance of the body caused Nola's eyebrows to rise: Chuck's head sat perched carefully at the top of the stretcher while his body was a few inches away from it.

"He was decapitated?" Ileana asked with a frown.

"In one clean swipe," Templeton said.

With surprise, Nola noted that the edge of the wound on the body's neck was indeed a clean cut. Most people, when they thought of decapitation, thought that it happened like that: with one clean stroke of a blade.

The reality was that decapitation with a sword or a knife was a messy process. It was less one clean swipe and more of a hacking situation. Knives and swords generally weren't sharp enough, and the force usually wasn't strong enough for it to be done any other way.

"That is unusual," Ileana said.

"Not as unusual as you think," Templeton said.

"What do you mean by that?" Ileana asked.

The phone on the opposite side of the autopsy suite rang before she could answer. Templeton quickly crossed the room and answered it. "Yes?"

She paused. "No, it's not ready. I haven't done any—" She paused again, turning to look at Ileana, her facial expression growing more annoyed. "Fine. I'll be right up."

Hanging up the phone, she turned to the others, a scowl on her face. "The feds are already here. They're taking the body."

"Were you able to do an initial examination?" Ileana asked.

"The feds told me I wasn't supposed to even look at it," Templeton replied.

Ileana smiled. "Yes, but my question remains."

For the first time since Nola had met the woman, she smiled. "My notes are in a file back in my office." She nudged her chin toward the back of the autopsy suite. "And I'm going to have to ask you three to go hide in there while the feds collect the body. I don't think it would be wise for them to know that you're here."

"We agree," Ileana said, striding toward the door.

Nola fell in step behind her, and Avad crossed the room as well.

Footsteps sounded from down the hall as Nola slipped into the room. She closed the blinds on the glass windows but stepped to the side so that she could see through the cracks. A moment later, two suited men stepped into the autopsy suite. Both looked to be in their late thirties, maybe early forties. One had thin pale brown hair and the other a rich dark black.

"Dr. Templeton," the one with pale brown hair said. "I'm Special Agent Chalet and this is Special Agent Krepp. We've come for the body of Charles Fitzpatrick."

Crossing her arms over her chest, Dr. Templeton speared them both with an annoyed glare. Apparently the doctor did not like people pulling bodies from her department. "You have the paperwork?"

Sean hustled in through the double doors holding a manila folder. He hurried across the room to Templeton and handed it to her. "Here you go, Doctor. I got the paperwork from them and had them sign it."

Agent Krepp took a step forward. "Okay, Doctor, if you could just show us which one of these—"

The doctor held up her hand while she read through the file. And she took her time reading it. When she was done, she turned to the men. "You seem to have forgotten to indicate which federal agency you're from. It's not noted on any of these forms."

Chalet gave her a condescending smile. "That's because this is a matter of national security, and it's best if you don't—"

The doctor shut the file with a snap. "I am not handing you that body without proper authorization. Either you put down exactly who you are and where you're from, or that body stays in my refrigerator."

The agents glared at her from across the room. "You don't want to make us your enemy, Doctor," Chalet warned.

She didn't back down an inch from the intimidating glares they were sending in her direction. "No, I don't. But I will if you force me to."

The three engaged in a staring contest before Krepp broke. "That was our mistake, Doctor. If you'll hand me the forms back, I'll fill them out correctly."

Not breaking her gaze from the other agent, Dr. Templeton handed the file back to her assistant, who scurried back across the room, handing it to the agents. One of them scribbled something on the form and then handed it back.

The assistant once again hurried back across the room and handed the file to the doctor, who glanced down at it. "The FBI? Now, was that really so difficult?"

"The body, Doctor," Krepp said.

With a grunt, Templeton walked over to where the body was and pulled open the drawer. She waved her hand toward it. "Here you go."

The men walked over and stared down in it.

The doctor raised an eyebrow. "Are you planning on carrying it out in your arms? Did you bring anything to take the body with you?"

The men blanched.

Templeton rolled her eyes. "Sean, grab them a body bag and a stretcher. Then assist the federal agents of the FBI with their body retrieval."

"Yes, Doctor, right away."

It took another few minutes to get the body situated in the body bag that Sean had laid out on the stretcher. Templeton and the agents stood back as Sean did all the work, carefully placing the head near the feet. Nola cringed at that, even though Chuck would no longer mind.

Then Sean pushed the stretcher back through the doors.

Chalet stopped at the doors, looking back at Dr. Templeton. "It was a pleasure meeting you."

The doctor just silently watched him in return. He shrugged and headed back through the doors.

As soon as the doors closed behind them, Templeton rolled her shoulders, a tremor running through her before she turned to her office.

Nola backed away from the door as Templeton pushed through. She made her way around the desk and then sat down in her chair with a thump.

She slid out the bottom desk drawer and pulled out a bottle of Jameson whiskey, placing it on the desktop before setting out four glasses. "Anybody want a drink?"

Nola and Avad declined, but Ileana nodded. "I think I could use a little."

No one said anything as the doctor poured herself and Ileana a healthy drink with shaky hands.

"What's going on Margaret?" Ileana asked.

Templeton took a long drink and let out a breath. "That's not the first body that's been found like that. And that's not the first time the feds have shown up to collect it."

Chapter Twenty-One

After dropping that little nugget about multiple bodies appearing without their heads, Dr. Templeton sat back and sipped her drink. The feds had been gone for about five minutes before she finally spoke. Placing her glass down on the desktop with a sigh, she nodded back toward the autopsy suite. "That's the second case that's passed through my office. And that's the second time the feds have shown up to collect the body."

"Always the same two agents?" Ileana asked.

"I'm not sure. I was out of town the last time they showed up." She walked over to the file cabinet to her right and pulled out the top drawer, leafing through the files inside before taking out a few sheets of paper.

She sat back down. Opening the file, she glanced between it and the sheet of paper that the agents had handed her before sliding them across the desk. "The signatures look the same to me."

Nola leaned forward and glanced at the papers. The signatures were, in fact, identical. Although, the last time, they hadn't indicated what agency they were from. And their signature was little more than a scrawl.

"I assume you followed up with the agencies?" Ileana asked.

"Yes. But it took a full afternoon of phone calls to find out they were FBI agents. I did verify that the agents had been sent here. But I don't like the whole situation. Something feels off."

"There have been two bodies?" Nola asked.

"Two bodies that have gone through my office. But bodies meeting the same description have been found in San Francisco, Utah, Texas, and North Carolina. So there's at least six bodies out there with the same MO. And those are the ones that I know of."

"There are other cases?" Ileana asked.

With a weary nod, Templeton took a sip before she spoke. "Two years ago, we had our annual medical examiners convention. I got to speaking with other MEs, and one mentioned a clean beheading. Something about it didn't sit right. Asking around, I found a few more cases."

"What about these other cases? Are there files from those?" Nola asked.

"Feds swooped in and grabbed those bodies too, even before an ID could be found. In this case, you're lucky that cop ran those prints. Otherwise, you never would have found your guy. But I'm afraid this is where the trail ends. There are no case files and no follow up. I tapped some of my sources in the FBI, and they haven't been able to find any cases this might be related to."

"Someone's covering this up," Ileana said.

"Clearly. But I'm not sure who they're covering for," Templeton said.

"What can you tell us about the cause of death? Death

by sword, especially a single blade, isn't common," Ileana said.

"Not anymore," the doctor replied.

"What do you mean by that?" Ileana asked.

"Well, historically, death by sword used to be a more common way of dying. Although decapitating someone with a sword was not common either in the old world. But it did happen. It takes a special sword and training to wield that kind of weapon and cause that kind of damage."

"But in the modern world, guns are much easier," Nola said.

Templeton nodded her agreement. "That they are."

"What kind of swords are we talking about?" Nola asked.

"There's a couple that could fit the bill. Basically, you're talking any kind of samurai sword that is kept at an incredible sharpness." The doctor nodded back toward the autopsy suite. "And it's actually a clean strike, so whoever's doing this, they're skilled, trained. There were no hesitation marks, not even on any of the other cases."

"Someone's gotten rather good at this," Nola said.

Templeton nodded. "Yes. Hesitation marks are common in killers when they first begin their work. Unsure of what they were doing or maybe slightly less committed, it takes them a few tries to smooth out their modus operandi. But this guy, he does one clean strike, no hesitation. He's committed. It's clear he's done this before."

"Has anybody opened a file on these cases? Has anybody started investigating them on a local level?" Nola asked.

With a shake of her head, Templeton shot that possibility down. "If anybody has, it's been on the down low because the feds swooped in, taking the bodies and making it clear that they had jurisdiction for these cases. So no one is going to be stepping on their toes. They wrapped these cases up tight. And most jurisdictions are pretty happy to have one less murder to solve."

Possibilities ran through Nola's mind. The most likely was that there was a law enforcement subject that they were trying to target who they didn't want anyone else muscling in on. Or it was possible the killer was someone who was an embarrassment for the federal government, maybe a former agent or soldier.

But it was also possible that they were simply being paid by someone to cover up these cases. Of course, that someone would have to have pretty deep pockets and quite a reach for them to be all over the country like that.

Which didn't make it impossible. It just meant that whoever was behind this had a lot of resources and a lot of pull within the federal government.

"Would you be willing to reach out to those other MEs? See what they remember about these cases?" Ileana asked.

Templeton looked across the desk at Ileana. "I can, but I'm not sure you should be diving into this one. I have a feeling you're stirring up a hornet's nest."

Ileana met her gaze. "The nest has already been stirred. But they're the ones who should be worried, not us."

Chapter Twenty-Two

The drive back to the estate was quiet. Neither Nola, Avad, nor Ileana were in the mood for conversation, all of them lost in their different thoughts.

Nola sat in the back of the SUV, trying different databases to see if she could find anything about death by sword. But there were precious few hits that were coming, and those that did were definitely not the same type of case that they were looking at. Those deaths were more of the hacking attempts at decapitation rather than a clean slice.

Nola paused for a second and then pulled out her phone. She looked up the number she was looking for and then quickly dialed.

Stan answered after only a few rings. "Hello?" he asked nervously.

"Are you going to work tomorrow?" Nola asked.

"No. I decided to call in sick. I've been . . . I've been trying to look for Bishop. I've been searching all of her different online personas and just basically trying anything I can think of to track her down."

"Have you found anything?"

The frustration was noticeable across the line. "No, not really. I thought I might have had a hit on the car, but it turned out to be the wrong one. I'm sorry, Nola. I just can't seem to find anything." The man's disappointment was as clear as was his worry.

"I have something I need you to look into."

Stan's energy levels seem to perk up. "Really? Great. What is it?"

Nola quickly explained about the body and the method of death. "There have been cases around the country. But the feds have swooped in and taken control of the bodies and the scenes. Can you see what you can find?"

"Sure. I'll run down everything I can. What does this have to do with Bishop?"

"The latest body they grabbed is the guy who abducted Bishop."

The line was quiet for a moment before Stan responded. His voice was more subdued. "Then I'll find everything."

"Good." Nola paused for a second. "I also want you to check out two federal agents. Their names are Krepp and Chalet. They're with the FBI."

"Okay, I'll give them a run through as well. How deep do you want me to go?"

"Deep. I want to know everything I can about these guys."

"Okay. It'll take me a couple hours. But I'll get back to you as soon as I have something." Stan said before he disconnected the call.

For a second, Nola worried that maybe she had made a mistake in asking him for help. After all, she really didn't know him. Normally this was something she would ask Bishop to do. She wasn't sure what the correct action was.

"That was good calling Stan," Ileana said from the front.

Nola closed over her laptop and placed it and her phone on the seat next to her. "We don't even know him."

"Bishop has mentioned him a few times. And I ran a background check on him."

"How deep?" Nola asked.

"Deep. The CIA can be a nest of vipers. I wanted to be sure that no one was trying to get to me through Bishop."

"What did you find?"

"Stan Mahoney seems to be a rarity, a good man. He's thirty years old. He's been a standout in schools, at least academically. He even skipped a grade. He wasn't much of a jock, and from what I can tell, he had a bit of a lonely childhood as a result. He's got a younger brother in the Navy, and his parents seem to dote on the brother. Stanley Mahoney, he's more of a loner. Not in the Ted Kaczynski way, but more in the shy way.

"He has a couple of online accounts for social media, but they're all pretty harmless. He seems to just go on to social media looking for something as an emotional pick-me-up rather than to cause any problems. He has no gambling habits. He's not a drinker. He has no known associations with any criminal types.

"And he's been a good friend to Bishop at the CIA. So I think it was a good thing to call him."

Nola blew out a breath, an unfamiliar uncertainty in her chest. "I just feel like my judgment is off. I don't know who to call because I just have this fear overriding everything I do." Now Nola understood why people said you shouldn't be involved in cases you were emotionally connected to. It was so hard to separate the emotions from the actions.

Ileana turned more in her seat so she could look directly

at Nola. "Stop that. Fear is a weapon. It's a weapon that bullies use to incapacitate their victims. You are not a victim. You have never *been* a victim. Your job is not to give in to the fear when people try to make you scared and fill you with terror. What is your job?"

Nola looked into Ileana's eyes. "My job is to return the fear to them."

Ileana nodded. "Don't forget that. When we find who is behind taking Bishop, we will be their greatest nightmare. They will be the ones who will be locked in fear."

Chapter Twenty-Three

After returning Ileana to the estate, Nola and Avad had gone to the strip club that O'Connor mentioned. It had been another dead end. No one there knew where Chuck had gone or who he was working with. And not a single one was concerned about him. In fact, loathing seemed to be the common denominator amongst all the people Nola spoke with.

Apparently, the man didn't make friends very easily or at all. Everyone they had spoken with so far had been less than upset that the man was missing. Neither Nola nor Avad had mentioned he was dead, in case that became a fact they could use later. The one person who seemed the most upset about his absence was his bookie, an overweight man named Paulie, whose "office" was the bar at Paradise Found. And he was only upset because Chuck owed him money.

Now back at the estate, Nola was feeling out of sorts. She reviewed the information that they received from the technicians at Bishop's apartment, but nothing there was pointing anywhere other than at Chuck Fitzpatrick, and he was a dead end. There were deep dives being done on Chuck's connections to see if there were maybe some links they could tap into, but that wasn't Nola's area either.

Once again, she was struck by how large a part of her own infrastructure Bishop took up. She basically was all of the data. She could make computers do whatever she wanted. Nola and Avad had some basic abilities, but nothing compared to Bishop.

But it wasn't Bishop's computer skills that Nola was focusing on right now. Right now all Nola could do was focus on how she had first met Bishop. And wondering why the hell she hadn't done better by the girl.

Her skin felt tight, and this massive house felt too small, too constricting. She needed to get out, but she couldn't go too far. A run. She needed a run. She'd always thought the estate was so big, with its rambling grounds and the wings on the house.

Right now, though, it felt like the walls were closing in on her. She had failed Bishop. She hadn't kept her safe. That was her promise years ago when she had taken Bishop in. She would keep her safe. She had never said it out loud to Bishop because she knew that there might come a time when something might happen to the young girl, and she didn't want to lie to her.

But in her heart of hearts, she had promised that she would keep the demons away. But she had failed, and now Bishop was gone.

And they had no leads on her. Whoever had paid Chuck had done so in cash. There were no cash influxes to his bank account, and no one believed he had the smarts for an untraceable account. There were simply no leads as to who hired him.

The truth was, the world would be better off without Chuck in it, but that didn't help Nola find Bishop. God, it was so frustrating.

"Nola?"

She whipped around at the sound of the small voice. Sofia, Rafe's daughter, stood uncertainly in the hallway with a picture in her hand.

"Hi, Sofia," Nola said, careful to keep the frustration out of her voice. "How are you?"

Sofia shrugged, pulling her gaze from Nola's and looking at the ground, but Nola caught the tremble of the young girl's chin. Both Sofia and Enzo really liked Bishop. She was that young, crazy aunt that was always coming over with ice cream and would curl up on the couch with them to watch shows. And both Sofia and Enzo had lost so much in their young lives. This place was supposed to be a haven for them. A place where they could escape to and could feel safe.

Bishop's disappearance had robbed them of that as well.

And Nola's anger at whoever had done this flamed even brighter. Taking Bishop from their lives had triggered a spiderweb of effects that kept spreading farther and farther out.

"What have you got there?" Nola asked.

Sofia shifted the paper from one hand to the other. "It's a picture. I drew it for Bishop. I thought when you found her you could give it to her." She handed it over.

On the page was a hand-drawn image of a group of people. Bishop was easy to pick out with her wild hair all around her head. And standing towering over them on either side was Avad and Rafe. Sofia and Enzo were in the middle with a little gray dog positioned in front of them.

And then on either side of them was one woman who was clearly Ileana. And the other was clearly Nola.

"This is beautiful, Sofia. She's going to love it."

Sofia looked up at her with her big brown eyes. "You're going to get her back, aren't you?"

Staring into the young girl's eyes, Nola didn't want to lie to her. But the hurt was so close to the surface along with the worry. And Nola couldn't bring herself to cause the girl any more pain, at least not right now. There might come a time when she'd have to break her heart, but she couldn't do it. Tough as she was, she wasn't that tough.

"I'll give it to her as soon as I find her," she promised

Flinging her arms around Nola's waist, Sofia hugged her tight. "I know you'll find her, Nola. I know you will."

Wrapping her arms around the little, Nola prayed that she was right.

Chapter Twenty-Four

Nola's breaths came out in even pants as she raced along the estate's fence line. After speaking with Sofia, it had become even more necessary for her to get out and work off some of her energy or she was going to explode.

She put herself through a grueling seven-mile run across uneven fields, up hills, and over a terrain that forced her to stay in the moment or risk injury. But while her body was starting to tire, her mind was still racing with fear, worry, and doubt. She should have encouraged Bishop to go work at one of those top computer firms, like Microsoft or Amazon or Google. Any of them would have been thrilled to have someone with Bishop's skills.

But she hadn't. In fact, she'd barely been part of the conversation when Bishop decided to go work with the CIA. Nola's missions had probably been a large part of the reason that she had decided to take up that particular field.

Nola had taken all of her demons and her rage and exposed Bishop to them year after year. Of course she'd then turned to the world of espionage for a career. That was all she knew.

Guilt dogged Nola steps. *I should have done better. I should have stepped away from her the first chance I got.*

But Nola shook her head at that thought. No, she wouldn't have been better off then. But she could have encouraged her to go into a different field. Maybe the blame went back even further. Maybe she should have tried harder to find her a different placement. For the first few years, it had been just the two of them before David and Molly came along. Maybe she shouldn't have even taken her in. She should have found someone else to do that.

By the time Nola made it back to the house, her thoughts seemed to be even heavier than when she had first started her run.

She took a shower and made her way down the stairs after getting changed. But hearing voices in the kitchen, she slipped out the back door and around to the side porch, not ready to make small talk and knowing that if something had shown up in the search, someone would have tracked her down.

The scene with Sofia slipped back into Nola's mind, leaving her feeling out of sorts. She shouldn't have gotten the girl's hopes up. But she simply couldn't bring more devastation to the girl's life if she didn't have to.

Besides, Nola planned on getting Bishop back.

And if she didn't get Bishop back, then Nola planned on taking out every single person who had a role in her disappearance, and Nola knew that she wouldn't come back from that.

She'd done a lot of amazing things in the last couple of years. And it was because the fear that held back most people didn't hold her back. She wasn't looking to die. That was not how she was built. But she wasn't afraid of it either.

She slipped out the back door of the kitchen and walked along the patio. The tire swing underneath the willow tree was moving gently up ahead. And as she pushed aside the tree's branches Molly looked up from the swing. "Hi, Mommy."

"Hi, baby girl."

Taking a deep breath, Nola looked at her little girl, at the pigtails on top of her head, her jeans and navy-blue sweater with the giant red heart. It was what she had been wearing when Nola had last seen her alive, the last time Nola had been whole.

"Do you know where Bishop is?" Nola asked her daughter softly.

Molly shook her head. "I can't see her right now."

Nola sighed, knowing it would never be that easy. When Molly had first started appearing, she hadn't even been sure if her daughter was a ghost or just a figment of her imagination. Off and on, throughout her life, she'd seen ghosts. It was not something she shared with many people. David knew, but she'd never even told Ileana. It seemed too, well, crazy to share.

"She's not dead, though, Mommy. She's still in your world," Molly said.

Nola let out a breath, her legs feeling weak. That had been her greatest fear. That she was already too late.

"You'll find her, Mommy. She's waiting for you to." Molly slipped off the swing and brought her hand up to Nola. But Nola felt nothing as her hand passed right through Molly's. Then Molly faded from view.

When she was fully gone, Nola felt the familiar ache in her chest. But it was smaller. Each time she saw her lately, the ache was just a little less. Nola knew the crater that had been created by the death of David and Molly had slowly been filling over the last few years.

Nola had resisted it in some ways at first. But she knew it was probably a good thing.

It had started, it seemed, down in Georgia with the disappearance of Anna Mae. Working with Rascal and meeting Anna Mae's little brother, they had started something. A healing. Or maybe they had just accelerated it. But Nola had accepted that it was happening.

Now when she looked at Molly, it was clear that she was a ghost. She wasn't fully opaque like when Nola had first seen her after she had died. Now, there was a little transparent sheen to her.

When Nola had first realized the difference in Molly's appearance, her gut had clenched at the idea that one day she would never see her again.

But it had been months now, and each time she had been a little bit more transparent. Molly was giving her time to say goodbye. And Nola desperately needed that time.

Nola hadn't grown up with a lot of people to love. She had no memory of her mother. And her father, well, they'd been more like roommates than an actual father-daughter pair. Growing up, the two people she'd had had been Beth and Nico.

But both of them had been taken away too soon. And then the next person that Nola had cared about had been Bishop. There was something about the girl that she hadn't been able to leave behind. And before she knew it, Bishop was living with her.

She had been with Bishop when she had met David. And to be honest, if she had met David before she had known Bishop, she wasn't certain that they would have gotten together. Bishop had helped her open her heart, so when she met David, she was ready to let someone else in.

And David brought them both into his world, giving them Ileana and Avad as well.

Bishop had healed part of her heart. She'd made it so that Nola was open to the possibility of falling in love, even though a large part of her denied that she would ever do such a thing. So Bishop hadn't just changed her life. She'd changed her heart.

Now Bishop was out there somewhere, hurt and alone. And she was counting Nola to find her. Nola would not let her down. With her dying breath, she would make sure that Bishop knew that she was loved and that Nola had done everything in her power to get to her.

Chapter Twenty-Five

Moving around to the side of the house, Nola took a seat on the patio, keeping the lights off. She wanted the dark. Cold air brushed against her skin. Nola closed her eyes, enjoying the peace of it for just a moment.

Small footsteps approached, but Nola didn't turn, as she knew who they belonged to. Cora slipped her head underneath Nola's hand, and Nola ran it across her fur. "Hey, girl. I'm afraid I'm not very good company right now."

Ignoring her words, Cora plopped her butt down and leaned against Nola's legs. Nola reached down and rubbed the front of her stomach. The two of them just sat there breathing in and breathing out.

And Nola finally felt some of her anger calm.

Cora was another one who had been through a lot. She had white blotches along her body where the fur would no longer grow. They were bite marks. She'd been in more than a few dogfights. Nola was pretty sure she'd been used as a bait dog to get other dogs to be more aggressive.

And then she had also been used to create puppies for a

puppy mill that no doubt sold off the dogs to whoever could pay the money without any thought going to what kind of life those puppies might live.

In a weird sort of way, Cora, Nola, and Bishop all had similar lifelines. And they had all ended up in the same place.

The door opened, and Nola knew it was Rafe stepping out onto the porch.

"Hey. You doing all right?" he asked.

"I'm not very good company right now," she repeated.

Rafe chuckled softly. "Oh, and normally you're the life of the party."

That comment brought a small smile to her lips. "True. But seriously, I just can't right now."

Ignoring her words, Rafe took a seat next to her and repositioned his chair so he could look at her. "What happened to Bishop isn't your fault."

Nola met his gaze. "What are you talking about?"

"You're sitting here blaming yourself for everrything that has happened to Bishop. You're trying to twist reality so that somehow you led her to the situation she's in right now."

His words echoed Ileana's from not that long ago. Apparently she wasn't quite as hard to read as she thought. "Didn't I? I should have encouraged her to go into some other field where she would be safe. Where none of this violence would touch her. She's had enough violence in her life."

"Yes, she has. And it's created who she is, just like your life created who you are and mine created me. You're not responsible for what's going on with Bishop right now. We don't know who took her."

"But she shouldn't be in this line of work. I should have—"

Rafe cut her off. "What, Nola? What should you have done? You found Bishop in a horrible situation and you pulled her out of it. And you tried to find a home for her, but she couldn't fit into that world anymore. The experiences that she'd had before you met her, they changed her. She was never going to be a normal kid after that. She couldn't be."

"How do you know this?"

"Bishop told me."

Shock flooded through Nola's system. "She talked to you about it?"

Rafe nodded. "Bishop understands who she is. She knows that her past doesn't define her, but she also knows that it's made her and influenced her into who she's become. Back then, there was no way she would have been able to go into a 'normal' family. She just wasn't equipped for that at that time. But living with you? That's what saved her."

Gently he took her hand and Nola didn't pull away. "Living with you was what allowed her to breathe. Living with you was what allowed her to sleep, knowing that if anyone came through that door at her, you would send them right back through it again. You made a scared little girl feel safe. You gave her time to heal. And you gave her a place to feel loved."

"And then I abandoned her," Nola said softly.

"No, Nola." Rafe shook his head. "Bishop never looked at it like that. More than anyone, she understands how when these events come along and blow apart your life, you can't control how you react to them. You can't change how you feel. She never blamed you for stepping away. She understood why you did. And her being part of this, her supporting you, that was her way of giving back some of the support that you gave to her. She's never been mad at you for that, Nola. In fact, she was glad that she was finally able to do something to repay what you'd given her."

"That's letting me off the hook too easy. I should have—"

Rafe reached out and took her other hand, holding them together in Nola's lap. "Nola, you lost two of your foundations when David and Molly died. You can't stand when you've lost two. You were too unstable. And you had Ileana and Bishop trying to balance you out as best they could. You're not to blame for the life that Bishop's chosen. She chose it so she could help people. She could have gone into Silicon Valley and made a killing with her skills. Instead she chose a job where the pay is not so great but allows her to help people. And that's why she does what she does."

"But what if that job has now brought her to this? What if that job is what caught the attention of someone who's now focused on her?"

"We don't know that's the case either. Right now, the truth is, we don't know why she was grabbed. We don't really know anything."

"And that's the problem. We have nothing to go on," Nola said, letting out some of the frustration that she felt that she was just sitting here while Bishop was in danger.

Her phone beeped, and she glanced down at it. It was a text from Stan. *I've got some background on the two federal agents. I need to send you some information and call you. Is there a secure email I can use?*

Nola quickly typed in an email address and hit send before standing.

I'll call you after it's sent, he replied.

"What's going on?" Rafe asked as he stood as well.

"Stan has some information on those two feds that took the body from the morgue. Hopefully he'll be able to give us a direction to head toward."

"I'll help you look," Rafe said.

Nola's first instinct was to tell him no, that she had this. But they needed all the help they could get. "Okay."

She turned toward the house, dropping her doubt, fear and worries about Bishop as she did so. Right now she was on a mission, and emotions were just going to cloud the issue. She'd given in to them. She'd let them have their room to breathe, but now it was time to get to work.

Now it was time to find Bishop.

Chapter Twenty-Six

BISHOP

Her head and thoughts feeling fuzzy, Bishop snuggled deeper under the blanket. Sleep was pulling at her, but she knew she needed to get up. She had to get to work. But she was so tired.

Slowly, the outside world started to seep deeper into her unconscious. She gripped the sheets, felt the smooth material against her hands. It felt so good.

But that was wrong. Her sheets weren't this smooth. These felt like silk. Her eyes flung open and she sat up in bed.

Heart pounding, she looked around wildly, but she didn't recognize the room. Everything came back to her in a rush: the attack at her apartment, being thrown in the trunk of the car, that guy attacking her again, and then being drugged.

Shaking, she flung back the covers, relieved to see that all that had been removed from her was her boots, which sat neatly next to the bed. The room was once again Asian themed, with heavy wood along the walls but a low platform bed with red silk sheets. Ancient, ornate fans lined the walls, and a bamboo screen sat in the corner.

She crept quietly over to the screen and peeked behind it, but no one was there. She checked the bathroom, but it was empty as well. Next she searched the room for cameras. She checked corners, lights, the bookcase, every possible location she could think of but she didn't see anything. If there were cameras, they were incredibly well hidden.

Pulling a chair over to the door, she propped it under the doorknob. Then she let out a breath, dropping onto the end of the bed, her legs feeling weak.

Don't hurt her. The words rolled through her mind. The guys who'd drugged her didn't want her injured. But why?

A noise by the bedroom door caused her to whirl around. A small envelope lay on the ground. Frowning, she walked over, picked it up, and slid out a heavy linen paper.

She flipped open the note.

Your attendance is cordially requested at dinner tonight at six. Attire is semi-formal.

Bishop stared down at it in shock. Semi-formal? What kind of craziness was this? She looked down at her jeans, T-shirt, and jacket and frowned.

Definitely not semi-formal, but she had no intention of going along with some crazy dress code. She was a prisoner, not a guest.

Sniffing the air, she wrinkled her nose. Of course, she did kind of stink. At that other room, she had done a quick wash just to get the blood off. She wasn't sure how long ago that had been, but she felt like she'd slept for a long while. She wouldn't mind not smelling herself.

A door across the room beckoned to her. She walked

over and then opened it a crack. It was a huge walk-in closet. Clothes on hangers lined the walls. There was shelf upon shelf of shoes and two tall built-in dressers. Whoever's closet this was had a lot of clothes. She did a quick search for a weapon, but there was nothing like that. There was, however, a black dress with big taffeta sleeves.

The dress was gorgeous and obviously expensive. She flipped a look at the tag and saw that it was her size.

That's strange.

She grabbed the next dress, a red strappy number, and pulled it down. It was also her size.

A cold chill broke over her, and she quickly checked all the remaining dresses. They were all her size and all brand new. A subsequent search of the clothes hanging on the racks and the drawers of underwear, socks, shirts, jeans, and everything else indicated that everything in that closet was in her size and also brand new with the tags still on.

Bishop stepped back, her skin crawling. There was no way that was a coincidence.

She backed out of the closet and sat on the bench at the end of the bed.

Grabbing the invitation, which she dropped on the bed before she searched the closet, she stared at it. There was no hint as to who it was from. But something strange was definitely going on here. This wasn't the Chinese trying to get a password from her. So what was actually going on?

Chapter Twenty-Seven

NOLA

Nola and Rafe had just reached the kitchen when Nola's cell phone rang. She answered it immediately. "Stan, what have you got?"

The CIA analyst's voice was shaky as he spoke. "I ran a background check on those two federal agents you asked about. They're dirty, Nola."

That wasn't exactly a surprise. "Dirty how?"

"Their names are Arthur Chalet and Jonathan Krepp. Chalet's been with the FBI for twelve years. Krepp's been with them for fourteen. They've both been assigned to the organized crime unit for the last five."

Nola scoffed. Agents with the organized crime unit being dirty, how unoriginal. "If they're dirty, how come they're still with the FBI?"

"Because nobody can prove it. They have a bunch of cases where critical witnesses just seem to go missing or critical evidence disappears. The FBI's even launched an investigation into them."

"When did they start the investigation?"

"Two months ago. But I think that Chalet and Krepp know that someone's onto them. I've traced a bank account to each of them that they've been slowly transferring all of their money into. I think they're getting ready to run."

"But not without one big payday," Nola murmured.

"That's what I'm thinking. And they did get a large amount just the other day: twenty thousand. In fact, they've gotten twenty thousand three times in the last year. And of course, it's put into their accounts in separate payments just under ten thousand dollars."

Nola nodded. Any payments above ten thousand would automatically trigger a look by the IRS. By keeping it just under, they were making sure they didn't raise any red flags.

"Do we have any idea where they took the body? Is there some sort of case that this is associated with?" Nola asked.

"Not that I can see. And I did some looking into the other cases that you mentioned. I can't be sure that it was Krepp and Chalet in all cases, but I did manage to get a look at the paperwork of two of them. While the signature is illegible, it seems to be the same illegible signature that they provided in Maryland."

"So it *is* them," Nola said.

"For the last five years, at least. But with this type of situation, they're probably at least the second group that have been called in."

Nola nodded. "You mean there was another team that you could track before them?"

"Two former FBI agents with the organized crime unit. They're both dead now," Stan said.

"Dead how?" Nola asked.

"One died in a car accident. And the other, hold on a second . . . Um, yeah, it was a boating accident. His body was found in pieces. He somehow walked into the propeller on the boat."

Nola narrowed her eyes. "Were there witnesses?"

"Yeah, for each one there was a witness. One saw the car drive off a cliff without even stopping. And the other saw the agent trip and fall right into the boat propeller while it was being worked on."

"And these witnesses?" Nola asked.

"I tried to track them down but wasn't able to. They're in the wind or they never existed. I couldn't find a trail for either of them."

Shocking, Nola thought. "What about Krepp and Chalet right now? Do you know where they are?"

"Not right this second. They've shut down their cell phones. According to their office, they have a week off. They seem to have gone dark."

Nola frowned, not liking the sound of that. "There must be a way to find them or to figure out who's paying them."

"I sent you the info on all the bodies, but I've also got Krepp and Chalet's past case files and notes. I started creating a spreadsheet with the relevant information. I can send it all over to you, see if maybe you can see something that I don't."

It was a long shot but it was also the only one they had. Nola nodded. "Good. Do it."

Chapter Twenty-Eight

BISHOP

Moving the chair from under the doorknob, Bishop placed it back where she'd found it. After checking the room again for cameras or hidden doors, she'd taken the world's fastest shower and pulled on a new shirt and socks along with her own pants boots and underwear. She was not wearing underwear some creep picked out for her.

Showering had nothing to do with that invitation. Ever since she had moved in with Nola, staying clean was an ingrained habit. She'd had too many years when feeling clean was merely a hope. Feeling clean gave her confidence and made her feel capable.

Now she patted her pocket where the string she'd taken from the other room sat. It might come in handy. The pen was already in her back pocket. A glance at the clock showed that it was just coming up on six o'clock.

She looked around the room, trying to see if there was anything she had overlooked in her earlier weapons search.

The table lamps were pretty heavy, but she couldn't exactly carry one of them around with her. The same went for the books along the bookshelves by the fireplace.

But there were a couple of glasses on a small bar over by the fireplace. If she broke one, she could use the glass shards. She should have thought of that sooner. She took a step toward them, but there was a knock on the door.

Pausing, she looked between the glasses and the door. There'd be no way to muffle the sound of the glass breaking, so she turned and took a deep breath. "Who is it?"

"My name is Melvin. I'm the house butler. I've come to escort you to dinner."

She pulled the chair away from the door as the door was unlocked from the outside. She waited, but the door didn't open. With surprise, she realized that Melvin was waiting for her to open it herself or to give him permission. She pulled it open.

A short, thin man with dark hair and even darker eyes stood at the threshold. Bishop nodded at him. "Melvin."

He gave her a small bow. "Miss Bishop. If you'll accompany me?"

She stepped outside and noted the guards that lined the hallway. Definitely no chance of making a break for it now. So, she nodded. "Lead the way."

Melvin stayed just in front of her, leading her down the long hall. Most of the doors were closed, but she caught a glimpse of an ornate dining room through one and an uncomfortable living room with what looked like extremely stiff chairs in another.

"Where are we going?" Bishop finally asked as they turned yet another corner.

"To the private dining room," Melvin said without turning around.

Bishop frowned at his back. "And who will I be dining with?"

"I'm afraid I can't tell you that. Ah, here we are." Melvin nodded to two men, who pulled open the double doors just ahead of Melvin. Melvin stepped to the side of the doorway and smiled, his arm extended toward the room.

Beyond him, Bishop could see a smaller dining area with a large ornate chandelier over the table. And standing next to the table was a man dressed all in black. Bishop moved into the room hesitantly, her focus on the man.

She didn't recognize him, and yet there was something familiar about him.

"Hello, Bishop," he said, stepping toward her.

Bishop frowned and then it clicked into place. She took a step back, her eyes growing wide. "You?"

Chapter Twenty-Nine

NOLA

The files from Stan arrived only five minutes later. Figuring it was going to be a long night, Nola had just made a new pot of coffee when her phone beeped to announce their arrival. She immediately forwarded the files to Avad. Then she carried the pot over to the table and placed it on a trivet.

Ileana, who was sitting at the kitchen table, lowered the phone that she had been holding to her ear. She nodded at Nola as she took a seat. "Margaret spoke with the other MEs involved in those other cases. It was the same situation for them. All they got was a cursory look at the bodies before the agents rolled in to confiscate them. But all agree that the heads were removed with a single swipe of a sword."

"Stan called. He's sent over a bunch of files for those two agents. I'm going to go through them and see if anything jumps out."

"I'll help you when I finish speaking with some of my contacts at the FBI. I want to get a better feel for these two agents myself," Ileana said.

"Good. I'll be in with Avad." Nola moved quickly down the hall and made her way to the security room.

The room was half armory, half monitoring station. Avad's little man cave within the estate. He sat at the computer monitors, scrolling through footage of street scenes.

Nola recognized the neighborhood around Bishop's home. "Find anything?"

Avad paused the recording he was looking at and shook his head. "Nothing. But I still have more to go through." He eyed Nola. "But you found something."

She sat down at the long wooden table in the middle of the room and flipped open a laptop. "I'm not sure. Stan sent me over all of the case files involving those two FBI agents. I was going to go through them and see if anything jumped out at me."

"Send me half of them. I'll go through them as well."

"I already did," she said, and then turned her attention to the task at hand: getting a better idea of who exactly these FBI agents were.

Hours later, Nola was still going through the files. Rafe and Ileana had each come in to help, although the two of them had left just a few minutes ago—Ileana to take a phone call and Rafe to get Sofia and Enzo to bed.

But Nola and Avad had stayed in the same spot, going through all of the research. Nola agreed with Stan that these two were obviously dirty. They had way too much money tucked away in foreign accounts. No government employee would be able to accumulate that much money in such a short amount of time. Not unless they had come into some inheritance along the way, and there was no evidence of that for either of these agents.

As to the source of the money, there were half a dozen possibilities, all of them related to some serious crime families. But Nola was going to need to cut those names down if she was going to figure out a connection to Bishop.

She flipped to a new file and did a cursory scan. It was from seven years ago. Reading the screen quickly, her attention shot back to a line halfway down the file. It listed the other agents who had been working with Chalet and Krepp on a case down in Memphis. Nola's eyes narrowed as she stared at one name, and then she grabbed her phone.

Avad looked up from his screen. "Do you have something?"

Nola stared at the screen. "I'm not sure. But it's the first connection I found with these two agents."

The call went straight through to voicemail. "I need to speak with you *now*. You need to drop whatever you're doing and get over here."

She disconnected the call and then immediately send a text message. *I need to speak with you asap.*

Three dots appeared, and then a reply came. *I'm on my way out. Can it wait?*

No. I need to see you now.

Three more dots.

Fine. I'm on my way.

Nola put the phone down and stared at the screen, not liking where her imagination was taking her. She couldn't handle a violation like this, and she really hoped that she was wrong.

Chapter Thirty

BISHOP
THIRTEEN YEARS AGO

The van smelled. Bishop sat crouched along the floor, staring around, not sure what exactly had happened.

Next to her, Ariel whimpered.

Bishop tightened her hold on her foster sister, who was only eight years old. "It's okay, Ariel. I'm here."

The words made Ariel cling to her even tighter. Bishop couldn't blame her. They were empty words. She didn't even know where here was besides an old, rusted dark-blue van.

There were six women in the van with them, including her foster mother. But Lenore didn't even look at her. In fact, she wasn't really looking at anything. She was too high for that.

Bishop had been with Lenore for six months. It actually had been a better situation than some of the other foster homes she'd been in. Lenore was a junkie, and she had lots of company at night that made Bishop lock her door and hide in the closet. But at least she had Ariel with her.

Ariel had shown up a month after Bishop. Lenore had managed to clean herself up well enough for the foster check. And for some reason, the state thought it was a good idea to give the woman another child.

Bishop had no idea what their qualifications were for letting someone take care of another living being. Within the foster system, it seemed to be only that the adult was breathing. She couldn't think of any other reason why someone would think a strung-out prostitute would make an excellent foster mother.

But then, she supposed excellence wasn't really their goal. They just needed to get the kids out of their care and into someone else's.

It had actually been going pretty well. Lenore ignored them, which was fine, and Bishop had taken care of herself and then once Ariel came along, she had taken care of Ariel as well. The two of them would even sleep in the same room, usually in the same bed, holding hands.

Bishop made sure she got to school, that she did her homework, that she ate, and that she had lunch for school. Bishop wasn't sure Lenore even knew that they went to school.

And then today, everything had changed. Two men had shown up after Bishop and Ariel got back from school.

They weren't Lenore's usual type of client. They were cleaner, and they looked healthier. In fact, one of them looked really strong. Plus, their clothes were really clean. They grabbed Lenore as Bishop and Ariel walked into the house.

The guy's eyes fell on Bishop, and the look in his eye

made it clear that they were not supposed to be seeing what was happening.

Bishop grabbed Ariel and sprinted down the hall.

But she had locked the front door. Her hands shaking, it took way too long for her to undo the locks, and by then, the guy had reached them. He grabbed each of them by the back of the shirt and pulled them from the door. "Where do you think you two are going?"

"Owen, what are you doing?" the other guy yelled.

Owen, who had a firm hold of them, half dragged, half shoved them back toward the kitchen. He stepped inside and shook each of them. "These two saw us. They were running for the door."

The other guy shook his head, looking at them. "What the hell is she doing with kids?"

"W-we're fosters," Bishop stammered out.

The guy holding Lenore grunted. "Who the hell would give Lenore fosters?"

Bishop completely agreed with the question but didn't say anything. She looked over at Ariel, whose mouth had fallen open, her eyes wide with fear.

"What do you want to do with them?" Owen asked.

"Well, we can't leave them here. And we can't have them going to the cops."

"We won't go to the cops," Bishop said.

The first man grinned. "Everybody says that. But eventually you'll go to the cops. Or the cops will come looking for you. Either way, you're coming with us."

After that, Bishop and Ariel had been loaded into the van with Lenore. Three other women and two other men were already inside.

The women were all restrained.

Owen restrained Bishop's and Ariel's feet but left their arms undone.

And for a split second, when he did it, Bishop could swear she saw regret on his face. But then he'd simply slammed the door shut.

They'd made two more stops for two more women, and then they'd started on a long drive. And it had been really long. So long that daylight turned into darkness.

They stopped once, but all Bishop could see was darkness out of the windshield. She was pretty sure the guys had just pulled over to the side of the road to pee. Only one of them got out at a time.

They didn't offer the same option to the women in the back. They just got back in the van and continued on.

It was daylight again before the van stopped. Ariel had fallen asleep sometime during the night, snuggled up against Bishop. Bishop had slept on and off, the rocking of the van making it difficult for her to stay awake. But that same rocking also slammed her head into the side of the van waking her right back up.

Bishop now swallowed hard as the van slowed and the driver rolled down the window, talking to someone outside before they continued on.

They'd arrived wherever they were supposed to be. She was sure of that. But she didn't feel any relief. She was sure that whatever was outside this van was definitely not going to be better than anything that had come before it.

The van pulled to a stop, and the two men got out. She could hear voices outside for a few minutes as they talked, and then the side door of the van slid open.

One woman who had fallen asleep nearly rolled out of it.

"Wakey, wakey," a man who Bishop hadn't seen before

said. He had a hard look in his eye, and he wore a gun at his waist.

Some of the women had already been awake and cringed away from him.

Lenore was awake too, and the drugs had worn off, but she was lethargic and shaking a little bit. She needed her next fix.

"Everybody out," the man ordered.

The women started to climb out of the van. Before Bishop or Ariel could stand, the back doors of the van opened.

The man who put Bishop and Ariel in there unsnapped the bonds around their ankles. "Don't try anything," he warned. "Come on."

Bishop nodded and helped Ariel out of the van.

Ariel gripped Bishop's hand tight. "I have to go to the bathroom," she whispered, shifting from foot to foot.

The mention of using the bathroom was enough to remind Bishop of exactly how full her own bladder was. She had been consciously trying not to think of it, but now that Ariel had said something, it was all she could think about. She started shifting as well.

The movement caught the attention of the man who had first opened the door. His eyes widened, and then he frowned as he stared at the two of them. "What the hell are kids doing here? We don't cater to that kind of clientele."

"Yeah, they were at one of the houses," Owen said. "They saw us. We had to bring them with us."

"Well, get rid of them," the man said with a wave of his hand.

Terror bolted through Bishop, and she stepped forward. "No, we can help."

The man raised his eyebrows. "Help how?"

"I can cook, and we clean really well," Bishop said.

The man scoffed. "I don't need some kids cleaning the place."

Owen shifted from foot to foot. "Actually, the place could kind of use a bit of a pick-me-up. It wouldn't be a bad idea to have someone in to clean it regularly."

The man stared at him. "And you think these two kids are going to do a good job?"

He shrugged. "I don't know. I mean, Lenore's place was looking pretty clean, and I'm pretty sure it wasn't Lenore."

The man stared at him. "Fine. They clean." His eyes roved over Bishop and Ariel. "And when they're old enough, they can join the stable."

He turned his back and then waved at the group of eight men who surrounded the van. "Get them inside, get them cleaned up, and then you each get to have a turn and see what kind of product we've got."

Bishop held tightly onto Ariel's hand.

Owen looked at the two of them. "You two come with me."

Bishop followed him as he led them into a tall two-story building. There was another building just a hundred yards to the right and another to the left. The ones across the street were abandoned storefronts.

She'd never been here before. And she wasn't sure why, but she knew they weren't in New York anymore.

"Where are we?" Ariel whispered.

Bishop shook her head, not willing to say the only answer she had for her.

Hell.

Chapter Thirty-One

It had been a year since Bishop and Ariel had been brought to the brothel. In that time, the two of them had seen way more than anyone their age should see.

Bishop had scoped out a small closet that the two of them slept in. It had locks on the inside that she bolted whenever the clients were there.

Usually, she and Ariel would clean the house and make food from around five a.m. to noon. After that, clients started to make their way in, and they would make themselves scarce.

A few months back, one of the clients had left an old computer, and she had pulled it into the closet. It didn't have internet access, but she had managed to play around with it a little bit and figured out a couple of programs that she could run and some games for Ariel to play.

It wasn't much by way of entertainment, but it was pretty good when they hadn't had anything like that for a while.

For the most part, the guys that guarded the place left

them alone. Owen, in particular, seemed to kind of keep an eye out for them. But he hadn't been around for the last couple of weeks.

In a weird sort of way, Bishop kind of missed him. He was a relatively friendly face.

The other women at the brothel didn't pay them any attention. They didn't really see much of them anyway. And usually when they did, they were either getting high or coming down from a high. It was the only way they could get through what they were forced to do.

But Bishop was getting worried. It had been a year, and she was thirteen now. She tried to wear clothes that were as baggy as possible to hide the fact that her chest was getting bigger.

And she'd seen the look from some of the guards. And she knew that in the not-too-distant future, she would be pulled into the brothel. She didn't know how she was going to handle that.

In her gut, she knew she wouldn't be able to do what the other women did. Which meant that they were going to force drugs on her until she was so out of her head, she wouldn't know what was happening to her.

She cringed at the idea of that. She'd rather die than go through that.

But her other worry was Ariel. Ariel would be alone once Bishop was taken away. Or worse, maybe they'd put her into the rotation as well, even though she was so young.

A couple of the guards had talked about how she might make a tasty treat. Either way, Bishop had to find some way to get the two of them out of there.

Today, she was going to slip out at around three p.m. She and Ariel never left the closet until five a.m., which was when everybody was ousted from the brothel. But she needed more information about the brothel during the other hours. She figured the afternoon was the safest, if anything here could be considered safe. So she was going to look around and see if maybe she could figure a way to get the two of them out.

She stared at the clock on the computer as time ticked on. Ariel was asleep next to her. Bishop tucked the blankets a little tighter around her.

She fell asleep in the afternoons, then she would wake up, and they'd have dinner, play some games and Bishop would read to her from one of the books that Owen had snuck them. Then after they played a few games of checkers, they would go to sleep.

Ariel was a good kid. Somehow, even with all of the ugliness around them, she was still innocent. Bishop had taken an old pillow and drawn a face on it with a marker.

Bishop had cut the fringe off on three sides so it only had fringe along the top, which looked like hair. She'd even drawn some ears. Ariel lay curled up with it next to her. She called the pillow Shelby. It wasn't exactly a toy, but it provided Ariel comfort, and that was all that mattered.

The clock on the computer shifted to 3:00.

Tremors rolled through Bishop, but she needed to see what was going on out there and maybe figure out a way to get out.

She'd heard that there was some sort of meeting at three o'clock that most of the guards had to attend. She was hoping that meant that they were leaving and there would be less guards on duty, which meant it would be a good time to look around. And generally there weren't a lot of clients around at that time either.

Bishop didn't like leaving Ariel behind, and with her asleep, the room would be unlocked. But there weren't a lot of options. She needed to find a way to get them out. That was more important than anything. She needed to do it alone. If Ariel was awake, she would want to go with her.

And she'd rather do it during the daytime. One of these nights, she was going to have to go out at three or four a.m. and gather some information from that time as well. That was probably a better time for them to escape, later in the night, when everyone would be tired.

But she wasn't quite ready to wander around this place that late. The brothel got really busy at midnight, and she didn't want to run into anyone. So three p.m. was her best bet.

She needed to do a quick run through and see where everyone was and then get back to the closet and just hopefully figure something out.

Standing up, she made her way to the door. She stood listening with her ear against it, trying to hear any sounds coming from the other side.

Bernice's loud cries came through loud and clear. Apparently she had a client with her.

Shutting out Bernice, she listened for the creak of the floorboards outside. Nothing. Slowly, she unlatched the lock and cracked the door open.

The hall was empty.

Two of the doors in this hall were shut, and she could hear noises behind them. Both Bernice and Hailey had company.

But Gemma and Candy's doors were open. Carefully, she slipped out into the hall and peeked into Gemma's room. Gemma sat on the bed, swaying softly, just staring at the wall.

Bishop slipped inside before she could think too much about it and made her way over to the window. Gemma's room overlooked the street. There were two guys standing down by the front door. The street itself was relatively empty. Few cars came down it.

She slipped out without Gemma having even realized she was there. She walked across the hallway to Candy's room. Candy wasn't there, so she slipped inside and looked out the back window.

There was a busy road about four hundred yards out on this side. She'd seen it over the last couple of months and wished that someone would just drive straight to the house and rescue them. But everyone on the highway just continued driving by.

But that busy road was where she was planning on taking Ariel. They would flag down a car and get help. She looked out the window and saw that there was only one guard standing out there.

There was a window on the side of Candy's room as well. She hustled over to it. There was a small alley outside and no one seemed to be there.

If she was able to get some sort of ladder, maybe they could lower themselves out and then wait until the guard in the back was distracted and make a run for it.

They were on the second floor, though, and it would be better if they could do that from the first floor because then they wouldn't need a ladder. She glanced over her shoulder at the door, debating. She needed to go down the stairs and see where everybody was.

Bishop hurried to the door and glanced outside. Gemma was still sitting on her bed, swaying and humming. Bishop stepped outside and walked carefully over to the stairwell.

Voices came from downstairs, but she didn't see anyone.

Hugging the wall, she walked quietly down the stairs, her heart racing.

There was no one in the front foyer, but she could see the shadows of the two guards outside.

Slipping down the hall, she heard a masculine voice coming from the dining room. She risked a glance inside, and her heart nearly stopped. There were twelve men inside. The meeting that they'd been talking about was happening here.

Standing at the front of the table was a man with gray-flecked hair, a strong forehead, and a hawk nose. And he looked at each of the men in the room.

"We'll be making the move on the O'Rourke's in a week. I need to know everybody in this room is prepared to do what needs to be done."

Each of the men around the table grunted their support.

Bishop was about to yank her head away from the doorway when a young boy standing against the far wall caught her eyes. His gaze latched onto hers.

Her eyes widened, and she let out a little cry before yanking her head back and covering her hand over her mouth. He'd seen her.

Quietly, but as fast as she could manage, she bolted for the stairs. She reached the top and glanced behind her but didn't see anyone.

She let out a breath and had just turned back to the hall when two hands grabbed her shoulders. "Well, now, who are you?"

Focused on the men downstairs, she forgot there were at least two men on the second floor. Her head jerked up, her eyes widening at the man standing in front of her. His pants were loose, his shirt hanging over his undone belt. He had brown hair. Licking his lips, he stared down at her. "Where have they been hiding you?"

Bishop tried to step back and tried to pull herself from his hands, but his grip only tightened. "Oh, no, little one. Pierre gets to try all the ladies in the house. I haven't seen you before, and I doubt anyone else has. So it looks like I'm first."

Bishop shook her head. "No. No, I don't work here."

Pierre grabbed her and yanked her into Candy's empty room. He slammed the door behind him and shoved her across the room. "You do now."

She rolled off the bed and got to her feet, backing away. But there was nowhere for her to go. There was a corner, and she was backed into it. Her head whipped from side to side, her heart racing. She couldn't let this happen. But she was trapped.

The man smiled at her and then lunged forward. He pushed her up against the wall. She let out a scream.

His hand covered her mouth. She bit it.

"You bitch." He backhanded her, and she went flying, slamming into the side table.

He grabbed her and threw her on the bed before dropping on top of her. Bishop screamed. "Get off of me!"

Pierre didn't say anything, too busy trying to undo his trousers.

Bishop tried to bring her knee up in between his legs, but he trapped her legs with his.

"No! No!" she screamed.

Then a shadow loomed behind Pierre.

Movement near his neck happened so fast that Bishop couldn't make it out. But she felt the blood as it sprayed onto her. His eyes widening, his mouth opened into a silent

O as more blood sprayed across Bishop's face. She turned her head, closing her eyes and mouth.

Pierre dropped on top of her.

She was shaking so hard she didn't think she'd even be able to open her eyes, but she finally managed to when the weight of Pierre was pulled off of her.

Opening her eyes, she scrambled up, her back hitting the headboard. The boy that she had seen downstairs stood next to the bed, a knife in his hand. He looked down at Bishop, and she stared back at him.

He wiped the blade on the sheets, retracted the knife blade, and slipped it into his pocket. "Are you all right?"

He was about Bishop's height, maybe a year or two older, and a little pudgy with acne all over his cheeks.

She looked up at him and then at Pierre, who lay on the ground, a pool of blood spreading quickly around him.

"It's okay. He won't hurt you again. I won't let anyone hurt you again." He extended his hand.

Bishop gripped it and let him pull her up.

Now Bishop stared into the face of that same boy, years later. "Jonas."

Chapter Thirty-Two

NOLA
NOW

Nola finished reading the file and found herself staring again at the familiar name. It wasn't possible. But the name was there in black and white.

Pushing back from the table, she went and got herself something to eat and tried to calm down her racing thoughts as she waited. She explained her thoughts to Ileana, who joined her in the kitchen. When she was done, she heard a car pull up out front.

Ileana raised a hand as Nola tensed. "Stay calm. This could be perfectly innocent."

Nola gave her a brief nod, knowing she was right, but her emotions were strung tight.

Avad walked to the front door and pulled it open.

Chandra stood with her hand raised, ready to knock. She let out a small laugh as she stepped past him and into the foyer. "Hey, Avad."

Obviously, Chandra had been on her way to somewhere fancy. She wore a show-stopping black dress that hugged every inch of her curves. A deep red velvet wrap hugged her muscular shoulders, and it slid down them as she looked at Nola and Ileana. "Now what's going on? I was on my way to a charity dinner. There are some big clients there that I was going to reel in tonight. And I'd really like to get to fishing."

"Bishop's missing," Nola said.

The mirth drained from Chandra's face. "Missing? What happened?"

After showing Chandra to the formal living room, Ileana quickly explained about what they'd found in Bishop's apartment. Too tense to sit, Nola positioned herself by the door, but Ileana glared at her and then the couch.

With a grunt, she left her position and took a seat next to Ileana. Avad took Nola's position by the door.

From her seat to Ileana's right, Chandra looked between the two of them. "Why didn't you call me sooner? What do you need?"

"We need to know about Special Agents Chalet and Krepp of the FBI's organized crime unit."

Chandra frowned, staring at her. "Chalet and Krepp? Who are they?"

Nola felt anger rise inside of her, but Ileana reached over and grabbed her arm. "You worked with them on a case down in Memphis. It was one of the last ones you worked before you left the government."

A look of understanding flashed across Chandra's face followed by a grimace. "Oh, those two."

"I take it you're not a fan?" Ileana asked.

Chandra shook her head. "No. In fact, I was pretty sure those two were on the take."

"And you didn't do anything about it?" Nola asked.

"It wasn't just one of my last cases with the government, it *was* my last case with the government. I spoke with my replacement and explained my concerns. But I doubt he did anything. You know how hard it is to build a case against an agent. I doubt that was the first act my replacement wanted to take on. Besides, it was a different agency. I was with Homeland at the time. But my superior did express their concerns to Chalet and Krepp's superiors."

"Why did you think they were corrupt?" Nola asked.

Chandra sat back, crossing her long legs. "Well, they were jerks, but that wasn't the reason—although it did make it easier to see them as being on the wrong side of the law. They just were a little too rough with some of the suspects. Rough to the point that it was counter to what we needed.

"When you're working with a witness, you need to finesse them into helping you. But these guys were like bulls in a China shop, at least with some of them. With others, they were choir boys. But the ones that they were rough with were the ones we actually needed. It was almost as if they were trying to mess up the investigation.

"Plus, there were a couple of things that just felt off. Dates and times that just weren't lining up. I don't remember all of the details right now, but I definitely got the feeling that they weren't trying their hardest to bring that case to a close."

"So if I told you they had foreign bank accounts that had lots of zeros in it, you wouldn't be surprised?" Nola asked.

"Surprised, no. Disappointed in the bureau? Yes." Chandra looked between all of them. "What does this have to do with Bishop? Did Chalet and Krepp grab her?"

"No, a guy named Chuck Fitzpatrick did. Do you know him?" Nola asked.

A frown marred Chandra's face before she shook her head. "No, the name's not ringing any bells. Who is he?"

"A two-bit hitman. He grabbed Bishop from her apartment," Nola said.

"So you know the guy's name and you don't have him yet? That's not like you. I expect you would have gone all Abu Ghraib on his ass by now," Chandra said.

"I'd be happy to, except the guy's dead," Nola said.

Chandra raised her eyebrows. "You?"

"Unfortunately not. Someone got to him before I could question him," Nola said.

"And let me guess: you don't have any idea who that might be," Chandra said.

With a sigh, Ileana leaned back. "All we know is that it's someone who likes to use a sword."

Chandra went still. "A sword?"

Nola narrowed her eyes. "You know something."

The lawyer didn't answer right away, and before she did, she shook her head again. "I don't know something, but I suspect."

Bringing her hand to her lips, Chandra's eyes shifted back and forth as if reading a file in her mind.

Both Ileana and Nola leaned forward. "What is it?" Ileana asked.

Chandra lowered her hand. "I can't say for sure that this is connected, but you're sure it was a sword that killed this Fitzpatrick guy?"

"Took his head right off his shoulders," Nola said.

A gasp escaped Chandra's lips as she sat back.

"This isn't the first time you've heard of this," Ileana said.

Chandra shook her head slowly. "No. There have been other cases."

Nola leaned forward. "Yeah, we pulled the files on those cases, but we're not seeing a connection, except that Chalet and Krepp, or people like them, took over the cases and made the bodies disappear."

"I'm not surprised. I'm betting they've been cleaning up their messes and making sure that there's no ties back to them," Chandra murmured.

"Back to who?" Nola demanded.

Swallowing hard, Chandra looked around the room. "Can somebody pour me a drink? This conversation's not going to be an easy one."

They moved from the living room into the kitchen. Ileana poured Chandra and herself a glass of wine. Nola turned down the offer, as did Avad. She didn't want anything cluttering her thoughts.

Ileana also brought out a tray of dips and fruit that they hadn't finished up earlier in the night. Chandra nodded her thanks as she grabbed a plate and loaded it up. "Thanks. I haven't eaten today."

Chandra took a bite and then wiped the side of her mouth. "I've been keeping an eye on the Wagner family."

The Wagners. The name slammed into Nola with the force of a train. "No, that's not possible."

Her eyes filled with regret, Chandra met Nola's gaze. "I'm afraid it is."

Avad frowned from over by the kitchen island. "Who are the Wagners?"

Visions of Bishop when Nola had first met her rolled through Nola's mind. "They're the scumbags I rescued Bishop from when she was just a child."

Chapter Thirty-Three

NOLA
TWELVE YEARS AGO

Nola stepped out of her office at Langley and walked along the hall, her hand itching to make the call. But she knew she needed to wait until she got outside. There were ears everywhere. She'd have to wait until she and her partner debriefed their supervisor about the latest case. It took thirty minutes.

Finally, the supervisor nodded. "Good work. I want you to guys take a couple of days off."

"Sounds good," Bill Jenkins said as he stood up.

Nola merely gave her supervisor a nod and headed for the door.

Bill picked up his pace to catch up with her. "Say, you got any plans for the next couple of days? You want some company?"

Nola rolled her eyes. Bill had been trying to get into her pants ever since they'd been partnered up three months ago.

And there was no chance that was ever happening. Not just because it would make work difficult but because he was one of those privileged kids who had somehow managed to get into the CIA. He had no real-world experience, and it was only his connections to his uncle, a senator, that got him in the door. He was an entitled jerk, and for some reason, he seemed to think that he was entitled to Nola.

"No," she said without breaking her stride.

He reached out and grabbed her hand, pulling her to a stop. "When are you going to stop playing these games?"

Looking him straight in the eyes, she grabbed his pointer finger and yanked it back to his wrist. "I don't play games."

He cried out, releasing her. "You don't need to be such a bitch about it."

"Apparently I do," she said before heading back down the hall and shoving the idiot from her mind.

She skipped the elevator and hustled down the stairs before making her way outside and into the parking garage. She quickly hopped behind the steering wheel of her old Honda and drove off the Langley grounds. She never made personal calls on the grounds. That was just asking to have your privacy invaded.

She waited until she was two miles from the campus before she pulled into a parking lot, and then she reached over to her glove compartment and pulled out her spare phone. She quickly dialed Chandra's number.

"Who is this?" Chandra asked.

Nola smiled. "It's Nola."

She could hear the frown in Chandra's voice. "Nola? I thought you were out of the country."

"I just got back. And I need a little help with something."

Chandra sighed. "Hold on, give me a second."

She could picture Chandra getting settled in behind her desk over in Homeland. "Okay, what have you got?"

"Human trafficking out of Chicago. The Wagner family."

Chandra grunted and then was silent for a few moments, and Nola knew she was checking the name on her computer. When Chandra let out a low whistle, Nola knew she'd found the right Wagner.

"Well, Elias Wagner has his finger in lots of different pies. He also appears to be an informant for the FBI. So if you're going to be building a case against him—" Chandra cut off, pausing for a second. "Wait a minute. You can't build a case against him. All of his crimes are US based. You have no jurisdiction here."

"This isn't a case, Chandra. This is personal."

Chandra was quiet for a moment. "All right. You're buying me dinner, and you can lay it all out. I'll bring my information and you bring yours."

"Deal," Nola said.

An hour later, Nola was sitting outside Grimaldi's at a table with a red-and-white tablecloth and a single candle. She'd only been there a few minutes when Chandra walked up with a smile. "Well, you are the best date I've had in months."

Nola grinned back at her. "You're the only date I've had in months."

Chuckling, Chandra took a seat. "We both really need to get better lives."

Nola grunted, not sure if she wanted a better life. She loved her job. She loved going to far-off countries and making sure that the ones other people couldn't touch got what was due to them.

And she had never really cared too much about having a social life, especially if it involved people like her partner, Jenkins.

The waiter came over and took their drink orders. Once he'd disappeared, Chandra leaned forward. "So what have you got?"

"A little girl that needs help." Nola explained to Chandra about how she'd tracked down Ariel, her friend from high school Beth's daughter, and how she'd disappeared from her foster home along with her foster mother and sister.

She was calm and methodical in her replay of facts. She didn't touch on the turbulent years she had spent looking, the sleepless nights, the dead ends and false leads. Nola had learned years earlier that Beth had a daughter, but when she joined the CIA and got cleared, she checked in on her. She just wanted to make sure that Beth's daughter had ended up with a good family.

She hadn't. She'd been bounced around from home to home until she simply disappeared, and no one had been looking for her.

No one except Nola.

All that, Nola kept to herself. Instead, she explained how she had finally tracked Beth's daughter to Wagner in Chicago.

Chandra listened quietly, and when Nola was done, she nodded. "There are eyes on Wagner's different establishments. Apparently he's got a couple of brothels that are pretty well known."

Anger flared inside Nola. "And they're allowed to just continue?"

"Like I said, Wagner's got some protection. But if we

find some kids in one of his brothels, well, that protection is going to disappear pretty quick."

"So when can I get information on those sites?"

"Right now." Pulling a USB stick from her bag, Chandra slipped it across the table toward her. "I brought it with me just in case. There are three potential sites. But they're well-armed. You're going to need help."

Placing her hand on the flash drive, she slid it closer to her and lifted an eyebrow. "Are you offering?"

Chandra nodded. "This Wagner guy, he's untouchable. And I've seen the bodies of some of the people that have crossed him. He doesn't deserve our protection. So hell yeah, I'm with you. As soon as we find a location I'm going to call in a team."

Nola nodded as she grabbed the flash drive and slipped it into her pocket. "Good."

It took two days for Nola and Chandra to get everything in place so that they could scope out the three possible locations in Chicago.

Once they did, it was shockingly easy to get into each of them.

Nola and Chandra had shown up as gas inspectors and while being led into the house had placed cameras that would allow them to see what was going on inside.

The first two houses had been a bust. They got recordings of plenty of illegal activity, but no kids. The camera in the third house, however, finally showed them what they were looking for.

The two girls had appeared just after dawn. The older one kept an arm around the younger one as she checked out the first floor to make sure there was no one around. Then the two of them set to cleaning.

Chandra leaned forward, her eyes narrowed. "They have them cleaning?"

Nola couldn't pull her gaze from the little girl. She looked so much like Beth. "It's better than what else they could have them doing in there."

Chandra grunted. "That's not much of a consolation. Okay, I'll bring in a SWAT team."

Nola stared at the two little girls on the screen.

The older girl was obviously looking out for the younger one, carrying the heavy buckets, making sure that she had everything she needed and staying close by her side. She would smile whenever she looked at Ariel, but when she turned away, a look of worry would cross her face.

Nola's heart clenched at the sight. That poor kid. Nola had had a rough childhood but not cleaner-in-a-brothel rough.

Next to her, Chandra was talking on the phone in low tones before she hung up. Nola looked over at her. "Well?"

"They'll be here in four hours."

Nola nodded. Four hours. Ariel had possibly been in there for at least a year. Four more hours would be all right.

Chapter Thirty-Four

Four hours stretched into five and then six. Nola and Chandra were sitting in an SUV just down the street from the brothel when Chandra finally got word that the team was on their way.

It was taking everything in Nola not to sprint down the street and grab those girls out of that house on her own. But she knew that she was a visitor on this particular mission. She needed to follow procedures or whatever they found wouldn't be used against Wagner.

And she wanted that guy to be behind bars for a nice, long time.

Chandra had even managed to get a warrant for the surveillance on Wagner's locations. They were now doing a simultaneous sweep of all three sites. That was what was causing them to take a little more time. Organizing three strike teams was a lot more difficult than just organizing one.

"They'll be here in five," Chandra said, closing her phone.

"And they know there are kids on site in this one, right?"

"They've been informed."

Nola nodded, and then the two of them waited in silence. They only had eyes on the first floor. But from the schematics of the place, they knew that there were four bedrooms on the second floor and one large closet.

She had a feeling that the second-floor closet was where the girls slept. The other bedrooms were too big, and she doubted anyone would waste that valuable real estate on someone not making them money. Plus, they had crept downstairs, which meant they were staying on the second floor.

The house itself was relatively quiet. She'd seen a few guards walk through, but no one other than the girls. The women of the house were no doubt sleeping off last night's activities.

A van pulled up behind them, and Chandra nodded. "Here we go."

Nola got out of the passenger side of the car and immediately went back to the trunk to pull out her gear. She slipped a bulletproof vest on over her T-shirt as Chandra went over to talk to the team.

A man hustled up out of the van and spoke with Chandra. From Chandra's body language, it was obvious she was not enjoying the conversation.

Chandra walked back to Nola, turning her back on the man. Nola held out a bulletproof vest. "What's going on?"

Grabbing the vest, Chandra grimaced. "They're a bunch of cowboys. That one even called me 'little lady.' Told me that you and I had to stay in the back and that we could go in as soon as the house was cleared."

"You reminded him about the kids?"

Chandra nodded. "Yeah."

Her phone beeped. Chandra pulled it out and answered it while she was strapping on her vest. "What?"

Chandra eyes grew wide as she looked at Nola. "Damn it."

A feeling of dread rolled through Nola. "What?"

Snapping the phone shut, Chandra quickly tightened her vest. "They didn't wait. The other two houses have already been breached."

Nola went still for a moment before she glanced at the house. "Someone's going to warn them."

"They probably already have," Chandra said.

With Beth's face in the forefront of her mind, Nola grabbed an M4 from the trunk and sprinted toward the house with Chandra right on her heels.

Chapter Thirty-Five

Yells came from inside the house. The two guards at the front opened fire as soon as they caught sight of Nola and Chandra.

The two them dove behind a car as gunshots rang out from inside the house as well.

"God dammit," Chandra said.

The SWAT van pulled up on the street in front of the house, and SWAT team members poured out.

Nola shook her head. This was a disaster. The guys at the brothel had been given the heads-up, and now instead of going in quietly as planned, they were doing a full-frontal assault.

Nola nodded to the alley between the brothel and the abandoned house next door. "Cover me."

Chandra nodded. "Go."

Nola took off at a sprint. Bullets chewed up the ground next to her and then stopped as Chandra took out the shooter who was standing in the second-floor window.

Nola bounded across the sidewalk and into the alley.

It looked like Nola had gotten lucky. None of the shooters was concentrating on the alley yet. She sprinted down the side of the alley to a small door leading into a basement.

She had no idea what was behind that door, but she knew that anyone who kept kids locked up in a brothel would not hesitate to use those kids as shields, if they didn't just kill them outright to make sure that they couldn't talk.

Nola kicked in the door and scanned the area. It was a basement. A couple of old bedframes sat in a corner and some boxes, but it was silent. She moved forward quietly but no one was there. She headed to the stairs and walked up slowly, her gun trained while her eyes shifted focus on the door up at the top of the stairs and also continued to scan behind her.

She made it up to the top of the stairs and paused. There were no sounds coming from directly behind the door, but she could hear gunshots in the distance. She turned the handle. It was unlocked. She slid it open a few inches and peeked outside. It opened into the hallway.

At the end of the hall, she could see that the two men who'd been standing at the door had now moved inside. Staying in the cover of the basement door, she aimed and took out the first one, catching him in the back of the head. The second one turned around, and she caught him in the neck.

Both men dropped.

She cast a glance down the hall into the kitchen and saw two more men were firing out the back. Apparently, everybody was now awake.

Female screams came from the second floor. Two women lay on the stairwell bleeding. The girls had last been seen in the living room to the left.

A scream rang out, young and high pitched.

One SWAT team member bolted in through the front door, the door Nola had just cleared. It was the leader, the one Chandra had been speaking with. The SWAT team leader headed straight for the living room on the right.

A second scream rang out. That was definitely a kid.

Nola bolted forward.

"Put her down, man," the SWAT team leader said.

"No chance. You let me go or she dies."

Nola skidded to a halt at the opening of the living room. There was a love seat, a couch, and two chairs sitting on a red floral rug.

And standing in front of the couch was a man with a gun to Ariel's head.

Chapter Thirty-Six

Movement from the corner of her eye showed that the other young girl was crouched down low by the side of the couch. She caught Nola's gaze, and then the girl looked at Ariel, as if telling Nola to save her.

Nola gave the girl a slight nod.

The guard held the gun to Ariel's head and screamed, "Back up now or I kill her."

The SWAT leader shrugged. "Then you kill her. But I'm not letting you out of here."

Nola's blood boiled.

A noticeable tremor ran through the little girl hiding behind the couch. Her mouth dropped open a split second before she darted forward, kicked the man in the back of a knee, and grabbed for Ariel. "Let her go."

The SWAT team leader looked like he was about to take a shot, but the man was moving too much. He didn't have a clean shot. He was as likely to hit the girl or Ariel as the gunman. But he still tightened his hold. His finger moved toward the trigger.

Nola charged the SWAT leader, dropping him to the ground.

His head slammed into the wooden floor with a thud. "What the hell?"

"You don't have a shot," Nola hissed. Then she scrambled off him and stepped in front of him, her hands up. The young girl who'd tackled the man had been flung away and now lay curled up by the fireplace. Her chest moved, but her eyes were closed.

Nola kept her hands up. "Okay, okay. Let's all just calm down," she said to the gunman.

The man with the gun looked anything but calm. His cheeks were red, his eyes glassy, and sweat pooled under his armpits. "I'm not going back to prison! I'll kill her and me before I let that happen."

"I believe you," Nola said as she reached behind her and slipped the knife from the sheath that she'd secured back there. "I wouldn't want to go back to prison either."

"You're going to get me a helicopter and get me out of here."

Taking another step forward, Nola nodded, keeping one hand up toward the man, the other one hidden behind her back. "I can do that. I *will* do that. I just need to know that you're going to—"

She flung the knife. It embedded itself in the man's thigh. His arm jerked away from the girl, and that was all Nola needed. She burst forward, wrenching the man's wrist and twisting it painfully.

He cried out, releasing the girl.

Nola kneed him in the groin and then slammed an elbow across the man's face before wrenching the gun from his hand. Turning it, she slammed the butt of it against his temple. He crashed to the ground with a groan.

Ariel had scrambled around Nola on hands and knees and over to the other girl.

The other girl was just sitting up. She blinked hard and then grabbed Ariel, pulling her into her and rocking her carefully. "It's okay, Ariel. It's okay." She looked over at Nola. "It is okay, isn't it?"

Inching the girls back toward the corner of the room, she stood in front of them and at the edge of the doorway to make sure that anyone who tried to get to the girls would have to go through her first. "It's going to be."

Chapter Thirty-Seven

It had been an absolute circus after they'd taken out the gunmen in the brothel. Ten people had been shot inside the brothel, six of them gunmen and four of them the women who worked there. Two of the SWAT team had taken bullets as well, although they would live.

The SWAT team leader was raising holy hell about Nola's actions.

Chandra had quickly ushered Nola away from all of it, telling her not to say a word and to let her handle it. Nola was more than happy to comply with that. She sat with the two girls and waited for their turn with the EMTs.

Neither girl spoke. They just sat quietly, holding on to one another.

Nola had snagged a blanket from one of the rigs and had wrapped it around the two of them. They both look so small.

"What's going to happen to us now?" the older girl asked.

"The EMTs are going to come over and check you out,

and then you're going to have to talk to some people and tell them how you came to be in this place," Nola said.

Ariel shifted, and the older girl hugged her a little tighter. Ariel buried her head into the girl's chest. "I mean what's going to happen to us? Are they going to put us into another foster home?"

Nola looked into the young girl's eyes. She nodded. "Probably."

Tears crested over the girl's eyelashes, and she reached up to wipe them away. "Is there any way they could put us together, at least?"

Nola wanted to say yes, that would definitely happen, but she knew that wasn't the case. "I don't know. But I promise you I'll make sure that wherever you go, it's to a good home not like the places you've been before."

"Okay," the girl said, the resignation in her tone making it clear how much faith she placed in adult's promises.

"What's your name?" Nola asked the older girl.

"Bishop. This is Ariel."

"Well, Bishop, Ariel, my name is Nola James. And I promise you that from this point on, your life is going to get better."

Bishop looked up at her with eyes way too old for such a young face. "Don't make promises you can't keep."

But Nola had kept that promise. Nola reached out to Beth's parents and told them about their granddaughter. After losing Beth, Nola knew that they had looked for her but were unable to find her. They had dropped everything and rushed to Chicago to take in the young girl.

Nola had been there when they arrived. Bishop and

Ariel had been put in a temporary holding facility. It was clean and safe, and Nola was there every day to make sure that they were all right.

Now Bishop sat with Nola on the front stairs of the home as they watched the meeting between grandparents and granddaughter on the front lawn. The social worker stood by, smiling at the happy reunion. Tears ran down the face of Mrs. Landry.

But Ariel looked unsure, taking a step back as Mrs. Landry reached for her. Ariel looked over her shoulder at Bishop, who nodded. *It's okay*, she mouthed. *They're good people.*

Ariel looked back at the Landrys and finally let her grandmother hug her. Her grandmother burst into tears. Mr. Landry, ever stoic, stood back, but Nola could see the tremor of emotion in his hands. Still tall and regal looking, with a little more gray at his temples, Mr. Landry looked over at Nola his gaze meeting hers. Recognition and appreciation passed across his face before he nodded.

Nola nodded back.

"They are good people, aren't they?" Bishop asked.

"They are. And Ariel is their granddaughter. Their daughter, Beth, she was my best friend."

"That's good. That she's got someone that's going to love her."

There was no jealousy, no bitterness in the statement. Bishop was a young girl with an old soul. She knew that this was better than any outcome Ariel could have gotten within the system.

Over the last few days, Nola had spent more and more time with her and Ariel. Ariel had talked about how Bishop was the one who had kept her safe. She didn't phrase it that way, but she talked about how Bishop always made sure that she ate, how Bishop always showed her whatever she needed to do, how Bishop always did this, and Bishop always did that.

It was clear that the reason that Ariel was safe today was because Bishop had been there to protect her.

Ariel looked back at Bishop, who waved slowly at her, forcing a smile to her face. The two of them had already said their goodbyes. Bishop had done most of the talking, saying how much Ariel was going to be loved and that she'd be in a real home. Then the Landrys had shown up, and Bishop had been the one who'd walked Ariel over to the social worker.

She'd kept that smile in place the whole time, still looking out for Ariel. But now Nola could tell she was trying her hardest to hold back her tears as Ariel took the hands of her grandparents and walked toward the parking lot. Without a word, Bishop moved to the edge of the porch. Ariel glanced back, and Bishop waved with a smile, even as a single tear rolled down her cheek.

Nola stood with Bishop as they watched Ariel climb into the back of the silver Toyota. Then Mr. And Mrs. Landry got in, and the car was moving. Nola stood with Bishop and watched until the car disappeared, neither of them speaking.

When Bishop turned back to her, Nola was surprised to see tears rolling down the young girl's cheeks. She hadn't made a sound. Blowing out a breath, Bishop wiped at the tears. "She's going to be happy, right?"

"Yes. She'll be happy. They'll take good care of her."

Bishop nodded. But she made no move to step away from the edge of the porch. And she didn't ask what was in store for her.

Nola studied the young girl. She knew the statistics.

Bishop was too old to be a cute kid who someone would be interested in adopting. She was reaching that horrible age for foster kids when no one wanted to take on a teenager. "I've been thinking about where you're going to go."

Bishop nodded. "Yeah, I've been kind of wondering that myself."

"If you want—and it'll probably only be temporary—but I was thinking maybe you could come live with me for a little while. I mean, I'm not much of a mom type. But you'd be safe and you'd have a home, if you want it."

Bishop looked over at her, and Nola could feel the calculation going on in the girl's head and also the desperate need to believe that something good might be around the corner. She nodded slowly. "Yeah, I think I'd like that."

Chapter Thirty-Eight

NOLA
NOW

Images of Bishop protecting Ariel rolled through Nola's mind, along with the condition of the women in the house. If Nola hadn't gotten to both girls, she had no doubt they would have one day been put up for sale like the other women of the house. The idea of it made her stomach bottom out and her skin crawl.

But it was that image of Bishop accepting Nola's offer of protection, of a home, that burned brightest in her mind.

"Why do you think this is attached to the Wagner family?" Ileana asked.

Giving Nola an apologetic look, Chandra looked between the other occupants of the room. "You all know how Bishop came to live with Nola, right?"

Ileana nodded, as did Avad as he moved closer. Nola started at seeing Rafe sitting in the other chair. Lost in her memories, she hadn't seen him enter the room.

Chandra continued. "The Wagners were the ones that had grabbed Bishop initially. It was the father, Elias Wagner, who'd been the head of the Wagner crime family. He dabbled in lots of different services, from drugs to prostitution to gambling. He pulled Bishop into one of his brothels. Nola and I got her out, along with another little girl."

Nola nodded, her skin feeling tight as she pictured those girls in that horrible house.

"They were supposed to lock Elias Wagner away," Nola said. After everything that had happened, she'd been assured Wagner would go away. She hadn't followed up, though, because Bishop had needed her, and she'd trusted the assurances that she'd been given.

"They did, for about three years. But he turned on some other crime bosses, made a few deals, and then he was out again," Chandra said.

"Where is he now?" Rafe asked.

"Six feet under. He died two years ago," Chandra said.

Nola frowned, trying to remember the details of the Wagner family, but she'd only done a cursory search of them at the time before she'd gone in. Now that she thought about it, there had been a child, but he was only about Bishop's age at the time of his father's arrest. She'd seen him only once or twice and from a distance. "So who's running the family?"

"It was believed that the family's lawyer took over the reins, but I've been keeping an eye on the Wagners over the years. And it looks like now the son is fully in charge."

Nola pictured the small chubby little boy. "What was his name?"

"Jonas. Jonas Wagner."

"Okay, but what makes you think that Jonas Wagner is connected to these cases?" Nola asked.

Chandra let out a sigh, grabbing a roll and breaking off a piece. "Jonas didn't exactly have an easy childhood. I kind of get the feeling that he might have been a good kid if he'd had a better life, a better father. But that die was cast."

Taking a bite of the roll, Chandra continued. "After his father's arrest, he was sent away to boarding school. He had a tough time there as well from what I can tell. He was picked on and bullied by the other kids because he was so small for his age. And it seems he didn't really spend a lot of time making friends in his earlier life. He had a breakdown when he was a teenager, and he was sent away to a mental institution for two years."

"A breakdown?" Ileana asked.

"When he was at boarding school, he became obsessed with samurai history. He read everything he could on their practices and mythology. Every paper he had a chance to, he incorporated samurais into it. It got to the point where he began to think that he was the reincarnation of a warlord," Chandra explained.

"So that's what got him sent away?" Rafe asked.

Chandra shook her head. "No, what got him sent away was when he grabbed an ancient sword from a display case at the school and tried to take off a classmate's head with it."

Well, that would certainly get you carted off, Nola thought.

"When they grabbed him, he was screaming about it being his destiny and him needing to fulfill it," Chandra said. "He was locked up for years. From what I could tell, he was caught in a full-blown delusion."

"How did he get out?" Nola asked.

"His father insisted. The elder Wagner was sick and knew he was dying. He wanted his son to learn the family business." Chandra paused. "From what I understand, part of that involved bringing over a sword master from Japan and giving Jonas lessons."

"The father fed his samurai delusion?" Nola asked.

"It looks like. After his father's death, young Jonas had a dojo built into each of his homes, and all of his homes were refurnished to give them a more Eastern flare," Chandra said.

"So, you think Jonas killed Chuck?" Rafe asked with a frown.

"Yes," Chandra said. "Once his father died, I think something snapped inside of Jonas. It was just after that that the bodies started appearing."

"How do you know all of this?" Nola asked.

Chandra met Nola's gaze. "Everyone has that case that sticks with them. The Wagner case was it for me. I've been keeping an eye on the Wagner family. It was just a horrible case. And that man never should have been allowed back out of prison. The fact that they cut a deal with him, it never sat right with me. So I just kind of kept my ear to the ground to hear what was happening. And I started hearing about how someone who had insulted Elias or Jonas Wagner turned up dead . . . decapitated with a sword."

"Was it ever linked back to Jonas?" Nola asked.

"No. In fact, very few people seem to know about his time in the mental institution. And the school, they've covered up the incident about the attack with the sword on the other student. I managed to get to one of the janitors before he got paid off. When I followed up with him, he refused to talk to me. But if anyone is behind this, I think it's Jonas."

Nola frowned. "But why? Why would they be interested in Bishop now after all these years?"

Chandra shook her head. "I don't know. But I think that's where you need to start. And I think I have someone you can ask about that."

Chapter Thirty-Nine

BISHOP

Standing across from her was a tall man, easily a foot taller than when Bishop had last seen him. But she could see the boy she had once known in his eyes and the scars from that horrible acne he'd had. It was him. It was Jonas.

He looked at her intently. "Years ago, I promised you I wouldn't let anyone hurt you. And I intend to keep that promise."

Bishop felt uncomfortable under the weight of his gaze. It took Bishop a moment to remember the promise he'd made. She shook her head, taking a step back. "Jonas, what are you doing?"

His expression switched from serious to joyous in the space of a second. "I'm pleased you remember me. I worried you might not. It's been so long."

He wasn't wrong about that. But when someone saves you from being raped, they tend to stick in your mind. "Of course I remember you, Jonas. You saved me."

"And I will always take care of you. I promised."

Bishop wasn't sure what to say to that. The look that Jonas was giving her, it was unsettling, as if he knew her, as if there was this strong connection between the two of them.

The truth was Bishop hadn't thought about him in years. After she had been rescued from the brothel, she'd completely shut out all of those memories. It was too difficult a time to visit.

But apparently Jonas here hadn't had the same approach. "Why did you bring me here?" she asked.

He shook his head as if disappointed. "You don't remember yet."

She frowned. "Remember what?"

"You and I are meant to be together. We were together a long time ago, and then our enemy tore us apart. But I won't let that happen in this lifetime."

There was a fanatical gleam in Jonas's eye that made Bishop more than a little nervous. Whatever had happened to him in the intervening years since she'd last seen him, he obviously had slipped loose of the sanity collar that most people wore.

"Why do you believe that we are meant to be?" she asked carefully.

"I don't just believe it—I know it." His eyes grew intense, and he took a step forward.

Bishop automatically took a step back.

His face fell. And then he seemed to give himself a shake. "It's all right. I know you don't remember yet. But once you do, you'll see how we have loved each other across time. And we are meant to be. But the only way for us to stay safe and to be with one another is for me to defeat our common enemy."

Bishop frowned. "I don't understand. Who do you think our common enemy is?"

Jonas's face darkened. "The one who took you from me. The one who took you from me eons ago. He has come back."

Her confusion only grew greater at that statement. She struggled to figure out who he was possibly talking about. She tried to remember if there were any men in the group who had broken into the brothel to rescue her and Ariel. She supposed there were a few, but it was Nola who had rescued her.

"I see your confusion. Our enemy has disguised himself as a woman in this lifetime. And under that guise, he has been able to walk this world without people seeing who he truly is. But I recognize him. I will always recognize the Dragon of Echigo, no matter what form he takes. And I will bring him to his end."

Bishop's heart clenched. "How? How are you going to bring him to his end?"

Jonas smiled. "I have been training for years for this moment. But first, my enemy, *our* enemy, will have to prove that she is worthy of facing me. I will set obstacles up for her to get through. If she succeeds, then she will face me one on one, and I will destroy her."

"And if she doesn't succeed?" Bishop asked.

"Then she will still be dead." Jonas offered Bishop his arm. "Now, I'm sure you're hungry. I had the chef prepare a Beef Wellington. It's really quite delicious."

Bishop's skin crawled at the idea of touching him. He was obviously insane. But she also knew she had to play along, at least for a little bit, until she could get word to Nola and warn her, even though she had no idea how she was going to do that.

But she would figure it out. So she curled her arm into his and forced a smile to her face. "That sounds delicious."

Chapter Forty

NOLA

Nearly forty minutes later, Chandra's car moved quickly down the dark country road with Nola behind the wheel and Chandra in the passenger seat. Chandra nodded to the well-lit driveway up ahead. "Turn in there."

Nola did and brought the car to a stop in front of the Tudor-style mansion. This neighborhood wasn't as expansive as where Ileana's estate was, but all the homes were on at least two acres and were well maintained. And each had a look that screamed old money.

Leaning over the steering wheel, Nola looked up at the well-cared-for home. "Apparently psychiatry pays well."

"Yes, it does. Dr. Blake Legion comes from a wealthy family. He's also made a lot of money in private practice. But he also donates his time to some worthy causes. We've become friendly through those associations."

"And it's a complete coincidence that he happens to have been the psychiatrist that worked with Jonas Wagner?"

Watching her from the corner of her eyes, Chandra smiled. "Perhaps not a complete coincidence. Like I said, I've been keeping an eye on the Wagner family."

"You can take the girl out of intelligence work, but you can't take the intelligence work out of the girl," Nola said.

Chandra laughed softly. "I guess so. It's just, like I said, there are cases that stick with you. And this was one for me."

"Are you sure that just dropping in on him is the best approach?" Nola asked.

"Catching him by surprise is going to be the only way we're going to get to speak with him. We can't let Wagner know that we suspect him. And I have a feeling that the doctor's communications might be occasionally checked to make sure he's being a good little boy."

Nola stared up at the house. "If he knows something, I'm going to get those answers. You understand what that means, right?"

Chandra swallowed. "I do. And I agree with you. We need to find Bishop. Because if Jonas Wagner has her, then she's not safe." She opened the car door and stepped outside.

Nola stepped out the other side and stared up at the house. *All right, doc, let's hear what you have to say.*

Chapter Forty-One

The gong of the doorbell rang out behind the thick heavy wooden door. Nola stood just behind Chandra, who was still in her charity dinner finery. A light flicked on in the hallway beyond the door before she heard the unlocking of the bolt.

A small man stood in the doorway with a dressing gown over his pajamas. His hair had turned silver and was closely cropped. He had a strong forehead and bright blue eyes as he peered at her. "Chandra? Is everything all right?"

"I'm afraid not, Blake. We need to speak with you."

For the first time, Blake's eyes fell on Nola. She met his gaze, unflinching. The look in her eyes made Blake's eyes widen.

"It's kind of late," he said, not opening the door any wider.

Chandra smiled. "I assure you, we wouldn't have come if it wasn't of the utmost importance."

Blake stood uncertainly in the doorway before he finally nodded and opened the door. "Of course, of course. Come in."

"Thank you, Blake." Chandra smiled at him as she stepped inside. Nola followed her in silently.

The doctor showed them to a formal sitting room to the left of the front foyer. The walls were done in dark wood paneling with a red Persian rug dominating the room. Navy blue velvet curtains framed a large window that overlooked the side yard.

"Please, have a seat." Blake gestured to a leather couch. Chandra and Nola took a seat as the doctor settled into a stiff-backed velvet chair.

Nola noted that the chair was slightly higher than the couch, giving the doctor a more elevated position. It was a power move, perhaps left over from his days of interacting with patients, but it was notable nonetheless.

"Now, what can I do to help you?" he asked.

Chandra took a breath. "We need to speak with you about one of your patients."

Blake was already shaking his head before Chandra had finished speaking. "Chandra, you know I can't speak about any of my patients. Doctor–patient confidentiality precludes me from—"

"We think one of your patients has abducted a young woman," Chandra replied. "You know that if you see any indication that a patient is going to harm himself or another, you are legally required to provide information to assist."

Blake studied her, shaking his head. "I don't have any patients that I know would harm themselves or others currently."

"What about in the past?" Nola asked.

"I've had patients that I have been worried about from time to time, and I have informed the authorities."

"What about Jonas Wagner?" Chandra asked.

Blake's eyes narrowed. "Jonas Wagner?"

"You treated him at Hartgrove Hospital. Don't you remember?" Nola asked.

The doctor flicked a gaze at Nola before turning his attention to the coffee table between them. "I'd have to check my notes. I'm not sure who—"

"We know that you remember Jonas Wagner. We know that Jonas Wagner is not someone that would be easily forgotten. Someone who thinks he's a samurai?" Chandra asked.

Looking up, Blake shook his head, his eyes pleading. "I can't tell you anything, Chandra."

Nola leaned forward, but Chandra put out a hand to hold her back. "A young woman is missing. The man who took her was decapitated with a sword. The woman who was taken knew Jonas Wagner years ago. Is there any chance that he mentioned her to you?" Chandra asked.

Blake looked between the two of them. "This young woman, is she biracial? With big curly hair?"

Chandra nodded. "Yes."

The doctor's shoulders slumped. "Damn."

Chapter Forty-Two

JONAS

Joy, pure joy rolled through Jonas as he sat across the long dining room table from Bishop. After all of these years, finally, they were together again.

She looked so beautiful in the dim candlelight. When he'd first seen her in that horrible house, he couldn't believe his eyes. She'd peeked through the doorway, and it had been like an angel staring straight at him.

That fateful day, he'd only gone with his father to work because he insisted that he begin to learn more of his business. Jonas had found the whole enterprise distasteful, but it was his birthright.

He'd come a long way since then in understanding how these women weren't good for anything other than their bodies. At least by giving them a place to live and a job, they were giving back to society—and his wallet.

But that day, he'd still been so naive, thinking that it was unfair for the women to be placed in such a situation. Of course, it was during that time that he had first seen Bishop.

He honestly thought she was a hallucination at first. This beautiful, innocent girl staring at him with those large eyes of hers.

After she disappeared from the doorway, he'd slipped out of the room, and it taken him a moment to realize she had gone back upstairs. Her cry alerted him as to where she was, and he'd hurried up the stairs, surprised that no one else had heard it.

Or perhaps they were so used to the cries of females in that place that they simply didn't react to them anymore. But as soon as he heard the cry, he'd known it was the girl. He hurried up the stairs, his heart pounding.

He wasn't a big kid. In fact, he was the smallest in his class. And he was not athletic like the other kids in his class either. But that day, that day he'd had more than enough strength for what needed to be done.

Stopping at the top of the stairs, he heard the commotion coming from the bedroom on the right. As he stood in the doorway, he'd felt a rage roll over him that he'd never felt before. The man lay on top of the girl, fumbling with himself as she tried to get out from underneath him. Her cries of "no" rolled through Jonas's mind again and again for years. Without a single conscious thought, he'd slipped his knife from his pocket and released the blade.

Before he knew it, he was standing next to the bed stabbing the guy in the side of the head and then in the throat.

Blood splashed across the girl, and she slammed her beautiful eyes shut. It took all of his strength to shove the guy off of her. He thumped onto the floor and lay still, blood pooling around him.

And the girl lay there trembling, looking so scared, a fallen angel in need of rescue.

When she opened her eyes, he extended his hand. "It's okay. He won't hurt you again. I won't let anyone hurt you again."

The girl took his hand, and he pulled her up. Then her eyes widened as she looked toward the doorway.

Jonas looked over his shoulder at a guard that stood there, his eyes growing wide as they looked from Jonas to the man lying on the ground. Then he disappeared from the doorway. Jonas looked back at her. "What's your name?"

"Bishop," she said softly.

And her voice was the most beautiful thing he'd ever heard. "I'm Jonas. And I'll protect you from now on."

His father had appeared after that and whisked him away before he could say much more to her. But he'd made sure that Bishop was sent books and candies and treats. For the next week, he'd sent her something every day, along with notes telling her all about himself and his life.

She hadn't written back, or at least, no one had given him any of the letters. But he knew from the moment that he touched her hand that they were connected somehow.

A week later, the feds showed up and emptied the place out.

He demanded that he get the girl back, but his father had slapped him across the face and told him not to be worried about a whore. Then he'd sent him away to boarding school.

Jonas wrapped his hand tightly around the stem of the wineglass. That was when he'd gone through his own darkness. Boarding school had been hell. He'd been the short chubby kid, picked on and bullied relentlessly.

But finally, he realized that all of it was just a test to see if he was ready to come into his greatness. And that was when he finally realized who he was. He'd once been a great warrior, and now it was time for the warrior to reemerge.

The day he realized that, he'd taken the sword from the display case in the front hall and brought it down across the neck of one of his bullies. But the sword was so dull, it wasn't able to pierce the skin. So he used it as more of a bat, hitting the boy over and over again before he had been pulled away.

The boy had been hospitalized, and his voice box was permanently damaged. He would never speak again. After all of the taunts and insults he'd let fly at Jonas, that was the least that he deserved.

But those dark times were in the past now. He had his angel back again.

She looked uncomfortable sitting at the end of the table, and she barely touched her food. But that was all right. She hadn't awoken yet to their path. She didn't have the same memories that he did from their long-ago life. They just needed to spend some time together, and the truth of them being meant to be would come to her.

He didn't ask her any questions during the meal, content to simply look at her, remember, and relive when he'd first met her. She was perfection.

Finally, he took his napkin off his lap and placed it next to his plate. "You look tired, my dear. I'll escort you back to your room."

He stood and walked over to her chair. His manservant Melvin quickly reached the back of her chair and pulled it back to allow her to stand.

Jonas extended his arm. Bishop hesitated for a moment before taking it. "Thank you."

The feel of her arm against his was the most thrilling thing he had ever felt in his life. He closed his eyes and inhaled deeply, taking in her scent. Then he opened his eyes and smiled, tugging her gently toward the hallway.

Bishop looked around, her eyes wide as she stared at the displays that they passed.

He stopped in front of one.

"This is the armor of Takeda Shingen, a Japanese warlord known as the Tiger of Kai. I managed to get it at an auction three years ago. It deserves to be here, where it will be honored for the legacy that it holds." He studied her to see if the armor or the name struck any flash of recognition, but there was nothing.

Bishop stared up at the ancient armor and then back at Jonas. "You know how to fight?"

He patted her hand. There was so much for her to learn. "Yes. I have been training for years. And now there's only one last fight that I need to partake in. And once I have defeated the one who stands in our way, we will be together forever."

Chapter Forty-Three

NOLA

Nola was up and across the room before Chandra could even blink. She grabbed the doctor by the lapels of his robe and yanked him to his feet. "You knew he was going after her?"

The man tried to grab onto Nola's hands and break himself free, but Nola shook him off easily. "You knew?" she demanded.

Blake's eyes were wide with fear as he she shook his head. "No, I didn't know. I never thought—"

Chandra leapt to her feet and grabbed Nola's arms. "Nola, let him go. Let. Him. Go."

Nola stared into the man's face. Sweat had broken out across his forehead. His eyes had widened, his nostrils flared. But they were all the signs of fear, not the signs of deception. She released him and let Chandra pull her back.

"Start talking," Nola ordered.

The doctor took a shaky breath, his gaze going to Chandra. "I will not put up with this."

Dragging the much taller Chandra with her, Nola took a step forward. "Talk."

Blake put up his hands. "All right. All right. I was going to tell you anyway. That wasn't necessary."

He put a hand into the pocket of his robe and pulled out a handkerchief, wiping his brow. "Yes, I worked with Jonas Wagner years ago when he was institutionalized. He was brought to the hospital after an incident at his school."

"Where he went after a student with a sword," Nola said.

Blake nodded. "Yes, exactly. He seemed to have suffered some sort of psychotic break. He believed he was the reincarnation of an ancient samurai leader. I can't remember the name. Anyway, he was convinced that the other student was his enemy and that the only honorable thing for him to do was to kill him."

"How much damage did he do?" Chandra asked.

"A lot, but the boy did live. Luckily the sword was old and dull. It didn't even break the skin, but Jonas hammered away at the boy, dislocating his shoulder and doing permanent injury to the boy's ability to speak."

"So what was he like when he came to the hospital?" Chandra asked.

"Not what we expected. We had been told that he attempted to kill a classmate, and we expected him to be violent, lashing out. But he was the exact opposite. He was quiet. He would sit in his room on the ground, his feet tucked underneath him, his head bowed, and he'd stay like that for hours, not moving."

"Catatonic?" Chandra asked.

Blake shook his head. "No, nothing like that. He was meditating."

Nola frowned. "That doesn't make any sense. If he has that kind of control . . ."

The doctor nodded. "That was what we were thinking as well. He did have an amazing amount of control, but part of it came from buying so completely into the delusion. Samurais were known for their control and for their dedication to their martial art. And he fully believed he was one, so he could sit like that for hours."

"Where does Bishop come into this?" Nola asked.

The doctor frowned. "Bishop?"

"The woman you described," Chandra explained.

"Yes." The doctor started to rise and then stopped. "I need to bring something up on my computer."

Nola nodded. "Go ahead."

Blake walked over to an antique secretary desk tucked into a corner of the room. He slid up the top and pulled out a laptop. Bringing it back to the coffee table, he pulled his reading glasses from the pocket of his robe, placed them on his face, and started to henpeck his way into his computer.

Nola moved behind him so that she could watch what he was doing.

On screen, he brought up what looked like patient files. "I keep some of my files on here. Not all of them, mind you, but just some that I think might be relevant or important at some point." He murmured as he stared at the directory. "Now where was it?"

He scrolled down before finally clicking on a folder. "Oh, yes, here we go."

Nola leaned forward and saw the name Wagner attached to all of the files within that particular folder. It looked like there were at least twelve different files.

The doctor scanned them and then clicked on one of them. It was a photo of a hand-drawn image.

Nola sucked in a breath as she stared at the younger version of Bishop. "What is this?"

The doctor gestured to the computer screen. "This is one of dozens of pictures that Jonas drew while he was in the hospital. He would draw her image over and over and over again. It calmed him. I asked him who she was, and he would never answer. I wasn't even sure that she was a real individual until tonight. I thought she might be a figment of his imagination."

"Would you say he was obsessed with her?" Chandra asked.

"Now that I know that she's real? Yes. Pictures of her, they covered his room. The one violent incident we had involving him at the hospital was when another patient grabbed one of his photos and ripped it. The anger that overcame Jonas that day, it was unreal. It took three order-lies to pull him back. The other patient was hospitalized for a month."

"Why on earth did you let this guy out?" Chandra asked.

Blake sighed. "I'm afraid that was out of my hands. I was outvoted by the board that runs the hospital."

"And let me guess, they are not physicians?" Nola asked.

Blake shook his head. "No. But I was assured that Jonas would be taken care of and that he would be watched so that he wouldn't be a danger to anyone else."

"Did you believe that?" Chandra asked.

He met her gaze. "I wanted to believe that. But the truth was that by the time Jonas left us, he had made some improvements. He didn't cling as tightly to the delusion of the samurai like he did before. I seemed to have gotten through to him that he could be enamored with samurais, he could even long to be a samurai, without actually being the reincarnation of one. So I think he was starting to create some space between himself and the delusion. And the meds were definitely helping."

Nola moved back around in front of the doctor. "And if I said that a number of bodies have shown up with their heads removed from their shoulders by a sword, would you say that was something Jonas is capable of?"

Blake's eyes widened as he looked between Chandra and Nola. "Is that true? Has that happened?"

Chandra nodded. "I'm afraid so."

Blake sat back heavily in the chair. "I don't know. But I definitely can't rule out the possibility that it's him."

"Do you know who Jonas Wagner's family is?" Nola asked.

"I didn't at first. His father came to visit him a few times, and he always had security with him. That wasn't all that unusual. We've had a number of patients from prominent families. But over time, Jonas let slip more and more about his father's work. And then I saw a few newspaper articles where Elias Wagner's name was mentioned, so I know who he is. And what he's capable of."

"So what would happen to a boy like Jonas going back into that type of violent environment?" Chandra asked.

"An environment that is fraught with violence? One where being tough and holding people accountable for even the smallest of transgressions was encouraged?" Eyes filled with concern met Nola's gaze. "Nothing good, nothing good at all."

"And if Jonas was now in charge of the family business, what would that lead you to conclude?" Chandra asked.

His mouth dropping open, Blake stared at her. "Jonas is in charge now?"

Chandra nodded. "It looks like it."

Blake shook his head. "Then I would say whoever crosses him is in a great deal of trouble. And if you're saying that these bodies have shown up and that they were decapitated with the sword, then I'm afraid that the space between Jonas and his delusion no longer exists."

Chapter Forty-Four

BISHOP

The samurai armor in the hall actually was impressive. But the guy next to her was batshit crazy.

Bishop remembered him as a child, but apparently he had taken a great deal more from their first encounter than she had. She had no idea what he was talking about when he mentioned that he had sent her gifts, so she murmured nonchalantly.

But his threat against Nola, that was very real, unlike the delusions that seemed to be racing through his mind. She needed to warn her. She needed to make sure that Nola was safe. Nola would be coming for her. But how was she going to warn her?

She studied the man next to her. He was strong and muscular, and his guards obviously respected him or at least feared him. And if he had been training for years, he would undeniably be skilled. She couldn't take the chance of him catching Nola unaware. "Is the fight really necessary? We're together now. Does it really matter that she is still out there?"

Jonas tugged her gently down the hall. "Of course it matters. She will always be a threat to us. She wants what is mine. And I will destroy her to keep both of us safe." He stopped at the door to her bedroom and then took her hand and kissed the back of it. "But do not fear. I will not let her anywhere near you."

He opened the door, and Bishop stepped in and then started to close it behind her. "Good night."

"Good night, my love," he said, that creepy stare focused on her face again.

As soon as the door was firmly shut, Bishop leaned against it, a shiver running over her skin. *What the hell am I going to do now?*

Chapter Forty-Five

NOLA

The ride back to the estate was a quiet one, but Nola's mind was full. She pictured Jonas as she had last seen him, realizing as the psychiatrist had spoken that she had actually seen him in the flesh once. It had been in passing at the DOJ. He'd been a strange little boy. But she hadn't gotten any violent tendencies coming off of him.

In fact, Bishop had mentioned once that he had protected her. Perhaps that protection had morphed into an obsession.

Which meant now she needed to find out where Jonas Wagner was. His family was based out of Chicago, but they had homes all over the country, so there was no guarantee that that was where they would find him.

"You all right?" Chandra asked.

Nola took a breath before answering. "I'm not sure. I feel like I should have done something to make sure that

Bishop was safe, to make sure that the Wagners didn't go after her."

"Why didn't you?" Chandra said and then spoke quickly. "Not that I'm blaming you. I'm not at all. But holding people accountable is kind of your thing these days."

"Yeah, these days. But the Wagners were before all of that. I spoke with my supervisor, and he assured me that Elias Wagner would be put away and wouldn't be able to hurt anyone again. But that wouldn't have stopped this threat. If it is Jonas—and I really don't have any reason to believe it's not—he wasn't even on my radar. He was just a kid, and I thought he was a harmless kid. His father was the one to blame, not him."

"But it looks like he's grown up into someone who is anything but harmless," Chandra murmured.

Nola nodded her agreement. "You said that you kept an eye on the Wagner family. What do you know about Jonas?"

"Not a lot. It took some doing to find out that he'd been in a mental hospital. They definitely didn't want that information getting out to the other crime families. In fact, he was put in under a false name, although it didn't take the staff long to realize who he was the son of. No one said anything. It was made clear that it would not be in anyone's best interest to do so."

That sounded about right.

Chandra continued. "The Wagner family went into a bit of upheaval after Elias was locked up. He ran things from behind prison walls, but it's never as easy to run things from the inside as it is when you're outside. The family attorney took on most of those responsibilities. From all reports, he was incredibly loyal to Elias. And when Elias passed away, the attorney took over. He was the one running the show until Jonas stepped in about two years ago."

"How did that happen?"

"That I don't know. I just know that the attorney receded a little more to the background, and Jonas came into the forefront. It's possible he's more of a figurehead than the actual leader, but as far as the other families know, Jonas Wagner is the one running the show. If they know anything about his samurai delusions, it hasn't slipped out. It's known that he has an affinity for Eastern decor, but I don't believe it's gone beyond that."

"And what about the family business? How's that done under Jonas?"

"Well, they haven't lost any ground, and in fact, they seem to be slowly pushing out one of the other families. So whatever Jonas and the lawyer are doing, it's good for business."

"I need to find him."

"I'll give you everything I have on the Wagner family, and I'll find out from a couple of my sources where he is now."

"Good."

"And I'll be going with you when you take him down."

Nola looked over at her and shook her head. "No. I'll be taking Wagner down alone."

"Absolutely not. Do you know how many people this guy's going to have arrayed around him? I'll be going with you. And I know Avad will as well."

Nola wanted to argue with the two of them. She didn't want either of them put into harm's way. But Chandra was right about the amount of security Wagner would have arrayed around him. "Fine. But you leave Wagner to me."

"I have no problem with that," Chandra said. "Just make sure he pays."

Nola nodded. "Oh, that I can assure you I will do."

Chapter Forty-Six

Pulling to a stop in front of Ileana's home, Chandra dropped Nola at the door. She didn't come inside, needing to get home and start making phone calls. She was going to clear her calendar for the next couple of days so that she had nothing in her way. Then she could help bring Bishop back.

As Nola stepped into the front foyer, she hoped that it was going to be that easy.

Rafe walked down the hall toward her. "How'd it go?"

"Good. We've got a name: Jonas Wagner. He runs a crime family out of Chicago. Him and Bishop actually have some history. It looks like he might be obsessed with her."

"Obsessed?"

"Yes. So I'll be going after him first thing in the morning. Chandra's looking for some leads on where exactly he is." She started to walk past Rafe.

He reached out a hand and stopped her. "I'll be going with you."

Alarm flashed through her, along with an image of Sofia

and Enzo. Nola shook her head, pulling her arm away. "No. This one's too dangerous. Sofia and Enzo need you. You're not coming on this one."

He turned toward her. "You don't get to make that decision."

Staring into his eyes, she couldn't help but remember how he'd taken care of her in Indiana. She'd enjoyed their time together and thought that maybe they had a chance for something.

But Bishop being taken made it clear that she didn't have a role in his life. His life was with Sofia and Enzo. Her life was in the darkness. There would always be a case that would pull her away. And she couldn't do that to Sofia and Enzo. She saw the look on Sofia's face. It was branded into her brain, how much she was hurting at Bishop being missing. Nola couldn't be part of their life and then disappear from it just like their mother had.

Nola stepped back, putting space between them in more ways than one. "I said you're not." She turned and walked down the hall, feeling Rafe's eyes on her the whole way.

Chapter Forty-Seven

RAFE

Rafe watched Nola walk away, concern rolling through him. Ever since she had learned about Bishop, she'd been more closed off than usual. She was more like the Nola he had first met.

The Nola who would risk anything for anyone.

And now she was going to risk everything for Bishop.

And she wouldn't let anyone else do the same, especially him. He knew she was keeping him at arm's length to keep Sofia and Enzo safe. But the truth was if something happened to Bishop, their worlds would be uprooted again.

And if something happened to Nola, then Rafe's world would be. And he couldn't go through that again. Pulling his phone from his pocket, he walked down the hall and slipped outside.

He quickly sent a text. *She's going to leave in the morning. Can you get here?*

Three dots appeared. *I'm already on my way.*

Another text appeared moments later. *Me too.*

Relief rolled through Rafe. He knew that as soon as Nola got a lock on a location, she would take off. And knowing her, that wouldn't be long.

Good. See you soon. He slid his phone back into his jeans and glanced down the hall, knowing that Nola would be annoyed that he was calling in reinforcements.

But she didn't have to do this alone. And she wasn't the only one who cared about Bishop or who cared about her. She had a team around her that wanted to keep them both safe. And Rafe was damn well going to make sure that they did.

Chapter Forty-Eight

NOLA

Plans and ideas rolled through Nola's mind as she walked into the kitchen. She stifled a yawn as she poured herself a large cup of coffee. Dawn had just broken. It was early, but Nola had already been up for hours.

She'd forced herself to sleep for two hours, knowing she needed at least one REM cycle to get through the day.

But the rest of the time she'd spent going over all of the blueprints for the homes that were linked to Jonas Wagner. All of the homes had state-of-the-art security. He kept body-guards around him twenty-four seven. And the estate grounds were highly secure as well.

It didn't mean it was impossible. It just meant it was going to be awfully bloody. She rolled her shoulders, feeling the weight of the fight to come.

Avad and Chandra were insistent on coming. In fact, Chandra had shown up last night, taking one of the guest rooms. Apparently, she was afraid that Nola would leave without her.

She wasn't wrong. Nola's inclination was to just pack up a couple of bags full of weapons, head to Chicago, and go in Rambo style.

But even she knew that that was not going to get the desired result. She needed to play this smart if she was going to get Bishop out.

The idea that Jonas had harbored feelings for Bishop all these years, had been thinking about her all these years, made Nola's skin crawl. She didn't want to think about what Jonas might be doing to Bishop right now.

She was relying on the fact that Bishop was smart. That Bishop was trained and could handle herself. Nola had made sure from a young age that Bishop knew how to take care of herself.

Of course, Bishop was grabbed from her apartment, a voice whispered in her mind.

Nola shoved it away. Bishop had been caught unaware. She hadn't expected someone to try for her, not at her front door.

But by now, all of her training had kicked in. She was looking for an exit, she was looking for weaknesses and security. She was analyzing the people who were holding her and trying to find the soft spots that she could prod.

Nola had to believe that was true. Bishop would keep herself safe until Nola could get to her. That didn't change the fact that Nola needed to get to her soon.

She took a long drink of coffee, feeling the heat soak into her bones. Then she placed the mug on the counter. It was almost 5:30. They were just waiting on the official word from some of Ileana's or Chandra's people as to where

Jonas was. Apparently, he hadn't been sighted in quite some time.

It took everything in Nola not to rush out to his nearest home and just beat one of his security guards until they told her where he was. But she held herself back, just barely.

A soft knock sounded at the front door.

Nola's head jolted up, her eyes narrowing. It was way too early for guests. She walked slowly to the front door, her hand on the weapon at her waist.

It was possible it was Rafe. He'd gone to drop the kids off at Avad's brother's last night. They would stay there while the rest of them went after Bishop.

The fact that Rafe had stayed the night with the kids to help them settle in was another reason that Nola wanted to leave quickly. She would prefer if Rafe wasn't part of any of this. His kids had been through too much. And if they lost Bishop and Rafe . . .

Nola shook her head. She couldn't let that happen.

She made her way quietly down the hall. Avad appeared at the top of the stairs, and he looked down at her. She noted that he already had his Beretta in his hand, which was more worrying. How come they hadn't been notified someone was approaching?

Nola nodded as he took cover, keeping his gun focused on the front door of the house. Slowly, Nola opened the door.

A tall, athletically built African American man in jeans and a pale gray fleece stood on the doorstep.

"Morning, Nola." Chief Rascal Nealon of the Delford Police Department in Georgia said with a smile.

Chapter Forty-Nine

Nola blinked hard, staring at Rascal. The two of them had met when she had gone down to Georgia to look into a missing person's case. With Rascal's help, she'd found Anna Mae Hayes and uncovered a human trafficking ring.

She and Rascal had stayed in touch, and she knew that he was now chief down in Delford, Georgia. Which meant that was exactly where he should be. She stared at him, trying to figure out what on earth he was doing standing on Ileana's doorstep at 5:30 in the morning. "What are you doing here?"

"I called him," Rafe said as he walked in the door behind Rascal.

Nola raised her eyebrows at Rafe. "Why?"

"To help get Bishop back," Rascal said as he stepped inside.

"Absolutely not. It's way too dangerous. And—"

Rascal cut her off before she could finish speaking. "Hey, this isn't just about you. I've actually gotten to know Bishop over the last couple of months."

The statement brought Nola up short. "You have?"

"Well, somebody doesn't return her texts very often." He gave her a pointed look before he shrugged. "So I started reaching out to Bishop to find out how you were doing. She keeps me updated on things. In fact, I tried to reach out to her the day after she went missing, and she didn't answer, so I called Rafe."

Nola looked between the two of them. "You two are friends?"

Rafe shrugged. "Bishop connected the two of us."

Nola looked between them before her gaze settled on Rafe. "And you told him what was going on?"

"Yes, I did. You trust him. I know that. And that's good enough for me. And Rascal is right: we need all the help we can get."

Nola shook her head. Part of her was relieved that they had more people coming with them, and the truth was that Rascal was good in a fight. Besides being the chief of a police department down in the South, he was also former military. He could handle himself.

That didn't mean she liked putting him in the path of danger. "Did you call anyone else that I need to be aware of?"

Rafe nodded. "Yep. I called Jack. He called from the highway. He'll be here in thirty."

Nola's jaw fell open. "Jack? Jack DiMeola? What?"

Rafe was already making his way to the kitchen. "I'll get breakfast started while you and Avad finalize the plans, and then you can fill us all in."

Nola stared after him, feeling like she'd lost complete control of the situation.

"Good to see you too, Nola. I'll go help with breakfast."

Rascal patted her on the shoulder before quickly making his way down the hall.

Nola looked up at Avad, who still stood at the top of the stairs. She could tell he was trying to hide his smile. "Not a word, Avad," she grumbled as she headed to the security room. "Not a word."

Chapter Fifty

The information came through on Jonas's whereabouts fifteen minutes later. It was one of Chandra's channels that provided it. Apparently, Wagner had been in DC and had just flown back to Chicago.

Which meant they had just missed him. Nola rolled her hands into fists. He'd been here, just a short distance away, while they had been searching for Bishop.

She had no doubt that Bishop had been held there and moved with Jonas back to Chicago. If Jonas was as obsessed with her as Blake suggested, then he would keep her close.

But she had to shove the worries and the anger and frustration aside and focus on the next step: taking the fight to Jonas at his Chicago home.

Of all the homes that Wagner owned, the Chicago one was the most secure. Nola knew that wasn't a coincidence. Which meant that getting to him, and more importantly, getting to Bishop, was going to be incredibly difficult.

She and Avad pored over the blueprints and talked back

and forth about how they were going to manage it for about twenty minutes.

While they were talking, she heard the front door open and voices in the foyer. She recognized Jack's voice and shook her head.

Avad looked over at her. "It is good that we have more people. We could probably use a few more, actually."

He was right, but she didn't like her people being in the middle of all of this. When she was in the CIA, and she went into a situation, she knew the people, but she wasn't emotionally invested in them. It made it easier to make decisions because she could base it solely on the facts at hand.

She worried that with this mission she'd be too worried about the safety of the people on her team. And while that was always a concern, it couldn't be the primary concern. After all, they were going into a dangerous situation. By its very definition, people were going to be placed in harm's way.

"I know, but I don't want them there."

"You know, before I came to America, I lost many members of my family."

Nola looked over at Avad and saw the grief in his eyes. He very rarely talked about his time in Bosnia. But it looked like he was in a sharing mood.

Avad continued. "It was difficult. But I realize now when I look back that part of the problem was that we were so busy trying to protect one another that we didn't protect ourselves. Our focus was split on the person next to us rather than the solely focused on the person we were fighting. Because of that, we hesitated when we should have stepped forward. We didn't move, instead looking to make sure that the person next to us was moving with us and was protected as well. Those kinds of decisions, those hesitations, it costs lives.

"I know that Ileana worries that this will push back all the progress you have made in coming back to the world since the horrible tragedy that befell your family, but Nola, you need to become that person again. Emotions get people killed. You need to lock them away. You need to be lethal and without compassion. That is the only way we are going to get Bishop back."

Nola looked deep into Avad's eyes and knew that he was right. She would take care of her team. She would keep them as safe as possible, but in order for all of them to survive, they all needed to check their emotions at the door and just do the job. She nodded. "Okay. Then that's what we'll do."

Chapter Fifty-One

RAFE

The kitchen was full of people. Rafe slipped another pancake onto an ever-growing stack. Conversations bloomed as the group got to know one another.

Everybody was trying to keep the conversation light-hearted, but there was a tension overriding the scene. They knew how dangerous the time ahead of them was.

But all of them had been in dangerous situations before. Of course, this time it was different. This time they were going into a situation with people they cared about to save someone they cared about.

Rafe was worried about Bishop, but he was also worried about Nola. She seemed to be slowly pulling away. He knew that was her defense mechanism. She needed to wall herself off to focus and to do what needed to be done.

But he worried that she was delving a little too far into that darkness within her. And he was more than worried that what she would face in the time to come would pull her so far into that darkness that she wouldn't be able to pull herself back out.

Or maybe he was more worried that she wouldn't want to.

"There you are. Just in time," Ileana said as she placed a pitcher of orange juice on the table.

Rafe glanced over his shoulder as Nola and Avad appeared in the kitchen. He searched Nola's face, but she didn't look over at him. He was concerned at the dark look in her eyes.

When she started to speak, his concerns only increased. There was no emotion in her voice, no feeling. She had shut all of that down.

"We've got confirmation that Jonas has moved back to his home in Chicago. We believe that is where he is holding Bishop. From what his former doctor says, he's obsessed with her, and he will keep her close."

"What's the Chicago home like?" Jack asked as he snatched a piece of bacon.

"A fortress. We've got the schematics and basic intel on the security. But we're going to need to head there and get a bird's-eye view to see it for ourselves. Once we've got that, we're going to come up with a plan and we're going to go in." Nola paused. "This is not going to be pretty. People are going to die. If you are not prepared to take someone's life, you need to step back now. There is no way we are getting in and getting out without a lot of blood being shed, and some of it may be ours."

Nola's gaze met everyone's eyes in the room before she finally focused on Rafe. "Some of you have people that are counting on you. You should seriously consider not joining us."

Jack reached over and stabbed a handful of pancakes

with his fork and placed them on his plate. "Good speech, kid. But we're all going. You've had our back for years. Now it's our time to have yours. And besides, we all really like Bishop."

"Love her, actually," Ileana said.

Nola's gaze shifted to Ileana. "You're not coming."

Ileana raised an eyebrow. "And why not?"

"Because you're, I mean you're . . ." Nola stammered.

"If the word you're looking for is 'old,' I will take you over my knee right now," Ileana said.

Nola's cheeks flushed bright red.

"I'm well aware of what I am capable of. Hand-to-hand combat might not be in my wheelhouse anymore, but you're going to need someone to run your team. That I can do."

Nola looked like she was ready to argue the point, but Ileana put up a hand. "I will take no arguments on this."

Nola looked at her. Avad nudged Nola's arm. "Nola."

She looked up at him, and whatever she read in his eyes kept her from further arguments. With a stiff nod, she said, "Okay. We're going to head for the airfield in an hour. Everybody eat up. I'll have dossiers for each of you to go over on the plane."

With that, she turned and headed out of the room.

The kitchen was quiet as Avad started to fill up two plates full of food.

Chandra walked over and took a plate with bacon from the counter that was right next to Rafe. "Is she all right?"

Rafe shook his head. "No. And she won't be until Bishop is back."

Returning his attention to the griddle, he turned his back on the group. What he said was true; he could feel it in his gut. She would not be all right until Bishop was back, and maybe not even then.

Laughter burst out from the table. Rafe glanced over to see Rascal laughing and a giant self-satisfied grin on Jack's face. Those two seemed to get on like a house on fire. The two of them were joking as they sat at the table and traded war stories like they'd known each other for years.

He couldn't help but miss his kids in the middle of all of this. Saying goodbye to them this morning had been difficult.

They knew he was going after Bishop. And they were worried for him and for Bishop and for Nola and for everyone who they had come to think of as their family.

He hated that this was being visited back upon them. They had finally made strides in school and at home and were turning into normal children. But since they had learned that Bishop had been taken, he had seen Enzo withdrawing.

He wished that they didn't even know. He wished that they had not overheard him talking to Ileana. It would have been better for everyone if they had just said he was going away with Ileana to help with work.

He didn't like the idea of lying to them, but he liked the idea of them being worried for him even less. He wanted peace for them, not more nightmares.

He knew Nola didn't want him to go. Part of him was touched by her concern, by her worry for the welfare of his children. But he could not turn his back on Bishop, no more than he'd be able to turn his back on Nola. Bishop was a spot of absolute joy in his and his children's lives.

She had become central to the kids' development. She had been the first one able to talk them into taking a trip to a movie theater. She'd been so excited and had promised them so much popcorn and candy and ice cream that when they were done, they barely thought about the fact that it was their first time going out in public since they had come to the country.

Rafe had worried that they'd be nervous or scared, but Bishop had managed to keep them so focused on the movie and her that they simply didn't have time to be scared. They were too busy enjoying themselves.

For that alone, he owed her. But each day, she'd made them feel more and more comfortable. Each day, she'd encouraged them to embrace life.

He knew that Bishop had a dark past and that there were dark times that she'd had to overcome, but it was hard to picture that when you saw her smile.

The idea that someone would try and harm her did not sit well with Rafe. He wasn't a man who was prone to anger. But the idea of someone hurting Bishop, *that* made him angry. And the idea of someone trying to take that bright spot of joy away from her and away from his children . . . No, he couldn't let that happen.

So there was no way he was going to stay behind while the others went after Bishop.

His gaze strayed toward the hallway. Not only did the idea of Nola being out there alone for this particular mission not sit right with him, she wasn't thinking as clearly as she normally did. Normally when she went on these cases, she was entirely focused on the mission at hand.

But right now, her need to get to Bishop was overriding her normally objective approach. And he didn't think that she would be watching her six. So he would need to do it for her.

In fact, as he looked around the kitchen, he had a feeling that everybody was of the same mindset. As much as they were here for Bishop, they were here for Nola too. She might have spent the last few years keeping people at an arm's length, but at the same time, she had showed up for them when they needed her to. She had been willing to risk everything to help them in their times of need.

And now they would do everything in their power to return the favor.

It was strange. Somehow by pushing people away, Nola had actually brought them closer to her.

The doorbell rang, and Ileana stood up. Placing his spatula down, Rafe started to head for the hall.

Ileana waved him back. "You're busy. I've got it," she said before she disappeared down the hall.

Rafe frowned, looking around at the group. Everyone was already here. He had no idea who that could be.

A few moments later, Ileana appeared in the hallway with a young man in his early thirties. He was prematurely balding and nervously pushed the glasses up his nose as he looked around the room.

Ileana nodded toward him. "Everyone, I'd like to introduce you to Stan Mahoney. He works with Bishop."

Chandra stood up and extended her hand. "Chandra Wilson."

Stan's eyebrows disappeared behind his thick frames. "Ms. Wilson. I've heard about you. It's a pleasure to meet you."

She gave him a nod.

Rascal introduced himself next, followed by Jack. Stan's eyebrows rose again at Jack's introduction. Apparently he recognized the name from the CIA's files.

From the stove, Rafe nodded over at him. "I'm Rafe."

Stan smiled. "Bishop speaks about you and the kids a lot."

Rafe's gut tightened. "She means a great deal to us."

Stan nodded, and Rafe could see just how much Bishop

meant to him too, although he doubted that the man had ever said it out loud.

"I was hoping I could help. I know Bishop does some work on the side. And I thought maybe I could offer my services? I took some time off of work, so they're not expecting me back." Stan looked around the room hopefully.

Another one that had been pulled in by Bishop's joy. Ileana steered him over to the table. "We would greatly appreciate your help. We're leaving in an hour for Chicago."

"Chicago?" Stan asked as he sat.

Rascal placed a stack of pancakes on a plate and set it in front of Stan. "That's where we think Bishop is being held. Eat up, and we'll fill you in."

Ileana retook her seat, overseeing everything, her eyes missing nothing.

Rafe was worried about her too. Bishop was as much her daughter as Nola was. And she could see the dark circles under Ileana's eyes that showed how much of an impact the abduction of Bishop was hurting her. But he could also see the steel in her eyes that indicated she would let nothing get in her way of getting Bishop back.

He was surrounded by incredibly strong women. He couldn't help but think about his own wife. She had been strong but in a different way than these women that he was with today. His wife would stare down the devil himself to protect their kids.

Chandra, Ileana, and Nola had the skills to take down the devil. And he was grateful that he had found this particular family.

Now he just hoped that he could put it back together after everything that was to come.

Chapter Fifty-Two

NOLA

An hour after getting confirmation that Jonas was in fact in the city, they were in the air. Ileana arranged for the flight and accommodations in Chicago. Nola sat at the back of the plane, reviewing everything she had on the young head of the Wagner crime family. She also reviewed the case file that the doctor had passed along. Apparently Wagner had deeply committed to the delusion that he was in fact a reincarnated Japanese warlord.

He even had a name: Takeda Shingen, the Tiger of Echigo. Takeda had been a real-life warrior, a descendant of the Minamoto clan. Takeda ousted his own father from power and took control of the clan. During his life, he had a nemesis of sorts, Uesugi Kenshin, the Dragon of Echigo.

He was widely regarded as a highly skilled tactician and martial artist. But he died under suspicious circumstances. His death came about during a military campaign, and it was unclear if he fell victim to a wound or disease. But after his death, his clan broke apart.

Nola grunted as she finished the history the psychiatrist's had compiled. Perhaps she should get someone to take a closer look at the passing of Wagner's father to make sure he wasn't helped along into the afterlife, as Takeda had done to his own father.

Despite his son's rather violent delusions, once his father sprung him from the hospital, he'd still hired one of the world's best swordsmen from Japan to come over and teach his son. It sounded like the father hadn't exactly discouraged his son's violent tendencies.

The master had stayed with them for four years, and even if Jonas had been a horrible student, he would no doubt have picked up some skills. And with his devotion to the delusion, he would be committed to recapturing those lost skills. Which meant he was going to be dangerous.

In fact, danger seemed to be something that surrounded Jonas Wagner. Bodies had piled up after he took control of his father's business.

His father had been diagnosed with an aggressive cancer, but that wasn't what killed him. He died of a pulmonary embolism, which could be brought about by injecting air into the bloodstream. Contrary to what was seen in movies, it was rather uncommon, but it could happen. And Nola couldn't help but wonder if the son had grown a little tired of waiting for the father, who'd had him locked away, to pass on the reins of control.

Not that she felt bad for Elias Wagner. With everything that the elder Wagner had done, his death had been way too peaceful a departure from this world. He'd been up to his eyeballs in human trafficking rings, prostitution, illegal gambling, and an assortment of violent crimes, all related to his illegal activities. A quiet death in bed was not the punishment he deserved.

After his father's death, Jonas Wagner had taken over control of his father's business and had seen it increase in all areas.

An agent's note attached to one of the files mentioned the family lawyer, Ivan Stetson. It confirmed what Chandra said earlier about suspicions he was running the show.

Nola flipped over to the file on Stetson.

He'd grown up in the streets of Chicago. The child of a single mother who'd worked as a prostitute in her younger days before becoming a factory worker later in life. The young Ivan had gotten into more than a few scrapes as a kid, but he'd still managed to pull good enough grades to get into college. In college, he'd done well enough to get into a state law school. And he'd managed to pass the bar on his first try.

Once fully credentialed, he went right back to his old neighborhood and started working for Elias Wagner, working his way up until he was the family's main lawyer.

He'd been with the Wagner family for close to forty years now. He would know all the ins and the outs of the Wagner enterprise. And if Jonas Wagner was as delusional as the psychiatrist suggested, not only would Stetson know, but the lawyer would also know that the criminal enterprise would need someone capable to pull the strings. It seemed unlikely that the lawyer had merely stepped aside after playing such a central role in the family when Jonas arrived to claim his birthright.

The question was: What did Ivan think about Jonas Wagner? Was he happy to let the boy act as the figurehead while he played the puppet master behind the strings? Or was he angry that someone else was getting the attention that he rightly deserved?

And how would all of that play into Wagner's abduction of Bishop?

Nola's gut tightened at the idea of Bishop being in the hands of these people. Bishop was tough, but she wasn't born tough. Nola felt like she, personally, had come out of the womb practically with combat boots on.

But there'd always been a softness to Bishop. Her toughness was created by what she'd experienced in her life; it wasn't encoded into her genes. If she hadn't been touched by any of her early experiences, Bishop would have been one of those happy souls who thought that the world was a beautiful place.

Early on, though, the world had decided to show Bishop exactly how dark it could be. She'd been born to an underage mom who put her up for adoption a week after she was born. As a biracial child, Bishop had struggled to be placed in a permanent home and had been passed from foster home to foster home. And some of those parents should have been arrested for what they'd done to the kids under their charge.

Nola didn't understand how people thought that the current foster system was a good one. There were some good-hearted souls who took people in to give them a good life and to give those kids a chance. But there were way too many who took kids in just for the money that the kids brought with them. And the checks on those behaviors were way too limited.

It seemed that everybody talked about protecting the children, except when it came to the children who needed the most protecting. They, apparently, were on their own.

Nola had come across Bishop only because she was looking for Ariel, Beth's daughter.

Even now, Nola couldn't figure out what had caused her to offer young Bishop a home, something she barely had at the time. She had an apartment she lived in, but she had no emotional attachment to it. In fact, back then, she didn't have an emotional attachment to much of anyone, save maybe Jack and his family. She had, however, just visited Jack and his family a few weeks earlier. Maybe that was what had inspired the offer.

Even so, she'd planned on only keeping the girl with her for a few weeks until a better situation could be found. But as the weeks then months carried on, a temporary situation had turned permanent. It had been tough when Nola had to go out of the country, but she had cut down a lot of those missions so that she would be home.

Then a short while later, she met David. So then Nola had been able to go out of the country while David kept an eye on Bishop. Once Molly came along, Nola switched all her activities to office duty. No more trips out of the country. It had been a tough transition, but worth it.

And over the years, Bishop had just blossomed. She'd excelled in school, throwing herself into her studies with gusto. With Molly, she had become the best big sister Molly could ask for.

Even when she moved out, it had been good because Nola knew that meant Bishop was feeling secure enough to take on her own place. And even though she moved out, she never really went too far. She still spent half the week back at home.

At least, until Molly and David died.

Then everything had shifted. Nola had crawled into a dark pit, and there was no room for anyone in it but herself.

Guilt that she hadn't been there for Bishop rolled through her.

But Ileana and Avad had been there for Bishop. They had stepped in and taken the girl in. The truth was, they were already part of her family before Molly and David passed away.

And these last couple of years, they had provided Bishop with the stability and the home base she needed. But now Bishop was out there somewhere, and she needed Nola's type of help.

And Nola was determined to give her everything she had.

Nola was pulled from her thoughts as Rascal took a seat next to her. He stretched out his legs in front of him and smiled at her. "How are you doing?"

"I'm fine," Nola said, closing her laptop.

Rascal shook his head. "No, you're not. I know you. I saw how determined you were to get Anna Mae back, and you didn't even know her. Now that it's Bishop, nothing's going to stand in your way."

"That's true."

It was impossible to miss the worry in Rascal's expression. "And that's what concerns me. You need to get Bishop back. *We* need to get Bishop back. But don't lose your edge. Make sure you're watching your corners. You can't go in there blind."

"I won't. I know what I'm doing, Rascal."

"No one doubts that. But you're used to doing these things on your own. And from what I read in that file"—he nodded toward the computer—"this is a big operation. You're not going to be able to take it on by yourself. You're going to need to trust the rest of us to help you."

"I do trust you," she said.

"To a certain extent. But you think that you're the only one willing to go that extra distance to save someone."

Nola shook her head. "That's not it, Rascal."

He frowned.

She let out a breath. "I know you would go that extra mile to save whoever needed it. I don't doubt that. I've never doubted that. I just don't want you to have to."

He stared at her for a long moment before his eyes widened, his mouth popping open. "You're protecting us? You think your life is worth less than ours?"

Nola shrugged, not meeting his gaze. "Not exactly. It's just, I suppose I've made my peace with death. I've accepted it, and maybe in some ways I look forward to it. After all, that's where Molly and David are."

Rascal was quiet for a long moment. "I understand that, Nola. I really do. But look around this place. You have people in this world that care about you. And the loss you feel about David and Molly, the people here would feel that about you. Your death is not something any of us want, and it's not something any of us would swallow easily. You are worth something. And your life, it's different now than it was right after Molly and David died. You know that."

Nola wanted to deny those words, but he was right. Bishop would be devastated if Nola was killed trying to save her. But Nola couldn't handle one of the people in this plane being killed either, because they all meant something to her.

And she couldn't handle one more death. She was strong. She knew that. But that was something that would push her over the edge. And she'd been walking along that edge for so long now that she couldn't take the chance of going over.

"I know. And I'm not planning on letting myself be killed. But I can't let any of you be either."

"Stubborn as always, I see."

Nola gave him a sad smile. "Yes. And stubborn enough to make sure that we get Bishop back."

Rascal reached over and squeezed her hand. "Of that I have no doubt."

Chapter Fifty-Three

The safe house was only twenty minutes from the airfield. It was a two-story colonial on the outskirts of Chicago. The neighborhood was an average neighborhood, not too fancy, not too run down. There were four bedrooms and two bathrooms for the group of them, not that any of them planned on doing much sleeping. It would be a home base simply to allow them to do recon of Wagner's place and then stage their attack. They'd driven from the airfield in three SUVs, not sure what the mission would require.

At the house, they unloaded their gear and stored it in the dining room. Rascal and Jack headed out for a food run as soon as they were done.

Nola took a seat at the dining room table and pulled up the schematics of the Wagner home again. "I'm going to go scout out the estate and see what I can find."

"I'll go with you," Rafe said, standing up.

But Nola shook her head. "I think it would be better if Avad came."

Rafe hesitated halfway up to standing. "Are you sure?"

"Yes, it would be better." She turned and headed down the hall as Avad was coming out of the kitchen. Ileana was right behind him.

"We need to go do reconnaissance on the estate. You up for it?" she asked.

Avad nodded. "Yes. I left the drones in the truck. We can use them as well."

"Good."

Ileana opened her mouth as if she wanted to say something, but Nola turned on her heel and headed for the front door.

She didn't look into the dining room where Rafe was talking with Chandra while Stan set up his equipment. She knew that she would see a hurt look on his face for rejecting his offer of help.

And she wasn't entirely sure why she had done it. Rafe was just as competent at surveillance as Avad. He would be just as beneficial on a reconnaissance mission.

Her choice had nothing to do with Rafe's skill, or lack thereof. It had to do with Nola's feelings.

She had grown closer to the man. And those emotions were just the sort she needed to wall off. He needed to stay in the rearview mirror. Bishop needed to be her focus right now. And with Avad, she could just focus on the job and not be hyper aware of his every movement.

But she couldn't help the little piece of her heart that wished things could be different. Another part of her wished she could kill every feeling that she had toward him.

Chapter Fifty-Four

RAFE

Rafe sat down heavily in the chair and watched Nola head toward the front door without even a glance.

Seconds later, Avad followed her, and he heard the front door close. He blew out a breath, running a hand through his hair.

"She'll be all right. She's done this kind of thing a million times before," Chandra said.

"I know. I'm not worried about her doing recon."

Chandra met his gaze with a nod and then stood up and patted him on the shoulder. "Well, I didn't sleep on the plane, so I'm going to go catch some Z's while I can. You should probably get some sleep too."

He nodded. "Yeah, after the food and Nola and Avad get back as well."

"Stan?" Chandra asked.

The CIA analyst looked up from his computer cases. "Uh, I'll sleep after I eat. I'm kind of hungry too."

"Suit yourselves." Chandra headed out of the dining room, stopping to speak with Ileana, who appeared just as she was heading up the stairs.

Rafe watched them for only a few moments before his thoughts returned to Nola. She was pulling away from him. From all of them. She was acting like she was doing this on her own.

Ileana stepped into the room. With a glance at Stan, who seemed lost in something on the monitors in front of him, Ileana slipped into the chair next to Rafe. "Are you all right?"

He thought about lying. After all, there was enough going on right now with him adding any drama. But the look in Ileana's eyes made it clear she would know if he was lying. Rafe shook his head. "I don't know what I am right now."

"You need to let Nola do this her way."

"But her way is closing off everyone around her. Her way is doing it on her own."

"Yes, it is. Nola is a highly capable individual. And by doing it on her own, she has been able to save countless lives. If this is what she needs to do, if she needs to push us away to save Bishop, then we let her."

"Do you really think that is the best approach?"

"I do. Many people think Nola's cold and unemotional. But she's not. She feels deeply. And it's because she feels deeply that she needs to lock those feelings away so that she can do what needs to be done. She cares for you. I see that. But right now she needs to focus only on Bishop. If she's blocking you out, it's because she remembers what happened to David."

Rafe winced, remembering that Ileana wasn't just talking about Nola's husband but her own son.

Ileana continued. "Losing them, it nearly killed her. She's lost too much in her life. And now she's started to care about people again, and then this came about. Whatever she needs to do to get the job done, we need to let her."

"And when the job is over?" Rafe asked.

For the first time, Ileana's eyes look troubled. "We pray that she hasn't walled herself off for good."

Chapter Fifty-Five

NOLA

Traffic was busy as Avad navigated through the unfamiliar streets. Nola hadn't been to Chicago in years. She'd always liked the city, though. There was a crispness to the air that wasn't in all cities. Perhaps it was the edge of danger that she always felt whenever she was here. After all, the only times she had come here were when it was related to a case.

Behind the wheel, Avad followed the directions on the GPS on his phone, working his way through the traffic to the other side of Chicago, where Jonas Wagner's home lay.

The Wagner home was situated on three acres. It had once been one of the oldest mansions in the area, but now it had been expanded so much that it barely resembled its original form. It was 27,000 square feet with ten bedrooms and fourteen bathrooms. There were three pools: two outside and one inside. A full-sized basketball court was also in the basement, along with a bowling alley and a dance club.

Nola shook her head as she read the description of the estate. It was truly a monster. Even without all the security precautions that were set up, finding Bishop was going to be difficult to say the least. And Nola still didn't have an idea about how she was going to work that.

Plus there were the security precautions to keep in mind. Wagner had cameras all over the grounds and more at the entrances. He had some cameras inside at the common areas but those were under control of the security inside. And then there was the human angle. They had over a dozen guards patrolling the grounds.

According to Chandra's connections, Jonas could call up another three dozen if he needed to. And Nola was pretty sure he would increase the number of guards given the precious commodity he now had in his possession.

She flipped to another screen, staring at a recent picture of Jonas Wagner. The kid had grown up better than she'd thought he would. Now he was tall and muscular. The picture was a surveillance shot, and there was an air of impatience and entitlement about his face.

Staring at it, Nola kicked herself for not making sure that the Wagners wouldn't be any problem for Bishop in the future. But she had once again placed her faith in the system, and it had let her down.

At the time, though, her and Chandra's bosses had been adamant that this was the final nail in the Wagner crime family coffin. And it should have been. They had turned over three brothels, which between them, had over three dozen women being held against their will.

The live bodies, however, wasn't the worst of it. There'd also been ten bodies found between the three backyards.

The coroner couldn't say for sure that the deaths were the result of homicide because the bodies were so badly decomposed. And the reason they were so badly decomposed was because they had been covered in acid before they had been dumped. The acid had eaten away all of the tissue, leaving them little more than skeletons.

Wagner's lawyers had argued that they were overdoses, and therefore, really the only thing Wagner had been guilty of was improperly disposing of a body ten times.

That wasn't the end of Wagner's lawyers' maneuvers, however. They had convinced the higher-ups that Wagner would be more beneficial to them as an informant then locked behind cell doors.

And the higher-ups grabbed that little carrot and ran with it.

For all of the counts of prostitution and racketeering that he had been charged with, Elias Wagner had only served three years in a medium-security prison.

When he was let out, he'd gone right back to his old ways. And this time it seemed he had federal agents keeping an eye out for him. It appeared when his son took over, the feds similarly looked out for him.

Nola had a feeling that the feds were looking the other way because Wagner's enterprise occasionally shared little nuggets of information with them.

She shook her head. People were getting killed, innocent bystanders or people who just got caught up in the wrong life, and the feds were looking the other way because hey, what did it matter if some lowly hooker died when there was a chance they might be able to get something on a low-level drug dealer from another crime family?

This was why the system was broken. Certain deaths counted more than others. Certain lives counted more than others. This was what had led her to doing what she did.

The man who killed Molly and David had been another

one the system was supposed to have taken care of. They had him dead to rights. But then the system failed, and when he got out, he went looking for payback against Nola. Instead, he found Molly and David.

That was what had led Nola to her mission to help those the system wouldn't help. Because no matter what people said about justice being blind, the truth was that blindfolds sometimes rose up, allowing Lady Justice to pick and choose who exactly got true justice.

"We're getting close," Avad said as he pulled off the highway, breaking into Nola's thoughts.

She stirred herself from her dark memories and returned her attention to the area around them. They were entering the more affluent suburbs that surrounded Chicago. Homes were set on larger plots of land, and the house sizes seemed to grow with each turn of a street that Avad took.

Nola stared out at the large McMansions and tried to figure out exactly how they were going to be able to do recon of Wagner's place. In these kinds of neighborhoods, someone driving by alone was suspicious. Slowing down or parking was out of the question. In these neighborhoods, people only went in when they were supposed to be there. There was no drive-by traffic.

But there was no help for it.

Avad drove down the street slowly, going past the mansion in question. There were two guards standing outside the fence at the front, along with an intercom and a guard hut next to it.

She spied two more walking the grounds, and that was all she had time to see before they were past it. But she'd held her phone up to the window so that she recorded everything, and she would review it once they had made a full sweep.

They continued down the street and then turned, heading around the block, although "block" seemed a rather puny term for the distance that they were covering.

It was easily a half mile, if not more, before they reached the next street, and then it was a full mile before they reached the next one. The estates here were truly massive.

Nola recorded all of it, looking to see if there was anything that might help them. The estate that backed Wagner's didn't have guards out front. It was a little more modest and a little more understated.

She quickly brought up the information on it. It was owned by a man named Miguel Santarro. He was ninety-two years old and spent almost all of his time down in Arizona. Apparently he needed the dry air due to a lung condition.

Nola quickly picked up her phone and called Chandra. "I need you to find out if the estate that borders Wagner's is currently occupied. It's owned by a Miguel Santarro."

"On it. I'll call you in five," Chandra said before disconnecting the call.

Nola and Avad continued around the block and then headed away from the estate, knowing that there was no way they could park the car and set off the drones without also setting off alarms.

They went two blocks over to a large park and pulled into the parking lot. Nola's phone rang as Avad turned off the engine. Nola answered quickly. "What have you got?"

"The estate's deserted. The electrical and gas readings indicate that no one's been there for at least a month or two," Chandra said.

"What about the security system?"

"It's a local hire that's in charge of it."

"I assume we can get around that?"

Chandra scoffed. "I'm insulted you even have to ask."

Nola nodded. "Good. It looks like we have our way in."

Chapter Fifty-Six

JONAS

Jonas was still basking in the glow from the dinner he'd had with Bishop. She really was perfection. He was about to slide open the doors when his manservant called from down the hall. "Excuse me, sir? Mr. Stetson needs to speak with you."

Jonas frowned as he turned. "Where is he?"

"Down in the security room."

Jonas turned and headed for the stairwell. He made his way down to the second lower level and along a concrete-lined hallway. The security room also doubled as a bunker that could be sealed off in case their estate was overrun.

His father had had it created years ago when he'd first gotten sick. Apparently he worried about the reaction of the other families when news of his ill health got out.

Jonas made his way into the security room, which held a row of monitors as well as an armory along the back wall.

He nodded at his lawyer Ivan Stetson who turned as he entered.

Ivan had been his father's right-hand man, and now he was Jonas's. He was sixty-four and Jonas had known him all his life. He'd never seen the man in anything but a well-tailored suit. Even now that his hair was pure white, it was slicked back, without a strand out of place.

"Well?" Jonas asked.

Ivan gestured to the bank of monitors. "You were right. She and that tall Bosnian guy drove by just a few minutes ago."

"You've got a tail on them?"

Gesturing to the console, Ivan nodded. "Yes. They stopped at a park. And then they took off again, driving back across the city."

"Make sure our people don't lose them."

"They won't. I've got three cars on it. They're changing every mile to make sure that they don't pick up the tail."

Jonas nodded. He'd expected Nola to find Bishop. No, actually he was counting on Nola finding Bishop. He leaned forward. "Do we have visual?"

Ivan tapped the guy sitting at the monitor, who quickly brought up the feed. Jonas watched as a car drove along the highway and started to exit. He smiled, loving the feeling that she had no idea that she was being watched.

The car continued on, and the image shifted to the second car, which was waiting on the exit. It was a smart move. They would have one car waiting at each exit just in case she got off.

He watched now as the car turned, making a left at the stop sign. His people followed her through the streets and then turned off. The image shifted again, and the last car took over the tail.

He watched as the truck pulled into a driveway.

The driver stepped out, and Jonas's eyes widened. The Bosnian guy was huge. For a minute, he thought it was actually the actor Dolph Lundgren.

He watched as Nola stepped out just as the tail car drove by, and he couldn't see much more as Nola turned and headed into the house.

But that was all right. He'd seen all he'd needed. And now it was time to begin.

Chapter Fifty-Seven

NOLA

Nola paused in the driveway, watching the brown sedan as it passed. She could have sworn she'd seen that car earlier.

"Avad, did you see that car before?" she called out.

Avad turned and watched the car as it headed down the street. "I'm not sure."

Frowning, Nola watched until it turned the corner. Once it was out of sight, she didn't feel any better. She was sure she had seen it before.

As Avad headed into the house, Nola stayed where she was, watching the street, waiting for something. Standing in the driveway, she paused to consider whether the feeling in her gut was real or if she was just imagining things.

The truth was, on the car ride back, she'd been so focused on getting information on the estate behind Wagner's that she hadn't been paying as much attention to their surroundings as she should have.

She cursed herself for her inattention.

This was why it was unwise to work on cases that were emotionally close to you. You became less observant and more obsessive. She wanted to come up with a plan and a way to get to Bishop, and she had put that ahead of making sure that they weren't followed.

Well, there was no help for it now. What was done was done. She'd just have to make sure that everyone kept their guard up. She headed into the house. As she stepped in, the scent of Italian food drifted down the hall toward her. It looked like Rascal and Jack were back with the food.

She made her way into the kitchen, and Rascal grinned over at her. "We have brought sustenance."

The pizza smelled delicious, and Nola's stomach growled in response. She walked over to the counter and grabbed a plate, putting a couple of slices on it and grabbing a bottle of water. "I'm going to send you guys all schematics of the estate behind Wagner's."

"Were you able to use the drones?" Ileana asked.

Avad shook his head as he helped himself to a few slices. "No. The park was too busy and it was too far to send them. Plus, we don't want to tip Wagner off that we're here."

Nola took a bite of her pizza, the warmth spreading through her. Man, she was hungry. Swallowing her first bite, she nodded to the group. "I want you to go over the maps of both estates and see if you come up with any ideas. We need a plan, and we need it fast."

Chapter Fifty-Eight

JONAS

The image on screen shifted as Nola's face disappeared from view. Jonas sat back in contentment. Finally.

It had taken him a long time to find out who the woman was that had taken his Bishop away from him. She had actually taken Bishop into her home. But her name had eluded him for years.

Finally, though, one of his contacts at the FBI had come through and told him that she was a former CIA agent. Apparently, she had been one of the top in her field, lethal beyond reason.

She'd cut back some of her activities after the birth of her daughter. Jonas smiled. But then the death of her daughter had sent her over the edge. She had essentially disappeared.

But he'd heard rumors about what she was up to. She'd taken revenge out on people who'd been victimized by the system. And she had cut a swath through those who stood in her way.

Jonas hadn't been sitting on his hands during that time either. Nola had honed her skills until she was a fine-tuned lethal machine.

And Jonas had done the same. He'd worked with master martial artists for years, perfecting his craft. All in anticipation of finally facing the one who had kept his true love from him.

She was a worthy opponent, and everything she had done to this point made it clear that she was who he needed to face. She was his dragon who needed to be slayed.

She had taken his beautiful Bishop from him, and then kept them apart all these years. But now, finally, he was ready to face her and to take her down.

But first, he needed to know that she was worthy. First, she needed to get through the gauntlet. She needed to prove that her love for Bishop was as strong as his.

"What do you want to do?" Ivan asked.

Jonas looked at the screen. He smiled. "Get the team ready. When it gets dark, send them in."

Chapter Fifty-Nine

NOLA

After she'd eaten her first slice, Nola had grabbed two more, picked up the laptop, and settled into one of the bedrooms, closing the door so that she could be alone.

Darkness had fallen as Nola ate and went through the schematics on the other estate. A tall brick fence separated the two properties, and there was a series of trees along the back that could offer cover.

The problem was the size of the brick fence: It was eight feet tall. It would not be easy to scale, and that meant they'd need to use some sort of ladder.

Nola knew that she could scale it, as could the others, but it would leave them open for someone to snipe them off because there was absolutely no cover on Wagner's side. She'd have to figure out a way to get around that.

Maybe Avad would have some ideas. He was good at those kinds of situations.

She could hear the others talking softly below. After an hour, she wiped her eyes, and her stomach growled again.

She'd already had four slices, but apparently her stomach was reminding her she hadn't really eaten much in the last few days. So she stood up and headed back downstairs to see what else she could find.

Hopefully there was still some pizza left, and maybe some of those garlic knots. They'd looked tempting, even though she hadn't grabbed any.

She reached the kitchen without running into anyone, but Jack was tidying up some of the plates and rearranging some of the food to discard the empty boxes. He looked up as Nola stepped into the room. "Hey, kid, how you doing?"

"Good. Any pizza left?"

Jack pointed to a box to his left. "Still a full pie."

He flipped open the lid, and Nola grabbed two more slices. She had planned on heading back to the bedroom, but Jack kicked out a chair. "Why don't you take a load off?"

Nola was tempted to turn down the offer, but it was Jack, so she took a seat.

He grabbed a slice for himself and took a seat across from her. "So how are you really doing?"

Nola shrugged, not meeting his eyes. "I'm good. I'm a little worried about how we're going to get in there. We need to create some sort of distraction so that they're focused on the front while we slip in the back."

"That's doable. But that's not what I'm asking, and I think you know it. Your emotions are all over the place on this one. You've never done a mission where it involves someone you care about."

Nola looked up at him. "No, I haven't."

"It's different. When it's someone you care about."

She heard the sound of experience in his voice. "You?" she asked.

He nodded. "It was when I first joined the CIA. My second mission. I fell hard for my partner."

Surprise rolled through Nola. "There was someone before Terry?"

"I don't know if I would say it was equal to that, but I had feelings for her and she did me. We were on assignment in Somalia. It was supposed to be an easy assignment. Go down to a café, meet with our contact, get a file from him, and then head out. There wasn't supposed to be any issue at all." Jack fell silent.

"What happened?" Nola asked.

"It all went south really quickly. Kim took her seat at the table to wait for the contact while I was the one playing lookout. It was a busy day. The street outside was packed, and the café itself was busy too. The contact arrived, and Kim laughed." He smiled.

"She had a great laugh. And that laugh pulled my attention back to the table. I keep thinking that if it were anyone else, I wouldn't have looked back for that laugh. But I loved seeing her face light up when she laughed. And so I looked.

"The gunmen came from across the street. The shots rang out before I even had a chance to clear my gun from the holster. Our contact, he was playing both sides, and he took out Kim while I was busy dealing with the guy across the street."

"That could happen to anyone, Jack."

He shrugged. "Maybe. But because it was Kim, I wasn't looking at it as objectively as I should have. My emotions were getting in the way. I was thinking about her as Kim and not as my partner. You're thinking about Bishop as your Bishop, and not as the target you need to extract. You can't do that. You can't think of any of us like anything except tools for you to use to get Bishop out."

"I can do that."

"Yeah, you can. But I know you. You will let yourself fall on a grenade to save the ones you love, but sometimes you need to pick that grenade up and chuck it somewhere first. Sacrificing yourself isn't always the first and best response, even though it's the one that may guarantee someone's safety. Sometimes you need to risk someone's else's safety for a better move."

"You think I can't do this?"

"Oh, I know you can do this. I have no doubt you can do this. I know that within twenty-four hours, Bishop will be sitting here amongst all of us. But I'm just not so sure you're going to be able to take care of yourself as well. Sometimes you've got to let the people you love get a little bit hurt so that you can save them and yourself."

Nola knew what he was saying. That she might have to look at Bishop without emotion so that she could pull her out and herself. But for someone who was so good at compartmentalizing her feelings, Nola was struggling with the idea of placing Bishop in harm's way.

"I know it's hard for you. But in the long run, that's the best guarantee you have of getting Bishop out. You put yourself and your own safety up there with Bishop's, and then both of you come out."

Rascal walked into the kitchen and then stopped still, looking between the two of them. "Sorry. Am I interrupting something?"

Nola shook her head. "Nope. In fact, I was just going to get everyone together in the dining room. We need to come up with a plan. I want us moving at first light."

Chapter Sixty

They had the vague outline of a plan. Nola wasn't incredibly happy with it. Of course, with the limited knowledge they had of the layout of the inside of the mansion, there was no way to get anything better.

The idea was that most of their group would slip over the back wall while there was some sort of distraction at the front. Ileana had offered to run the drones to distract the guards and pull their attention away from the back wall, giving Nola and the others enough time to get over the wall and hopefully across the yard before the guards were any wiser. Jack would play sniper up in the trees on the Santarro estate to provide them cover.

Stan would loop the security cameras to block out the feeds while also allowing himself and Ileana to see what was going on inside the estate. The hope was as soon as they got into the system, they would get eyes on Bishop, and then Stan could direct them there.

But it still was dicey.

They'd spent two hours going over the schematics and

trying to figure out what would be the best way in, and that was the best they had. And Nola was afraid it wasn't going to be good enough.

Part of her wondered if maybe she should just slip out by herself and try to get into Wagner's home on her own. After all, she worked better when she was by herself.

At the same time, a voice inside her head—which sounded remarkably like Jack—warned her that it wasn't wise to simply go it alone on this one. There was too much riding on the outcome. And she couldn't trust her own judgment as to what the next move should be.

It was a rough deal for her to accept the fact that her own judgment was now circumspect. For years, she had counted on her judgment to get her out of sticky situations and at times to get herself into them.

But she was aware enough to know that Jack was right: She was too close to this. There was an urgency inside of her to get to Bishop that wasn't there with her other cases. So she had to be a little more cautious than she normally would be because that recklessness inside of her could and would affect all of her decisions, and that wouldn't be good for any of them.

After everyone except Avad had called it a night, she headed upstairs, intent on getting some sleep. She knew she needed at least a few hours before all of this began. They were going to go at three a.m. The rest of the house was quiet. Avad was on the first watch.

Stepping into the shower, Nola quickly washed off the day and then got into the clothes she'd be wearing for the attack. She didn't want to have to waste time getting changed later.

She lay down in the bedroom that she was sharing with Chandra. There were two twin beds. Chandra was breathing softly, already off in dreamland on the other one. Nola had always envied her ability to drop off to sleep almost instantaneously.

Nola lay down and closed her eyes, but sleep eluded her. Instead, she thought of when she had first met Bishop and those first days when it had been the two of them in her small apartment. Neither of them seemed to know how to relate to the other. Nola had barely been a child when she was young, so she didn't know how to talk to Bishop. And Bishop had been through so much in the last year that she was just kind of getting through each day. Plus, she was missing Ariel something fierce, and Nola had no idea how to bridge that gap between them.

But slowly, day by day, they had closed the gap. It had started with ice cream sundaes one night, and that link had been added to with movie marathons and trips to the bookstore.

Slowly, the two of them figured out a rhythm that worked between them. They hadn't been mother and daughter. Bishop had been through too much and seen too much to need or want that kind of complete oversight. But Nola had become the adult in her life that she could count on. The one she could go to when she needed to and the one who would always tell her the truth.

David coming into their lives had been another adjustment. But he had won Bishop over rather quickly. In hindsight, Nola knew that Bishop had taken to David so quickly because she could see how much Nola trusted him. And Bishop trusted Nola's judgment.

And now it was that judgment that Nola herself was questioning.

She tossed and turned, picturing Bishop, her imagination going to overdrive, and finally she sat up. She wasn't going to sleep. Who was she kidding thinking that that was going to be an option? Quietly, she slipped out of the room and down the hall. At the top of the stairs, she put on her boots and then walked down to the first floor.

The flip of a newspaper page came from the kitchen. Avad always read the news, no matter what city they were in. And he always read the news on a physical newspaper. There was no digital version for him. She rounded the stairwell and headed down the hall toward him.

He looked up from the kitchen table, not seeming at all surprised to see her. "Couldn't sleep?"

Nola shook her head. "I tried, but it's just not working. Why don't you go and get some sleep? I'll stay up and keep an eye out."

Avad nodded. He gestured to the monitor in front of him. "I put some motion sensors along the backyard and in the front. Just as an extra precaution."

"Are you expecting trouble?"

He shrugged. "I'm always expecting trouble. You said you thought you saw that car earlier, correct?"

Nola pictured the brown sedan. "To be honest, I can't be sure."

"Well, let's hope that it was nothing. But just in case, we've got the sensors."

Nola looked at the monitor, seeing the lights that were all a steady green except for one that was blinking.

She frowned, looking at it. "Avad." She pointed at the light.

He stared at the screen for only a split second before looking to the front of the house. "We've got company."

Chapter Sixty-One

It was possible that it was just some sort of stray dog that had walked across the motion sensors, but Nola didn't think so. The other lights on the monitor began to blink, confirming that whatever was out there was more than one stray dog.

Without a word, Nola and Avad moved toward the front of the house. Nola was in front, her gun leading the way. She nodded to the stairs. "Go wake everybody up," she whispered.

Avad placed a hand on the banister, about to head upstairs, when gunfire burst through the front of the house. Bullets blasted through the door and the windows, raining splinters of wood and shards of glass across the foyer.

Grabbing Nola, Avad threw her to the floor and covered her with his body. Nola lay crouched underneath him, hearing the incredible volley of weapons that was being unleashed. *No need to wake everyone now,* she thought as her mind raced for options for her and Avad.

There had to be at least four gunmen, all with automatics.

Gunfire erupted from upstairs now, aimed toward the front lawn as her team returned fire. The attackers shifted their aim, now focused on the second floor.

Avad quickly crawled off Nola, and together the two of them stayed low against the ground. Glass cut into Nola's palms as she crawled along the floor toward the living room.

She slid along the wall by the front window and peered outside. There were four gunmen. As she studied them, she pulled two glass shards out of her palm and dropped them to the floor. Then she pressed her palm against the side of her hip to staunch the bleeding.

Two gunmen had taken refuge behind one of their trucks and was firing at the windows upstairs. A third lay unmoving on the front lawn and a fourth was pulling himself along the ground out of sight behind one of the other cars.

Nola took aim at one of the men behind the truck and caught him in the foot. He let out a cry, leaning forward and exposing his head. Her bullet went right through the top of his skull.

A crash came from the back of the house.

Nola nodded at the other car that pulled up front. Four more men jumped out.

"You got this?" she asked Avad.

He nodded, already pulling the trigger and catching one of the men in the middle of the chest before he'd even reached the sidewalk.

Her palms now slick with blood from the shards of glass, Nola hurried down the hallway. She kept flat along the side of the wall, her gun once again leading the way.

Taking a breath, she peeked into the kitchen just as a gun barrel appeared to the left of her head.

She grabbed onto the wrist that held the gun and shoved it away while bringing a front kick up between the man's legs. He cried out as she connected with his family jewels. Instantly, she brought her left elbow up, catching him underneath his chin while slamming his gun hand into the side of the doorway.

The man four feet behind the guy let off three shots at Nola. One crashed into the doorway right next to Nola's head. She grabbed the man she was holding and pushed him toward the gunman. Two of the bullets slammed through the man's back—one went straight through and tore through Nola's jacket but missed her.

Using the guy she held, she bum-rushed him across the floor, plowing into the other gunman and slamming the two of them into the counter.

The gunman in the back let out a cry.

Nola slammed a hook into the right side of his face before bringing her own gun up. She pressed the barrel to his temple and pulled the trigger. Then she stepped back, letting both of them drop.

Taking a step back, she flicked a glance at the back window. It shattered as gunfire burst through, raking the back wall of the kitchen. Nola dove for the ground.

She crawled toward the hallway but, hearing footsteps coming behind her, quickly twisted onto her back and brought her weapon up again. As the first man appeared in the doorway, she let off a shot, catching him in the thigh and then in the right eye.

He fell forward as she scrambled backward. She'd just managed to get into the hallway as more gunshots cut into the threshold of the doorframe she'd just crossed.

Getting to her feet, she fired blindly into the kitchen. A grunt sounded from farther in the room, and then the gunfire stopped for a moment.

Sliding down the wall, she peeked around the corner and saw that a man kneeled on the ground, blood staining his shirt. Her blind shot had caught him in the shoulder.

She raised her gun and pulled the trigger catching him in the throat. He fell backward out the door.

The front door burst open. Nola whirled around, bringing her weapon up and pulling the trigger, but all she got was an empty click. She was out.

But worse, she was caught out in the open.

"Nola!" Rafe yelled as he released a barrage of gunfire from the stairwell. He took out the man at the door. A second guy stormed in, and he met the same fate as the first.

More gunfire sounded from the rooms upstairs, telling her that at least some of her team was still doing well.

Then the gunfire quieted from the living room where Avad was, and it went silent upstairs as well.

Rafe hurried down the stairs, handing Nola a Beretta as he kept his focus on the area surrounding them.

"Avad?" Nola called out.

"All clear out front," he replied.

"Rascal? Jack?" Nola yelled.

"I'm clear here," Rascal called down.

Rafe nodded toward the kitchen. "I'll check the back."

Nola nodded as Chandra appeared at the top of the stairs. A quick scan showed she was uninjured. A sigh of relief rolled through Nola. But it was only temporary as she caught sight of the expression on Chandra's face.

Chandra met her gaze. "Nola, Jack's been shot."

Chapter Sixty-Two

Nola hurried up the stairs, worry rolling through her. She never should have let Jack be a part of this. She burst into the room that Jack had been staying in with Rascal.

Stan sat in a corner, looking completely shell-shocked. In fact, he was probably going into shock. Chandra draped a blanket over his shoulders and helped him stand, pulling him from the room.

Jack sat up in the bed, leaning back against the headboard, his face sweaty and pale. He grimaced as he met Nola's gaze. "Got caught unaware. It's nothing. It's a through and through."

Nola's gaze shot to his arm, which Ileana who sat next to him, had wrapped in a white pillowcase and was now tying the ends of. "We need to get him to a hospital."

Snorting, Jack shook his head. "No chance. We all know that the cops are going to be here in about ten or fifteen minutes, and if I go to the hospital, they're going to have to report a gunshot wound. We need to get moving."

He wasn't wrong. But gunshots weren't something to play around with. "Jack, your arm—"

Jack cut Nola off before she could finish. "It's nothing. Everybody here has been stitched up in the field. Hell, I could probably do it blindfolded. Now let's get moving before the cops show up."

Rascal hurried up the stairs. "I just checked the scanner. The gunfight was called in. The cops are on their way."

Meeting her gaze, Jack wouldn't let Nola look away. "No emotions, remember?"

The conversation between the two of them rolled through her mind. She held his gaze for a long moment before nodding. "Right. Patch him up the best you can. We'll stitch him up in the car. Grab everything that we need, and let's get moving."

Nola hurried down the stairs, leaving the others to take care of the second floor as she made a beeline for the dining room. She quickly started packing up all of their weapons. She noted that two of the gun cases had already been taken out to the car.

After she'd finished packing one of the duffel bags and zipped it up, Avad appeared, grabbed it, and headed back outside. Rascal and Rafe hurried down the hall from the kitchen where they'd packed up the few things they had with them.

Pausing on his way out to the car, Rafe stood in the doorway. "You need anything?"

Nola shook her head. "No, I can get the last of it. I'll be right out."

Rafe nodded and headed for the door. Nola shoved her computer into her case and zipped it up.

A phone rang from somewhere behind her. She stopped, looking around. Avad and Rafe were outside with Rascal.

Chandra had taken Stan out to the car and then disappeared back upstairs to help Ileana.

The only phone of her team on this floor was her own, and it certainly was ringing. She stepped out of the hall and tilted her head, listening. The call was coming from the kitchen.

Avad appeared at the front door and headed up the stairs. "I'll get Jack."

Nola nodded, heading in the direction of the kitchen.

The kitchen was a disaster. Four bodies lay where they had fallen, one half out of the kitchen door.

The ringing was coming from the two bodies in front of the kitchen sink. She paused for a moment and then realized it was the guy on top. Rifling through his pockets, she found his phone in the exterior pocket of his jacket. She pulled it out. On the screen it simply said: THE BOSS.

Nola debated for a moment whether or not to answer it. But Wagner obviously knew that she was here. He'd sent a team after her. She tapped on the screen. "Hello?"

A deep chuckle sounded from the other side of the phone line. "So you did survive. I had hoped you would."

Nola stared at the four bodies and the growing pools of blood. "Well, your welcoming committee seems to suggest otherwise."

"Oh, they were just . . . let's call them an appetizer. After all, I needed to make sure that the indomitable Nola James lived up to her reputation."

"And what reputation is that?"

"Oh, I know all about you, Ms. James. I know about the cases that you've been taking on for the last couple of years ever since your husband and daughter died. I know the body count that you have created, and it is quite a body count. Very impressive."

Rafe walked into the kitchen and raised an eyebrow. Nola met his gaze as she spoke. "And I assume this is, of course, Jonas Wagner?"

Rafe's eyes widened.

"Of course it is."

Nola nodded at Rafe.

He disappeared back out the doorway. Nola followed him, knowing that the cops would be here soon, and she needed to be gone. But she also wanted to hear what Jonas had to say. "So what is this appetizer all about?"

"You and I have been tussling together for a very long time."

Nola had no idea what to say to that. She had no idea what the man was talking about. The only time she had even seen him he was a child. "I don't see how that's possible."

"Yes, of course. You have no memory of our former lives either. You see, you and I were once great enemies. We met on the battlefield time and time again. And you killed my true love, keeping us apart."

Nola frowned, not sure what the heck he was talking about. It must be part of his samurai delusion. Did he think she used to be a samurai as well? "Oh, I did?"

"Yes, you did. And in this lifetime, you're trying to keep us apart again. But I won't let you."

"Where is Bishop?"

"She's here with me. She's safe as long as you do what I tell you to do."

Scanning the dining room for anything left behind, she made her way to the front door. "It seems odd to be threatening your true love."

"Our love exists beyond just this physical plane. Now, to win her freedom, you must fight fairly."

Nola scoffed. People often talked about a fair fight, but the truth was there was no fairness in fighting. It was rare that opponents were evenly matched. One was always stronger or one was faster or one had a better weapon. True equality in fighting was a myth. It was something that was sold to young kids and naive people across the world.

A fight was as dirty as humanity got. When it came to your life or the lives of others, you would pull no punches to make sure that they were safe. Or at least, Nola wouldn't. "Sure, we can have a fair fight."

Jonas chuckled. "You're lying. But that's all right. I expect no better than that from you. Here are the rules: You will come to me at my home. You will fight my people, and when you have bested them, then you will face me."

"Why bother with all the early fights? Why don't we just get to the main event?"

"Because you have to prove your worth. You have to prove that you are worthy of fighting the master. You have been given too much credit, too much fear. You haven't *earned* it. So you will present yourself at my home, and you will fight without guns."

"And if I choose to bring a gun?"

"Then I will kill Bishop."

Nola went still. "I thought you said you loved her. That you were soul mates."

"We are. And we will see each other again in our next lifetime. But better that she die at my hand than for you to fight dishonorably in her name."

Nola shook her head at the warped logic as she stepped out of the house. Another white guy with delusions of grandeur and a savior complex. The man who'd grabbed Bishop and pulled her from her home was talking about fighting with honor. It was absolute garbage.

And it was absolutely the rule she needed to follow. "Okay, I'll meet you. When and where?"

"You know where I live. You were here earlier. And leave that giant Viking of yours at home. This fight is only for you. Do you accept?"

Making her way down the path and to the driveway, Nola slipped into the passenger seat of the car with Rafe behind the wheel. She nodded. "I accept."

Chapter Sixty-Three

BISHOP

Something was happening. Bishop knew it. She could feel it in the air. She'd heard a lot of people moving around outside tonight. She didn't know what they were doing or where they were going, but something was up.

She had laid down on the bed but only ended up staring at the ceiling. Jonas was crazy. He was going to kill Nola. She had no doubt of that. Or at least, she had no doubt that he was going to *try* to kill Nola. She wasn't entirely sure he was capable of doing it.

But she couldn't let herself be used in a way that would hurt Nola.

There was a knock at her door followed by the sound of the lock sliding out. Sitting up in bed, she stared at the door, not sure what to do as she glanced at the clock. It was close to one in the morning.

The knock came again. She scrambled out of bed. "Who is it?"

"My name is Ivan Stetson. I am Jonas Wagner's lawyer."

A lawyer? Bishop shoved her feet into her boots as she sat on the end of the bed. "What do you want?"

"To speak with you," he said. "And preferably not from behind this door."

Pausing for a moment, Bishop debated her options. But the truth was, she didn't have any. The door locked from the outside. And it was already unlocked. Pushing herself from the bed, she crossed the room and pulled the door open.

A man in his mid to late sixties stood there. His hair, which was a bright white, was combed back from his head and slicked in place with oil. He wore a crisp navy-blue suit with a pale blue tie. Gold cufflinks flashed off the edges of his white shirt. He smiled at her. "Miss Rhodes?"

Bishop nodded slowly. "Yes?"

"I've been asked by Mr. Wagner to escort you to a safe location."

Bishop looked around the room. "This isn't safe?"

The man hesitated for a moment. "There are some activities that are going to be occurring over the next few hours that may become a little dangerous. It would be best if you were located somewhere that was more protected."

"And where's that?"

"We have a special location in the basement for these types of events. If you will accompany me?"

Bishop thought about refusing. After all, if he was asking, she could say no, right?

As if reading her mind, Ivan smiled. "Do not mistake my politeness for the need for actual permission. You are coming with me one way or another."

The two large men behind him pushed back their jackets to reveal the guns at their waist.

Bishop stared at them and then looked back at the lawyer. "I don't think Jonas would like it if one of your goons shot me."

Ivan chuckled. "You are absolutely right. Smart girl. He wouldn't. But he would like it even less if he lost you."

He nodded at one of his men. The man pulled a rag from his pocket then dumped some liquid from a bottle that he uncorked from his other pocket and stepped toward Bishop.

Putting her hands up, Bishop took a step back. "Okay. I'll walk. No need to break out the chemicals."

Ivan smiled. "Excellent. If you'll allow me." He extended his arm to Bishop.

Bishop looked at it like it was a snake. "I don't think I will."

Ivan inclined his chin. "If I were in your shoes, I probably wouldn't either. Now let's be on our way. The show's about to begin."

Chapter Sixty-Four

NOLA

Avad led the way, driving them a few miles away from the safe house. Nola watched as the police cars streamed by them, heading the way they had come.

She pictured the scene back in the house. Chicago had seen its fair share of violence, but that scene was definitely going to draw a lot of attention. She just hoped that it didn't interfere with what needed to be done for Bishop.

Avad pulled to a stop at the back of the parking lot of a supermarket. Rafe pulled the other SUV to a stop next to them, while Chandra pulled in behind them. "I'm going to check on Jack," Rascal said as he stepped out of the back of the SUV.

Nola started to open the door, but Rafe reached over and grabbed her arm gently. "You okay?"

She paused with the door partially open. "I'm good."

"That was Jonas Wagner on the phone?"

Nola nodded. "Yeah. He confirmed he has Bishop at his

home. And he wants me to go meet him there for some sort of, I don't know, tournament of champions."

"What does that mean?" he asked with a frown.

Nola nudged her chin toward the other car. "Let's go talk to everyone else, and I'll explain it all."

Rafe looked like he wanted to say more, but finally, he nodded. The two of them got out of the car and headed to the one with Jack in it. A peek in the back seat showed that Stan was monitoring the police channels, the blanket still wrapped around him. The back door was open, and Ileana was stitching up Jack's arm while Chandra spoke on the phone a few feet away. Nola frowned. "Who's she talking to?"

"One of my connections in the Chicago field office. We didn't have time to wipe down the safe house. Our fingerprints are going to ping. I'm having a team from the DoD take over until we get Bishop clear of all this," Ileana said.

"You can do that?" Rafe asked.

Ileana jabbed a needle into Jack's arm. "I can do a lot of things. Making that mess back there go away will be difficult, but I will make sure the blame is pointed back at the Wagner family. It shouldn't be too hard. After all, he did send them."

It was nice to know that Ileana still had that kind of pull. Nola turned her attention to Jack. "How you doing?"

He gave her a goofy smile. "Good. Good. I had a bunch of painkillers and a fifth of vodka. I'm feeling great."

Nola raised an eyebrow at that. "Ileana?"

"He's good. The painkillers should make sure that he's not feeling too much pain for the next couple of hours. They'll wear off by morning, though. And he definitely shouldn't be climbing any fences tonight."

"That's okay. He's not going to need to."

Jack raised an eyebrow at that. "We're not back to this nonsense about you going in alone, are we?"

"Sort of." But before Nola could say more, Chandra joined them.

"All good?" Rafe asked.

Chandra grimaced. "'Good' would be stretching it, but a team's being dispatched to take over the scene. Tomorrow morning, though, we're all going to need to answer some questions."

"Anyone know what those answers will be? Because I'm thinking the truth might be a bit of a problem," Rascal said.

"What, you think telling a bunch of cops we were using the place as a safe house before we declared war on a Chicago crime family might not go over well?" Jack asked.

"I'm thinking no," Rascal said with a shrug.

"That's tomorrow's problem. Tonight's is that Jonas has invited me to his home." Nola quickly explained about Jonas calling and what he'd said about wanting to face her one on one after she'd gone through a gauntlet of obstacles he placed in her path.

All of them looked at her stonily when she was done, with almost identical expressions on each of their faces. Expressions that said *no way in hell are you allowed to do that*.

Nola put up a hand before any of them could speak. "He will kill Bishop if I don't follow his rules."

"How will he even know if you have a gun on you?" Chandra asked.

"Well, I'm pretty sure when I shoot someone with it, it'll be a dead giveaway," Nola replied.

"You can't go in there unarmed," Rafe said.

"I won't be. He said I can't bring a gun. But he's all invested in samurai mythology. I'm betting that any samurai weapons would be free game. That leaves me with swords,

259

daggers, staffs. I'm pretty sure that I can bring any weapons, just not a gun. And I plan on doing exactly that." She looked at Avad.

He nodded. "I have some things in the back of the car. I'll get them."

Nola had known that he would. Now Rafe was shaking his head at her. "We're not going to just sit here and wait, hoping that you make it through these ridiculous death matches."

"And I'm not expecting you to. Jonas inviting me in is actually a good thing," Nola said.

"How the hell is this a good thing?" Chandra asked.

Nola smiled. "You guys said that we needed a distraction in order to get over the back wall. Well, it looks like that distraction is going to be me."

Chapter Sixty-Five

JONAS

His sword strapped to his side, Jonas let his fingers trail over the scabbard. He felt downright giddy. Finally, it was time for the showdown that he'd longed for all his life. This was why he'd been brought here. This was why he had been born at this time, so that the tiger could finally defeat the dragon.

The door to the dojo slipped open, and he looked behind him as Ivan stepped inside.

"Is she safe?" Jonas asked.

Ivan nodded. "I escorted her down to the bunker personally. She is resting comfortably in the bedroom down there."

"And did you provide her with food and drink?"

"I did, although she expressed her displeasure at being moved."

Jonas sighed. She didn't understand yet what was at stake. She was still reeling from all that she had been through in the last few hours, and it had been quite a bit. He could understand her being out of sorts.

But he would make it up to her after all of this. Once Nola James was taken out, they would be free to live in peace. He thought he'd start with a vacation down to the Fiji Islands. It would be a wonderful way for them to start their lives together. "Good, good. Any sign of Nola?"

"Not yet." Ivan paused. "Are you sure this is the best course of action? We could just take her out from afar. It would be easier."

Jonas whirled around and brought the tip of his sword to Ivan's neck. "Are you questioning my destiny?"

Ivan put up his hands, lifting his chin a little bit to avoid the blade. "No, nothing like that. I have no doubt in your abilities. But being it is a foregone conclusion how the fight will end, I thought it might be best for everyone if we just skipped right to the end."

Jonas studied him for a long moment and then shook his head. People in the modern world had no appreciation for the time it took for goals to be achieved. They wanted everything right now. But nothing worth having happened quickly.

And his defeat of Nola had been years in the making. He wouldn't be rushed. He would savor this time before his victory. After all, it was the journey that mattered.

He knew that he would succeed. He had no doubt of that. It was finally his turn. He was meant to be the successor this time round. Nola James's days were numbered. Actually, it wasn't days anymore. Now it was down to hours. "I appreciate the sentiment, but I won't be robbed of this moment."

He removed the sword from Ivan's neck.

Ivan rubbed his neck, even though Jonas had been very

careful not to even nick him. "Very well. If it's all the same to you, I think I'd like to watch from the bunker as well."

"Of course, of course. You should stay down there with Bishop. But when the time comes, I would like for the two of you to be here to witness my final triumph."

"Of course. I'll escort her myself. I'm looking forward to it." He gave a small bow and then crossed the room and headed out the door.

Jonas watched him go a smile on his face as he pictured what was going to happen in the next few hours. He sliced his sword through the air, listening to the sound it made as it twirled and listening to the sound of it slipping through the air. In his mind, he could see the blade literally cutting through the molecules that were unseen to the human eye.

He brought the sword to his side and looked up. *I am an instrument of death. And today I will sing beautifully.*

Chapter Sixty-Six

NOLA

The plan was fought over, debated, and finally accepted by everybody in attendance. No one was happy with it, but everyone accepted that it was the best that they were going to do. She would take one of the SUVs and drive in alone while the others went to the Santarro estate behind Wagner's. Jonas had only mentioned Avad, so they weren't sure if he even knew about the rest of them. There was a chance he didn't, which could work to their advantage. And right now, they needed all the advantages they could get.

Ileana, Stan, and Jack would use drones to keep an eye on what was happening in the back and to let the others know when they could get over the wall.

The other three would scale the wall, and their only job would be to find Bishop.

That was the biggest argument that they'd had.

Chandra, Rafe, and Rascal all argued that they should also help Nola. But Nola knew that that couldn't happen.

She needed to do this alone or forfeit Bishop's life, and she simply couldn't take the chance of that. Finally, the others agreed, although grudgingly.

Playing sniper, Avad would clear the way for the infiltration team while staying out of sight. Once Stan had control of the cameras, he would slip over the wall after the others. Stan stood in front of her now, the blanket still wrapped around her. He leaned closer. "I think I might have a way to communicate with Bishop," he whispered.

"Why are you whispering?" Nola asked.

Stan shot a look over his shoulder. "Because I'm not sure if it will work. And so I don't want to get anyone's hopes up."

"And you want me to go in and get Bishop no matter what."

Stan's mouth opened a little and his cheeks flamed.

Nola reached out and touched his arm. "It's okay. I'm glad someone is thinking only about Bishop. Now what is this way of communicating?"

"I need you to say the word Galahad." Before Nola could ask he hurried on. "I figure whatever's going to be happening will be being watched and maybe Bishop is one of the people watching. It's a program we created. It was just something we did when we were bored. I'm not sure if she even remembers it. But if she does and can reach us, it could really help."

"Galahad. Got it."

"Um, good luck," Stan said before gripping the blanket tighter to him and climbing back in the SUV.

Avad walked over to her and nodded. "The weapons are in the back of your car."

Nola nodded, and he looked down at her. "Don't hesitate. Anyone who steps in your path, you take them down without pause."

"I will," Nola said, as it was a promise she could easily keep.

He gave her a nod back and then stepped away, allowing Ileana in. She hugged Nola tight and then stepped back from her. "You are fearless, do you hear me? Fear will get in your way. Shove it aside. Fear will only bring about that which you are most afraid. Its job is to weaken you. So you will have no fear, do you hear me?"

"Yes."

Ileana squeezed her hand and then stepped aside. Chandra moved in and pulled a blade from her back pocket. "This is my lucky throwing knife. I want you to take it with you."

Nola raised an eyebrow. "You have a lucky knife?"

Chandra frowned. "You don't?"

Nola grinned and slid it into her pocket. "Of course I do. Thanks, Chandra."

Chandra stepped back, and now it was Rascal's turn. He stepped up, taking a deep breath. "You are one of the most ornery women I have ever met in my life."

"Thanks?"

Rascal hugged her tight. "And you better be stubborn as hell when it comes to someone trying to take your life, you hear me? You fight like it's the devil himself that you're going up against."

"That should be easy. I think Jonas Wagner may actually be the devil."

With one last hug, Rascal stepped aside. Rafe, who'd been leaning back against the other SUV, walked over to Nola. Silently, the two of them headed over to the driver's-side door of the SUV Nola would be taking. The others made a point of giving them some space.

Stan had waved at her from the back seat, looking worried. Jack had already said his goodbyes and was passed out in the back of the van. Nola wasn't sure how much help he was going to be even when it came to just the drone work. But Ileana said she'd use a stimulant if she had to get him on point. Nola almost felt bad for what Jack was going to have to go through.

Rafe opened up the car door for Nola. "I'd say take care of yourself, but I don't think you will."

"That's not really the point of all this."

His jaw tight, Rafe nodded. "Then I'll say this: You go through each and every one of them. You don't pause, you don't hesitate, you don't take a moment to think about whether or not it's the right course of action. You trust your gut. When you go with your gut, you're the most impressive fighter I've ever seen. So trust what your instincts are telling you. If they tell you to drop, drop. If they tell you to jump, jump. Don't second-guess yourself, Nola."

"I won't." She reached for the door handle and placed one hand on it.

"Nola," Rafe said.

She'd turn back to him. "Yes?"

He leaned forward and tipped her chin up and kissed her gently on the lips. "I think I'd regret it if I never did that. Give him hell."

The warmth of his lips still on hers, she nodded. "I plan to."

Chapter Sixty-Seven

The drive from the parking lot to Wagner's estate took twenty minutes, although Nola took a longer route so the others would be able to get into the Santarro estate and set up before she arrived. Unlike earlier in the day when she and Avad had traveled here, there was very little traffic out at this time of night to slow her up.

Even though Nola had agreed to allow the others to get set up before she arrived at the Wagner estate, it took everything in her not to punch down on the accelerator and get this tournament of death started.

But that would be reckless, and that she could not do. Because she needed to keep Wagner's attention on her long enough for the others to get Bishop out. So she took her time driving. She used the drive to calm her breathing and to center herself.

She shoved all worries about Bishop and the team that she had left behind out of her mind. Those worries would just get in the way now. Now what she needed to do was focus on the job ahead. She breathed in. She breathed out, slowing her heart rate.

A few blocks before Wagner's estate, she pulled over to the side of the street and went to the back of the truck. She pulled over the weapons bag Avad had left her and loaded herself up.

Unsurprisingly, he'd given her a lot of toys to work with. She had a dozen throwing knives, which she strapped around her waist. She had two metal clubs that she twirled to get the weight of and smiled, knowing that they would do the job pretty well. A good hit with one of them could shatter a bone.

She had a couple of more knives, which she stashed at various locations on her body, including one knife that she was a big fan of. The end of it slipped around a finger, and the knife itself looked like a raptor claw.

That would come in handy.

She put sheaths along her forearms that would protect them from any strikes. And she did the same to her thighs and around her waist. It was as close to armor as she could manage.

Pulling her hair back into a tight ponytail, she took a breath. Then she grabbed a bottle of water, took a quick swig, and slammed the back of the SUV shut. It was time.

Chapter Sixty-Eight

BISHOP

The subterranean level that the lawyer had brought Bishop down to wasn't nearly as posh as the upstairs level. It looked more like a military bunker than part of an ostentatious mansion. Concrete blocks lined the walls, and even the floor and ceilings were made of concrete. They had passed through what looked like a giant blast door to get here.

Jonas was seriously paranoid if he'd created something like this in the basement of his home.

The room she'd been shown to was a guest room. Someone had tried to soften it up by covering the concrete walls with velvet fabrics and throwing down a thick rug on the floor. But the room still felt cold, and it wasn't just the temperature.

Bishop had searched every corner of the room looking for any possible escape, but there was nothing. She was basically in a well-appointed cell.

She hopped up on the edge of the bed, her feet braced

on the bench below her, her boots tapping away on the upholstered fabric as she nervously looked around the room. She could not just sit here and wait to be rescued or be damned to this life. She had to do something. Hopping off the bed, she paced, trying to figure something else out.

There was a knock at the door, and then it opened. She whirled around as the lawyer stepped inside. "Miss Rhodes. I thought you might like to join me in the control room to watch the festivities."

Control room equaled computers. And computers meant maybe a way to communicate.

Bishop nodded. "Actually, I would really like that."

Chapter Sixty-Nine

NOLA

The phone rang as Nola pulled onto Wagner's street. She slid her thumb over the screen. "Yes?"

"We see you coming down the street. My men will search you to make sure that you didn't bring a gun."

"All right." She noted where five men stood in the street, their guns aimed at her. Apparently the gun rule only worked one way. "They seem to be armed."

Jonas chuckled. "Just long enough to make sure that you're following the rules. They're not part of this fight unless you make them part of it. Now, pull over."

Nola did as she was ordered, easing the car into the curb.

"Get out."

Setting the phone down, Nola gripped the two metal bars from the passenger seat. *Let's hope that bastard wasn't lying,* she thought as she opened the driver's-side door, keeping her hands in view. She stepped out with the metal bars at her side as she walked toward the men.

They didn't tense at the sight of the weapons in her hand. That was a good sign. One of them stepped away from the other. She nodded at the man who stepped toward her. "So what's your name? Galahad?"

The man ignored her question and nodded to the hood of her car. "Empty all metal and weapons onto the hood of your car."

Placing the bars down first, she pulled off her belt with the throwing knives and then added the rest of her knives to the pile.

A man came over and ran a wand over her to see if there was any more metal.

She tensed a little as he went down to her ankles, but the wand never sounded.

He nodded and stepped back, speaking into a radio before nodding at another man, who spoke into a phone and then looked at Nola. "You may take back all of your weapons."

Apparently she'd been right about the weapons. And Jonas hadn't been lying about the rules for this little engagement.

She quickly strapped all the weapons back on her and slid the two metal bars into the carrier along her back.

Once everything was secure again, she looked at the men. "Now what?"

The man nodded down the road. "Now you walk. You'll meet your first opponent shortly."

Nola didn't like the idea of giving her back to a group of men with guns, but she supposed there was no helping it.

She nodded and started to walk down the road.

Chapter Seventy

BISHOP

The control room was just down the hall from the bedroom that Bishop had been shown to. Although Ivan had called it a control room, it was less a control room and more of an entertainment room. There were rows of recliners, and they all faced a large screen.

Right now, the screen showed a view of a street where five men stood, all of them armed.

Ivan gestured to the row of seats closest to the screen. "Why don't you take a seat? Are you hungry? We have water, popcorn, snacks. If you want something a little more filling, there's some sandwiches set up at the buffet as well."

Was she hungry? Her stomach felt like a hollowed-out pit. These guys were going to try and kill Nola, and they thought she might be a bit peckish? She shook her head, her focus on the screen. "Where is that?"

"Just outside the estate."

If that was Jonas's normal security, it was strange. The

five men were spread out across the road. "What are they doing?"

"Waiting for the festivities to begin," Ivan said before he walked over to the buffet and started filling up a plate.

What did that mean? She was tempted to ask the question out loud, but she was pretty sure she wasn't going to get a satisfying answer. Pulling her gaze from the screen, she studied the room. The recliners were plush, and all had tables set next to them to allow someone to set down their food and drinks. There were three rows of eight recliners, four on each side, with an aisle of stairs in between.

In the corner of the room along the back wall, which also had heavy red drapes covering the concrete, was a man who sat with two monitors set up in front of him and headphones on. Every once in a while, he would hit some keys on his keyboard, and the scene on the screen would shift. She moved along the back to look at his screens. Instead of one view of the street, he had multiples, as well as a few of the exterior of the house.

That computer could come in awfully handy. She was going to have to figure out a way to get access to it. And right now that didn't seem possible because she didn't know what exactly was going on.

The man caught her looking and gave her a hard glare.

She stared back at him for a long moment before he looked away back at his computer, and then she continued on. The computer guy wasn't someone she was worried about. She was pretty sure if it came down to it, she could take him out at least.

The security that came with Ivan was a different story. Both were armed and thickly muscled. Plus, there was an additional guard with a gun at his waist who had already been in the room when they entered. Taking all of them on would be suicide, or at least really painful, so that was out, at least right now.

Bishop knew that she was at least two levels below ground. And there was that blast door. She prayed that it hadn't been shut or that there were no plans to shut it because she didn't know how, if she was going to make a run for it, she'd be able to get through that. In fact, she knew she wouldn't be able to. So she needed to be sure that thing was open before she tried anything.

"The show's about to begin," Ivan said as he took a seat, a giant ham sandwich on the plate in front of him.

His two security guys had loaded up their plates as well, and they sat in the second row of seats behind their boss.

Bishop moved closer to the screen as a car came into view at the end of the street. She squinted her eyes, trying to get a look at who was in it and struggled to hold in the gasp when she recognized Nola behind the wheel.

She'd come. She was doing whatever it was that Jonas had instructed her to do.

No, Nola. Just keep driving. Don't stop, she begged silently.

But the Nola on the screen didn't listen to her. She slowed the car to a stop and then slowly stepped out.

One of the men approached her. "So what's your name? Galahad?" Nola asked.

Bishop's head jerked up. Stan. She'd talked to Stan. That was their code word. Hope burned in her chest.

She and Stan had worked out this program where if one of them ended up in a bad situation, they could contact each other through a secure texting program that they had developed. It was untraceable. It couldn't provide an exact location of where someone was, but whoever could access it could give them information that would allow someone hopefully to find them.

It had been a stupid idea they'd had one afternoon when things were quiet. It had been fun to create the program, but Bishop had never imagined that she would ever use it for real.

She couldn't believe that Stan was actually a part of this. He was so nervous. But she supposed Nola hadn't given him a choice in the matter. She winced a little, imagining that meeting and hoped that Stan hadn't come out of it too scarred.

Bishop looked around the room. Now she just needed to get a hold of someone's phone. That should be doable.

On screen, Nola emptied all of her weapons onto the hood of her car, and the small burst of hope from earlier shriveled.

With each weapon that she placed on the car, Bishop's heart dropped even farther. No, no, no, no, no. What was she doing? She couldn't just hand over all her weapons without even fighting. That wasn't Nola.

Ivan looked over from his spot on the couch. "Oh, don't worry. This isn't part of the fight. This is just kind of like a registration."

Bishop stared at him, not understanding what he was talking about, before her gaze returned to the screen. One of the suits ran a security wand over Nola and then gestured for her to take back all her weapons.

Bishop stared in disbelief as Nola loaded back up again. "She's allowed to keep all of them?"

"Jonas wants this to be an actual battle. It's not fair if his men are armed and Nola isn't. So she gets to face each of them with whatever weapons she can bring with her, just no guns."

Bishop stared at the screen, her jaw hanging open. Was he insane? And a small glimmer of hope began to build once again in her chest. If Nola had an array of gunmen set against her, her chances were slim to none.

But if she had to fight her way through? Well, Bishop had seen Nola fight.

And when Nola had something to fight for, she was even more lethal. The guys arrayed against her were only fighting for a paycheck.

Bishop's appetite finally returned. She stood up and headed over to the buffet and grabbed a sandwich. Nola was coming to get her. And she needed to be ready. And she'd barely eaten in the last twenty-four hours.

She took a seat at the opposite end of the row from Ivan, placing her plate on the table next to her. A glance up at the screen showed Nola walking down the street. And Bishop couldn't help but think she looked like a gunslinger at high noon.

Come on, Nola. You can do this.

But Nola wasn't the only one with a mission. She needed to get one of the phones off the people in this room. With Stan working with Nola, she'd have a way to contact them without anyone knowing. It would be untraceable, which was critical because she had no doubt they were monitoring all the cell phone chatter in the area to make sure no one was riding to Nola's rescue.

But how was she going to do it? As if in answer to her prayers, one of the security guys got up and headed to the buffet with his empty plate. Bishop quickly slipped out of her seat with her full cup of Pepsi. She head over the buffet as well, only watching it from the corner of her eyes, as if fixated on the screen.

It didn't take a lot of acting.

She moved closer to the security guy and then took one more step. Her cup crashed into his chest, and she jumped back while turning the cup and dumping the contents on his jacket and pants.

"What the hell?" the man yelled.

"Oh my god, I'm so sorry. I was just . . ." She gestured to the big screen.

The man growled.

Bishop grabbed a handful of napkins and started wiping down his jacket. "I'm really sorry. Let me just—"

He snatched the napkins from her hand. "Get away from me."

Bishop quickly backed away. "Sorry." She slunk into the back row of the control room, keeping her hand placed on the phone she'd grabbed from the man's pocket.

Step one complete. Her eyes shifted back to the screen. She hoped Nola was just as lucky, although she doubted Nola's challenge would be as easily accomplished.

Chapter Seventy-One

RAFE

They had gotten into the Santarro estate without too much bother. Chandra had used her connections to get the codes for the security system, and they were now set up in the family room on the first floor.

Jack had been moved inside, and they had tapered off some of the painkillers so that he could man the drones. Rascal had gone and set them up outside while Jack set up the monitor along the kitchen island with Stan's help.

Rafe found himself pacing along the back wall of windows, staring at the estate's backyard. He couldn't believe that they'd let her go alone. It was insanity. He should have fought harder to make sure that at least one of them went with her. What was he thinking? What were any of them thinking?

Ileana moved up softly next to him. "She's going to be all right."

He stopped his pacing but didn't look at her, keeping his

gaze on the brick wall in the distance. "You don't know that."

"Yes, I do. I have known Nola for a lot longer than you have. I've known her longer than anyone here. I knew her before she even met my David."

Rafe pulled his gaze from the fence to look at her. "What was she like back then, before David, before Molly?"

Ileana smiled. "She was a force. She was this burning light to see that justice was done. It is a rare attribute in the intelligence field. There were some rather difficult situations that Nola was placed in that I thought for sure she would not be able to get out of, but she did each and every time. Not uninjured, of course, but she managed to get out. For a long time, I couldn't quite figure out how, but then I realized it was because she didn't care."

"What do you mean?"

Rafe had seen how much she cared about Bishop, about his kids, about Ileana and Avad, he'd seen how much she cared about him too.

"Most people, when they go into battle, their goal is to take on the enemy, but part of their goal is also to protect themselves. They're always consciously aware of their own mortality.

"Nola is, of course, aware of her own mortality as well, but she is not hampered by it. She does not pause to consider the possibility that this could be her last moment. I have a feeling that a long time ago, Nola accepted that death was a part of life, and she does not fear it. She's not rushing toward it, to embrace it the way I feared she had been just after David and Molly died, but she doesn't fear it, and that makes her a formidable opponent."

"That's not easing my worries."

Ileana smiled. "It should. Because Nola fights with lethal

efficiency. She shuts all those emotions down, and she just does what needs to be done without thinking, without contemplating the ramifications. She's the most instinctual fighter I've ever seen. And she will come through this."

Rafe paused, staring out into the dark night. "But at what cost? What Nola will we get back? Is it possible that she'll dive too deep into the darkness and be unable to resurface?"

A crease appeared between Ileana's eyebrows as she shifted her gaze to the wall of windows, as if she, too, was searching for a glimpse of Nola. "That I do worry about. After David and Molly, the darkness, it threatened to swallow her whole. By taking on the cases that she did, she was able to pull herself out, to funnel that darkness into a righteous cause.

"But I don't know what this will do to her. After meeting you, the kids, Rascal, and linking up with Jack again, it changed something in Nola. She became lighter. The darkness, it was still there for Nola, it will always be there, but it was held at bay.

"But in order to do what needs to be done, she's going to have to drop that wall between herself and the darkness. She's going to have to *be* the darkness."

"And what happens if we can't pull her out of it this time?" Rafe asked.

The troubled looked on Ileana's face grew deeper. "Then I'm afraid she will no longer be ours."

Chapter Seventy-Two

NOLA

The road was quiet. Nola knew that the home directly across from Jonas had only its staff these days. The couple that owned the home were on a tour of Europe.

The neighbors on either side were similarly out of town.

That still left staff, and Nola wasn't sure what Jonas's plan was to keep them from calling the cops. She hoped that it wasn't anything lethal.

Of course, if he waited until she got into the house, then it was possible they would be able to keep the noise down. These homes were so far apart from one another that sound wouldn't travel very well.

Nola walked slowly down the street, scanning from side to side. She could feel the eyes of the security on her back. The hair at the back of her neck rose, although she didn't think any of them had pulled out one of the guns that they kept at their waist. But the possibility that they could made her uneasy.

Avad was somewhere nearby with a high-powered sniper rifle, keeping an eye on them. He would stay as long as Nola was in view. It was the best that any of them could do as backup besides just coming in and taking out the security.

But that would sign Bishop's death warrant, and Nola wasn't willing to take that chance.

She still had Dr. Legion's warning running through her mind: *He's fully committed to the delusion now. He believes that this life is just one of many. He will do as he said, which makes him extremely dangerous.*

She couldn't take that chance with Bishop's life.

Jonas Wagner. It was still difficult to connect that little boy with the man who had orchestrated all of this. She didn't remember much about Jonas from that time period. Her focus was entirely on Bishop and Ariel. But that little boy had obviously traveled down his own dark path for him to create something like this. Although, she supposed she'd seen worse transformations over the year.

"It's okay, Mommy. He's going to follow the rules," Molly said as she appeared next to Nola, her hands in her pockets as she walked by Nola's side.

"What makes you say that, sweetheart?" Nola asked, still keeping up her vigilance.

"He really does believe he's a samurai. He wants to fight you. He wants you to win so that you can face him and he can beat you."

In a weird sort of way, that was comforting. At least she didn't have to worry about a bullet in her back. Unless, of course, Molly was actually her own delusion, in which case, it was a false assurance.

Molly cocked her head to the side with a smile. "You

think I'm a delusion? That's good, Mommy. That means you're growing too."

Nola wasn't sure about that. "Where are they?"

Molly nodded toward the open garage. "There are two waiting for you in the garage. They want to wait until you're inside so that the neighbors don't hear anything."

Just as Nola had been thinking. "Did you see any guns?"

Molly shook her head. "No. Like I said, he's following the rules, Mommy. He's not going to let any of his people destroy his chance. He's been waiting for this for years."

Nola rolled her shoulders. "Then let's not make him wait any longer."

Chapter Seventy-Three

RAFE

They had set up a drone along the neighbor's fence line. It wasn't a great image. But it was enough for Rafe to see Nola walking confidently down the street.

Rafe's chest clenched as he watched her. He hated letting her go in alone. He understood it and even supported it, but he still hated it.

He wondered if this was what Mariana had felt every time he'd walked out the door to go to work. She'd always been so worried for him. And he'd laughed off her fears, telling her that he would be fine, even though each time he stepped out that door he'd known that there was a good chance he might not come home that night.

He'd always thought that she was softer than he was. But to be able to deal with this feeling every day, that took a certain kind of strength that he hadn't recognized before.

"Avad's in place?" he asked as Ileana walked up next to him.

They were in the main room. Rascal and Chandra were walking a perimeter. Rafe had just set up a sniper's nest upstairs with Jack. He was feeling better, although he still wasn't 100%. Jack and Avad, when he returned, would keep watch while the others went over the wall.

"Avad's in position. He's got a full view of her. He said that the guards are following Jonas's rules, even though they do have guns. None of them have reached for them."

Rafe nodded, turning his gaze back to Nola.

She was scanning the street, but she tilted her head to the side for a moment longer than she'd done before, and he knew that she was seeing Molly.

He didn't have any fear of ghosts. He'd grown up with a grandmother who'd told him about the ghosts that she'd seen all throughout her life.

The fact that Nola saw her daughter was actually a comfort in a way. He knew how devastated Nola had been by her daughter's and husband's death. The idea that Molly was still able to offer her comfort in small ways, Rafe appreciated that.

Nola had just reached the driveway and was walking along it.

Rafe tensed, knowing that as soon as she went into the home, they'd lose all visuals of her. The home was situated about a quarter mile back from the road. Nola grew smaller and smaller as she walked toward it, her steps unhurried but determined.

The garage door lay open. He watched as she stepped inside and the garage door slid shut behind her.

Ileana let out a breath. "It's up to Nola now."

Chapter Seventy-Four

NOLA

As soon as Nola was clear of the garage door, it slid quietly closed behind her. No one jumped out at her as she scanned the space, her nerves on high alert. It was not a small space. It easily fit twenty cars of various makes and models, two powerboats, a half dozen motorcycles, and a couple of Ski-Doos in the corner. But no people were in view.

The cars all sat in rows, but the garage was extra tall, allowing for a crane device that could be used to move some of the cars without driving them.

Along the right wall was a mechanic's dream setup. Nola noted all of the heavy tools set on a pegboard against the wall. She quickly cataloged the size and shape of the tools in case she needed them.

The garage itself was quiet. No sound came from inside, so she stopped still, giving herself a moment to familiarize herself with her surroundings. The cars were relatively close together, which was going to make fighting difficult in some areas.

Her metal batons wouldn't do any good that close. She'd have to go for the small daggers or maybe the throwing knives. She calculated scenarios and situations as she started to walk slowly through the cars, noting the door along the back that led into the house.

Molly had disappeared just as she stepped into the garage. A rustle of material was all she heard before she threw herself to the ground.

A knife embedded itself in the Ferrari next to her.

It had come from somewhere to her right. Lying flat against the garage floor, she spied two feet in thick black boots about six cars over.

Scrambling back on hands and knees, she slid along the edge of the car, heading in that direction.

Keeping low, she hurried toward the spot where the boots had been. She stayed hidden behind the cars as she moved. She reached the bumper of the car where she had seen him and peeked around the corner, but there was no one there.

She cursed silently. She hadn't heard him move. But he knew where she was, and she had no idea where he'd taken off to. She lay down on the floor looking underneath the cars but saw no sign of him.

A scream came from overhead.

Nola's head jolted up as a man came flying at her from the roof of a car. She rolled out of the way as his feet stomped into the ground where her head had just been. He hurried after her and slammed a kick into her ribs.

Nola grunted at the hit but managed to grab his boot and use it to turn herself around. She slammed one of her boots into his groin.

She reared back and hit him again in the same spot. His head bent forward.

Keeping a hold on his leg, she arched herself up wrapped her left leg around his neck and yanked him to the ground.

He crashed into the concrete floor with Nola's leg wrapped around his neck. He tried to reach back and grab her but she easily dodged his attempts.

While not letting up the pressure on his neck, she slammed her fist into his ribs over again and again. Slowly, his scrambling hands at her leg eased until they stopped entirely. With one more tug at his neck, she released him. He fell heavily to the floor.

Nola scrambled back and grabbed the knife that had been knocked out of her hand when she rolled and slowly got up, scanning the area.

Keeping an eye on her surroundings, she placed her fingers at the man's neck. He was still alive. She debated for a moment. Did she kill him now or let him live? She didn't want him popping back up again down the road and having to fight him again.

But he was completely unconscious. She couldn't bring herself to take his life. Not yet. Not until she knew what the rules were.

She sat up but stayed crouched, waiting for the second guy. Molly appeared between two cars to her right. She pointed farther into the garage.

Staying hidden behind the cars, she made her way slowly in the direction Molly indicated. Crouching down low enough to see under the cars, she scanned the area for the man but didn't see any sign of him. Where was he? Was he hiding behind the tires?

"Mommy, get down!" Molly yelled.

Nola flattened herself to the ground as two arrows slammed into the tires of the classic Ford Bronco next to her. She rolled underneath it, out of the archer's view.

He'd taken the high ground. From the angle of the arrows, she knew there was only one spot that he could be: the car elevator.

Nola's mind whirled as she pictured the garage, an idea already forming. She rolled out from underneath the car on the other side and kept low as she slunk away from the car elevator.

She had seen the controls for the elevator about halfway down the garage, against the back wall. If she could get to those, she could bring that guy back down to earth.

Of course, she had to cover completely open space before she did that. And that she definitely did not like.

She spied welding equipment along the side of the wall. A car door lay next to an old bumper and some other parts of a car.

Nola hurried over to an Aston Martin, staring at the car door, another idea forming in her mind. Taking a deep breath, she sprinted over to the car door. An arrow just missed her right foot, and her pulse rocketed.

She grabbed the door and hefted it up, keeping it on her side, her head ducked down.

Arrows rained into the car door but couldn't penetrate all the way through. She reached the long bench against the back wall and slammed her palm into the button that controlled the elevator.

The whirring of gears told her it was working. A glance around the door showed that the elevator had slowly begun to lower. Step one down.

On the bench, a container of antifreeze sat along with oil and other supplies. She quickly grabbed the antifreeze and a rag and then hurried back behind the cars.

Her assailant had stopped firing once the elevator had started to move.

Nola uncorked the antifreeze once she got safely behind the cars and then started to move, listening for her opponent.

This assailant wasn't as quiet as the last one. She could hear him moving. Weaving in and out of the cars, Nola carefully left a trail of antifreeze.

Then she grabbed her throwing knives once she was done, as she spied the individual for a moment above the hood of a red Ferrari. Taking a deep breath, she raced in between cars, her attention focused on where he'd just been.

His head popped up. She chucked a throwing knife at his head. He let out a yell as he scrambled forward into the space between the cars. She released the second knife and caught him in the shin. He let out a cry, stumbling and crawling behind a car.

Nola smiled. She pulled the matches from the pocket of her pants, lit a match, and brought the flame to the rag she'd stuffed in the antifreeze container, then she tossed it over the car.

The antifreeze ignited, creating a wall of flame behind the archer. His head jolted as he turned to look at it.

Which was the distraction Nola was waiting for. She slid across the hood of a stingray Corvette and slammed her foot into the side of the man's head. His skull crashed into the side of a souped-up Hummer.

Nola dropped to the floor and then kicked him under the chin. He went flying back, his head crashing into the Hummer again before he lay still.

Looking around, Nola didn't hear or see anyone else. Molly peeked out from behind the cars. "That's all there was, Mommy."

As if to confirm her statement, the door on the far side of the room opened, beckoning Nola farther into the house.

It was an invitation Nola wasn't going to turn down.

Chapter Seventy-Five

BISHOP

The mood in the control room went from excitement to concern to what Bishop considered to be serious stress. It was hard for her not to keep her smile back. Apparently these guys thought that Nola would be taken out in the garage.

But they had underestimated her.

Bishop had watched the scene unfold with her heart in her throat. She could barely contain her terror as that guy leapt out and threw that knife at Nola. And then she had could hardly keep in her cheer when Nola finished off the second guy.

"Why didn't she kill him?" one of the bodyguards asked.

"I don't know," the lawyer replied, his gaze focused on the screen.

It was hard to keep the disgust off her face as Bishop watched them. She knew that they thought of this as some sort of movie or maybe something like a pay-per-view fight.

They didn't seem to get—or maybe they just didn't care—that lives were on the line.

But Bishop was glad that Nola had left both those guys alive. She could have killed both of them. She'd chosen not to.

Because she didn't need to. That, as far as Bishop was concerned, was true strength.

On screen, the door to the house opened, and Nola made her way toward it.

Bishop slid out the phone again and typed quickly. *Nola made it through the first encounter. She took out two of their guys in the garage. She's heading into the house.* She slid the phone back into her pocket.

She couldn't help Nola, but maybe she could help the others when the time came for them to come in.

Bishop stared up at the screen. *Come on. Give me something that can help.*

Chapter Seventy-Six

NOLA

The dark doorway beckoned. Nola made her way slowly across the garage, keeping her eyes peeled for any movement and her ears cocked for any sound.

But it was quiet.

She grimaced and rubbed the side of her chest where the man had kicked her. That was definitely going to bruise pretty good. But overall, she'd come out okay. Still, she had a feeling that those two had been the least skilled of the group she would be up against.

She had to admit that Jonas had a serious *Enter the Dragon* kind of vibe going here. As she approached the open door leading farther into the house, Nola moved to the side so she wouldn't be an easy target.

"They're in the hallways, Mommy. They're waiting for you," Molly said.

Nola acknowledged the information with a simple nod

of her head. Then she took stock of her weapons. She still had everything but two of the throwing knives.

Unless they did some serious renovations, the hallway would be wider, which would give her more room to maneuver. She pulled out the batons as she peeked through the doorway.

The hallway was indeed wider, about ten feet across. There were no doorways or hidden alcoves in this stretch of the house, but it was long. It curved to the left about twenty feet ahead.

Taking a deep breath, she stepped through the door. Keeping her eyes peeled, she walked slowly, her footsteps muffled by the thick carpet. She paused as she approached the corner and listened but didn't hear anyone on the other side. She didn't see anyone either, but there were two doors in this hall.

Around the corner, the first door was on the left side of the hall. It was locked. Of course, that only meant she couldn't get in. It was entirely possible someone was waiting inside until she passed so they could sneak up behind her. She'd need to keep her head on a swivel. She moved farther down the hall, trying the other door, but it, too, was locked. Up ahead was a circular staircase leading up.

Nola eyed the staircase suspiciously. It was metal, which meant that as soon as she stepped on it, there'd be no way to muffle her steps.

But there was also no other way open to her unless she wanted to go back and hang out in the garage. There was a reason that she had been told to go in this direction. They wanted her upstairs for the next challenge.

Nola peered up the stairwell but didn't see anyone. Taking a breath, she slid the batons back into their holders. They'd be of no use on the stairwell.

She climbed it as silently as she could but still winced every time the metal creaked. She reached the top of the stairwell without any incident. But she knew her reprieve wasn't going to last.

Her foot had just touched the hardwood on the main level when a man bolted out from the left, seemingly out of nowhere. He'd been behind a curtain. He swung a bat at her head.

Nola ducked and tackled him around the waist, slamming her shoulder into his hip while simultaneously pulling back on his calves.

The man hit the floor with a thump.

Nola kneed him in the groin and then flipped his left leg over her head, trapping it with her knee as she reached up for his throat.

Keeping his leg locked, she pressed her forearm to his throat as he wailed at her, trying to throw her off. Nola ignored the blows. She wanted to go for her knife, but that would mean taking the pressure off his neck and the hand that held the bat. And she couldn't do that. Just a few more seconds and he would be out.

But she didn't get those seconds.

A second attacker dressed all in black ran down the hall toward her. Flicking her gaze between her oncoming attacker and the one under her, she waited until the very last moment. As the second attacker dove for her, she rolled off the first man, grabbing the shirt of second and then, using his momentum, sent him flying up and over her as she rolled. He slammed into the metal stairwell behind her. His back cracked audibly on impact.

The first attacker rolled to his hands and knees, coughing. Nola got to her feet and slammed her knee into his face. His head whipped to the side and he dropped.

Nola didn't have time to appreciate the quick victory. Two more men hustled down the hall toward her. But these two weren't rushing in like the other two had done. They took their time as they moved forward, and that told Nola that these guys had a little more training than the two thugs she had just taken out.

She straightened eyeing both of them. The one on the right darted forward, throwing out a right hook.

Nola twirled into the man's chest, wrapping her arm around his extended arm and continued the arc of his throw. He let out a cry as he was flung across the space and into his partner.

His partner shoved him away and bolted forward going to grab Nola around the waist.

Dropping to the floor, Nola wrapped her arms around the man's ankle, slamming her shoulder into his knee.

The crack was loud as his knee dislocated. Slamming an uppercut into the man's groin, she darted back to her feet and finished him off with a hook to his cheek. He collapsed with a cry, not unconscious but wishing he was.

The man who'd first thrown the hook to her head shook his head and then rolled his shoulders as if resetting.

Nola skirted around the man moaning on the floor as the guy brought up his fists.

The move almost made Nola smile. This fight was actually kind of fun.

The man shot out with a right cross, followed by a left, but Nola easily deflected both. At the third punch, Nola slipped to the side and latched onto the man's wrist, yanking him forward. Unprepared for the move, the man stumbled, losing his balance.

Stepping farther to the side, she latched onto his wrist and then rolled her forearm along the man's elbow until it pointed straight at the ceiling, then she brought her forearm down on it. The man cried out as his arm protested the pressure.

It was an exceedingly painful move, forcing the elbow to head in a direction the bones were not created for.

And Nola knew with a little more pressure, she would break his elbow. So she raised her forearm a little bit and then slammed back down into the man's elbow. There was a satisfying crack.

She grabbed him by the hair and slammed her knee into his face. He collapsed to the ground, no longer a threat to her. She stepped by him and made her way slowly down the hall, but no one else appeared.

Looks like round two goes to me.

Chapter Seventy-Seven

BISHOP

She's through the second challenge. Bishop typed quickly, trying to keep herself from cheering. She hadn't found anything that would help the others, so she figured the least she could do was keep them updated on Nola's progress.

The lawyer and his security had grown more and more quiet as Nola made her way through each of the men set against her.

Apparently they thought they were in for an enjoyable little show where they got to see a woman get the crap beaten out of her. But that same woman slowly and carefully taking out each of the obstacles in her path hadn't been what they were looking for.

Bishop grinned. That was Nola: always destroying people's hopes for an easy victory.

The lawyer stood up and glanced around the room before his gaze fell on Bishop. "Who is she? Where'd she train?"

Trying to keep the smile from her face, Bishop shrugged. "I don't know. She's just Nola."

The man narrowed his eyes at her. "All right, come on, you're going back to the room."

Bishop frowned. "What? Why? I want to see this."

"Well, you might, but I'm not staying around for the end of this. I have a feeling I know how this is going to go. And I don't intend to be a part of it."

While she thought that was a smart move on his part, she couldn't let him take her back to that other room. She wouldn't be able to report to the others what was going on.

"Can't you just lock me in here? I mean, I won't do anything. Where am I going to go? And that way I can watch what's going on."

The lawyer hesitated for a moment and then shrugged. "You know what? Jonas wants you to see this. So yeah, you stay here. I'll put some guards on the door. But don't even think of leaving."

"Absolutely," Bishop said quickly.

The lawyer nodded to his security, and they headed for the door.

Bishop pulled out the phone and quickly typed. *The lawyer and his two security guards are leaving.*

Chapter Seventy-Eight

RAFE

Rafe was watching the camera feed from the back room, but there was absolutely nothing to see. There were three guards back there, but none of them had moved toward the front of the house during Nola's entrance as they had hoped.

They were coming up with a second plan, which involved Jack and Avad taking out each of the men as they reappeared.

Stan was over in the corner of the room doing something on the laptop. He looked up as Rascal stepped back into the room. "Bishop just sent another text. Nola got through level two."

"That's our girl," Rascal grinned. Even Rafe had to smile.

The front door opened, and they turned as Avad stepped inside. He nodded. "I heard the new plan. I'll get into position."

Without waiting for a word from anyone, he headed up the stairs.

After watching him go, Rascal turned back to Rafe. "He's a man of few words, that one. I can see why him and Nola get along so well."

Rafe scoffed. "Yeah, two peas in a pod, those two."

"Guys?" Stan asked, excitement in his voice.

"What's going on?" Rafe asked as he and Rascal moved toward him.

"It looks like the lawyer is getting antsy. He's leaving Bishop alone in the control room and taking off with two of his security. He's leaving the estate."

Raising an eyebrow, Rafe looked over at Rascal. "You feel like taking a drive?"

Rascal grinned. "Oh, I definitely feel like taking a drive."

Chapter Seventy-Nine

JONAS

The man lay on the floor, holding his leg, a grimace of pain across his face. Jonas leaned closer to the screen and then hit the control on the remote to rewind the footage. He watched as Nola grabbed the man's ankle and slammed her shoulder into his knee all over again.

He paused the image just as the man was screaming in pain. Jonas shook his head. It had been a poor showing by his people thus far. Nola had taken one hit in the garage, but since then she had cut through his people like it was nothing.

A small trickle of fear rolled through him, but he shoved it away. He was not that poor, defenseless adolescent boy he had once been.

That boy had been pitiful. He'd always been in his father's shadow and always found himself wanting when his father's gaze fell upon him. It wasn't until he truly embraced who he was that he had found the strength within.

I am a warrior, he thought, straightening his spine. *That is my true birthright.*

And warriors didn't crumble at the sight of opposition. They embraced it. They looked forward to the challenge to come.

He nodded. Yes, he would face Nola James, and his victory would finally be complete.

And the next challenge wouldn't be so easy for her. The opponents she had met thus far had been leftovers from his father's crew. They were tough men, strong men, and fearless men for the most part, but they weren't well trained. They relied on the fact that most people didn't know how to respond when a punch was thrown at their head.

Nola James wasn't one of those people. She didn't flinch. She didn't cower away. She responded. And his men weren't prepared for that.

But that was all right. Because he now had the information he needed for how he would fight her.

He would not hold back. He would not give her an opportunity to slip past him. She didn't hesitate, and he had to be the same. He would give her no chance, no refuge from his attack.

And killing her would be a true honor.

Chapter Eighty

RAFE

Waiting two blocks away from the Wagner estate, Avad, Chandra, Rafe, and Rascal were in the Durango they had borrowed from the Santarro garage. As soon as Stan had indicated that the lawyer was leaving, they knew they needed to grab him.

Stan and Jack were still back at the estate, keeping an eye on things. Ileana and Chandra were each in one of the other rentals. Ileana would make the initial stop. Jack spoke through the radio. "Okay, they're coming up on the turn now. Get ready. Ileana, get into position."

Jack had sent a drone out to keep an eye on the Mercedes as it left the Wagner estate. The fact that this was all going down at night meant they could use them with a much lower chance of discovery.

Ileana pulled out onto the street. Chandra waited a moment before pulling out behind her.

As soon as the Escalade holding the lawyer drove by, Rafe started to count. At five, he pulled out behind them.

"Don't get too close," Rascal warned.

Rafe nodded, easing off on the gas.

Up ahead, Ileana was slowing down so that there was less space between her car and the lawyer's.

Chandra pulled up into the lane next to them and drove, matching the speed of the Escalade as Rafe closed the distance from behind them.

"Now," Jack said through the earpiece.

Ileana slammed on her brakes. The Escalade did the same as Chandra swerved to the right, boxing them in.

Rafe pulled to a stop right behind them. Rascal was already bolting from the car. Avad came out from the trees, his long gun focused on the driver. Chandra had her weapon up as she leaned across the passenger-side door.

The Escalade's windows were all down to enjoy the evening air. As the driver went for his gun, Chandra let off a shot, and the man cried out, more from fear than any pain. She'd hit the dashboard, not him.

Avad and Rascal bolted forward, their weapons practically inside the Escalade. "Nobody move," Rascal ordered.

The white haired man in the back seat looked up at them calmly. "What do you want? We don't have any money."

Rafe glared at the man. "We don't want money. We want information."

Chapter Eighty-One

NOLA

Calming her heart rate, Nola walked down the hall. Molly was nowhere to be seen.

Nola was conflicted about Molly being around for any of this. She didn't want her daughter seeing her like this. At the same time, her presence had been undeniably helpful.

Simultaneously, she knew that her worries and thoughts were definitely crazy. Her daughter was already dead. Nothing she would see here could harm her, or at least she didn't think it could.

The hallway widened up ahead. It was framed in heavy thick wood with similarly thick-planked wooden floors. This hallway held four doors, all of them closed. She tried each one as she passed. All were locked, but the potential for someone to slip in behind her still remained.

"They're waiting for you up ahead," Molly said, appearing next to her as if summoned. "They won't try to trick you, Mommy. He wants to keep this fight fair."

"No fight is fair," Nola mumbled. Here, despite Jonas's protests, that was even more evident. Jonas knew the layout, he knew the players. Meanwhile, Nola was walking in blind. Plus, Nola would be fighting Jonas after she had been through God knew how many of his men. Meanwhile, Jonas would be fresh as a daisy. No, this fight would not be fair, no matter what Jonas proclaimed.

"They're in the room down the hall to the left," Molly repeated.

"How many are there?"

"Three." Molly paused. "But you will only be fighting two."

Nola's heart rate picked up. "Is Jonas there?"

Molly shook her head. "No. He's waiting for you after this."

"What about Bishop?"

"She's safe. For now. But I don't like that man, Mommy. He'll hurt her if he has to. He's not right."

"No, sweetheart, he's not." Nola paused as she reached the end of the hallway. She glanced to the right and to the left. All the doors on the right were closed, but at the end of the hall, a set of double doors were wide open, inviting her to step through.

Looking down at Molly, Nola paused. "Go stay with Bishop."

Her daughter tilted her head as she looked up at her with a frown. "But she can't see me."

"I know. But I'd feel better if I knew someone was with her."

Molly nodded, looking up into her mother's eyes. "Be careful, Mommy. These ones are more dangerous." Then she disappeared from view.

Nola sucked in a breath, the pain of seeing Molly disappear yet again stronger than the pain in her side from the kick earlier. She rolled her shoulders and then her neck, listening to the crack. She released all her fears, all her emotions. Then she turned the corner and headed for the open doors.

Chapter Eighty-Two

RAFE

Rafe and the others wasted no time getting the lawyer and his security guards cuffed and back to the Santarro estate. Now the three men were uncomfortably situated in the basement. The two goons were blindfolded, gagged, and strapped to chairs in a corner.

The lawyer was positioned center stage on a chair without a gag. It was only Rafe and Avad down here with them. Now Rafe pulled the blindfold off the lawyer's eyes.

The man blinked a few times, looking around. "Quite a setup you've got here. What is this, amateur hour?"

Rafe leaned back against one of the metal pillars. "We had to come up with the situation quickly."

Ivan looked around the room, his gaze stopping an Avad. "You're the Viking. You're working with her. That means the rest of you are working with her." He chuckled. "Jonas missed that."

"You thought she was going in alone?" Rafe asked.

With a slow nod of his head, Ivan's gaze shifted between Rafe and Avad before he glanced at the ceiling. "I was assured that she was a loner. And that no one else would be involved in this."

"Well, you were misinformed. Now we need to know the layout of the estate," Rafe said.

Not a trace of fear was on the lawyer's face, but there was a calculation in his eyes. "What's in it for me?"

Avad glared at him, his arms braced behind his back. "Less pain."

Ivan looked up at him. "You know, if you're ever looking for a new job, I'd hire you in a second."

Rafe took a step forward with a growl.

"Hey, hey," Ivan said, leaning back in his chair. "No need for that. I'm a lover, not a fighter."

Rafe scoffed, knowing that this man had been the force behind the Wagners' increase in criminal activity over the last few years. This "lover" was responsible for lots of deaths. "You talk to us, then we'll let you go."

"Yeah, he doesn't look like he wants to let me go," he said, tilting his head toward Avad.

"Maybe, but he doesn't make the decisions." Rafe shrugged.

The lawyer eyed Rafe. "You're not an American, are you?"

Rafe shook his head. "No."

"And neither is he. And that Black fellow, he sounded like he's from the South. The older woman, she's from what, the Middle East? Then you've got the fashion model, she's an American. A very good-looking one. So what, you're some sort of international group of operatives? Why are you focused on Jonas Wagner? Did Nola James hire you?"

"Something like that," Rafe said.

A look of understanding crossed the lawyer's face. "No, this isn't about money. You all care about her. It's written over your faces."

Rafe crossed his arms over his chest. "We want to know the layout of Wagner's home."

The lawyer nodded. "And what are you going to do with Wagner when you're done?"

Rafe didn't say anything, not sure how to answer that question, but Avad did. "We're not going to do anything. Nola is."

Ivan laughed. "So you think she's going to win this little game of death? I have to admit, when Jonas first suggested it, I thought he was crazy. I mean, how is some broad going to be able to take on each of his fighters? But then I saw her in action. She is formidable."

"You have no idea," Rafe said.

"Actually, I didn't. I mean, I knew she had been on some sort of one-woman vengeance spree. But the guys she's taken down, they weren't really fighters, you know? I mean, one was a lawyer, another was an accountant. Last guy we heard about he was what, a restaurant owner? None of those guys were really all that tough. But she's got something. Jonas was right about that, at least."

And there, Rafe heard the desire in the lawyer's voice. And it wasn't aimed at Nola. "You *want* Jonas gone."

A shrug was the only response Ivan could manage with his hands restrained. "Being I'm amongst friends, sure. I want him gone. That kid, he's not all there. I mean, honestly, he never should have been given the reins of the family business. But Elias was clear: He wanted his son in charge. He thought the power would keep the crazy away."

Ivan shook his head. "I guess crazy runs in the family.

Jonas isn't all bad. He makes a good figurehead. Or at least *made* a good one for a little while. But he's gotten more and more unbalanced. So if something were to happen to him, yeah, I wouldn't exactly be upset."

"So why haven't you made something happen to him?" Rafe asked.

A deep chuckle emerged from Ivan. "Because I'm not stupid. The other families would figure it out. But this situation, Jonas has been building this for years. This has got nothing to do with me. And if he doesn't make it out, well, that's not really a concern of mine."

"So you'll give us the layout of the house?" Rafe asked.

The lawyer nodded. "Yes, and then you'll let me go?"

That was the last thing Rafe wanted to do. This guy was responsible for as much if not more crimes than Jonas.

But he wasn't in law enforcement anymore. None of this was sanctioned. They had no right to hold him. Right now they were the kidnappers, and none of them was willing to take the giant leap into being murderers. "If your information pans out, then yeah, we'll let you go."

The lawyer smiled. "Well, then I'm going to need a pen."

Chapter Eighty-Three

NOLA

The door stood open, calling her forward. As Nola approached, she noted there was no furniture in the room. And the wooden floors stopped at the door's threshold. Instead, there were pale cream mats laid down on the floor. On the far wall, she could make out two crossed swords hanging on the wall along with other Asian-inspired prints and scrolls.

It's his dojo, she thought as she approached the door.

She thought about slipping to the side to peek at the room's layout before she stepped in. But her gut told her that wasn't necessary.

So she stopped in the middle of the doorway and glanced to her left, where an older man stood on a small dais. Two younger men, both dressed in black flowing pants without shirts, stood before him, their arms braced in front of them. The men were coiled muscle, and each couldn't have been older than their mid-twenties.

The older man inclined his head toward her. He wore a double-breasted white coat and long flowing black pants, the same as the two younger men. "Welcome, Nola James."

Nola stepped into the room.

One of the younger men flared his nostrils, looking like a bull about to charge. But the older gentleman put up his hand, and the man relaxed.

"Your final battle will be here before you meet Jonas Wagner. If you survive, I will direct you where you need to go."

Nola glanced around the room. "And you're okay with all of this?"

The man shook his head. "I owed Jonas's father a blood debt. This is how I will pay it." He gestured to the two younger men.

"What are the rules?" Nola asked.

The two men step forward. The older man nodded. "The rules are simple: survive."

One of the men charged. Nola whipped the metal baton from her back and aimed at the man's head, but he ducked, continuing forward.

She brought up her foot, but the man caught it and sent her flying back. She hit the ground with a thud and rolled as the man went to stomp where she'd just been.

From the floor, she reached out with a roundhouse kick toward his knee, but he jumped high, avoiding it. She rolled backward and onto her feet, standing and facing the man.

The other combatant stayed where he was, just watching. Apparently, they were going to fight her one at a time. Nola wasn't sure if that was a good thing or a bad thing. Sometimes having to fight two attackers made it easier: you could use one against the other.

But attacker number two was a worry for another time.

She kept her focus on attacker number one while making sure she kept a watchful eye on the second one in case he decided that he wasn't going to wait.

The man across from Nola wasn't going to be as easy to take down as the other individuals.

Nola slashed forward at his head with her baton. The man ducked to the left as Nola expected, and she slammed a round kick into his ribs.

He returned the favor with a cross to her face that jolted her head back.

Yeah, this fight was definitely not going to be as easy as the other ones.

Chapter Eighty-Four

RAFE

With the paper Ivan had written on grasped in his hand, Rafe hustled up the basement stairs. Avad was taping the mouth of the lawyer and double-checking their restraints on his thugs to make sure that they couldn't get out. He stepped into the hallway and hurried down the hall toward the main room.

Ileana moved away from the kitchen island where she had been waiting. "Well?"

Rafe held up the paper. "I have it." He handed it over to Stan, who quickly scanned it and put it onto the computer.

Moving from their post by the windows, Rascal and Chandra looked over his shoulder. "So Bishop's in the basement?" Chandra asked.

Rafe nodded. "Yeah, apparently Jonas has created a panic room that's about the size of some people's homes. There's a control room down there, which is where he last saw Bishop, although it's possible she was placed in the bedroom down the hall from it. I've marked both of those on the map."

"What about security?" Rascal asked.

"Pretty tight. There's electronic surveillance as well as human surveillance. And Jonas has brought all his people in because of the situation today with Nola." Rafe ran a hand through his hair. "It's going to be pretty dicey."

"Do we know where the guards are stationed?" Chandra asked.

"Some of them I marked off on the map, but a few of them are roaming. They could be just about anywhere. And there's some that are stationed in a small room off the garage. They'll wait there until they're needed."

Rascal nodded. "Okay, so we have to make sure that the guards in that room don't know anything's happening as we go through the rest of the building."

Chandra tapped Stan's shoulder. "Can you do something with the electronic surveillance so they can't see us coming in?"

Stan nodded. "Yeah, I should be able to keep you guys covered once I get into the system. But I don't want to get into it until you guys are on the way just in case I tip someone off. They could have a trip wire in their system that tells them about a breach."

"Is there any way to tell ahead of time if they have that kind of protection?" Rascal asked.

Stan shook his head. "No."

"Then we'll deal with it," Rafe said. "Now we need to figure out the quickest route down to Bishop. There's some sort of blast door there that they can shut if things go sideways. We need to make sure that they trigger that before we can get to her and get her out."

Ileana nodded. "We'll make it work. Chandra, you're good at strategy. Figure a way in."

"I already have an idea," Chandra said, her attention focused on the screen.

Ileana nodded her head toward Rafe, and they headed toward the windows that overlooked the backyard. Ileana dropped her voice. "What condition are the lawyer and his security in?"

"Untouched. I think the lawyer is hoping to walk away from this scot-free."

"Did you promise him that?"

"I said I would release him, yes."

Ileana nodded, glancing out over the backyard. "All right, then. We'll release him once we have Bishop back."

"Not before?" Rafe asked.

Ileana shook her head as she met his gaze. "No, he's going to be a bargaining chip in case I need him to get *you* all out."

Chapter Eighty-Five

NOLA

As Nola's head snapped back, she knew a good fighter would take advantage and go in to finish in that moment. But the kid in front of her was cocky. He wanted to prolong the fight, make his master proud.

Stupid.

Before he could make his next move, she slammed her foot into his chest, sending him sprawling. She continued forward, striking a baton into his ribs. She twirled it around the top of her head to bring it to the side of his head when he caught the arm and slammed an elbow into her chin. She shifted her head, avoiding a full hit, but pain still radiated across her jaw.

He wrapped his arm around the arm he'd grabbed and pressed against the elbow. She had a choice: either hold on to her baton and break her elbow or let it go.

She let it go.

The baton rolled across the room, out of her reach. The

man pulled a small dagger from his belt and jabbed toward her ribs.

Nola just managed to shift to the side, avoiding the thrust. She slammed her elbow back and into his face, then wrapped her arm around his neck and slammed a knee into his chest.

He lashed out with the knife and caught her across the thigh.

The cut wasn't too deep, but it stung nonetheless.

She slammed her elbow into his jaw again and then ducked under his arm. She wrenched his arm back and took out his legs, then stomped on the back of his shoulder and yanked his arm up, stripping the knife from his hand as she did so.

He screamed as his arm was yanked out of its socket. Without mercy, Nola kicked him in the back of the head and stomped on the back of his ankle to make sure he wouldn't be able to continue fighting. He cried out.

The master clapped his hands. "Very good. Nola James, you have won the first contest."

After a glare at Nola, the man who she'd just fought crawled to the side of the mat.

The second man stepped forward. With her chest heaving, she felt blood rolling down her leg. Apparently that cut was a little deeper than she'd realized.

The second attacker wasn't taking any chances. He grabbed a throwing star and chucked it at her.

Nola dove to the side and managed to avoid the first star, but the second one lodged in her ribs. With a grunt, she took it out and returned it to the man, followed by two of her throwing knives.

All three missed as the man dodged them and bolted toward her.

He threw a roundhouse kick at her that she saw from a mile away. She grabbed onto the leg and twirled with it before slamming her forearm into his knee. She kicked out the leg he was standing on, and he crumpled to the floor and then rolled backward.

Nola winced in pain as she lurched to the side and agitated the injury caused by the throwing star.

The man stood up and glared at her before he ran to the other side of the dojo with a heavy limp. He grabbed one of the swords from the wall and turned toward her.

Nola pulled the remaining metal baton from her back and held it in front of her other hand in front of her face.

She shut out everything except for her focus on the opponent in front of her. The pain in her side, the pain in her leg, Bishop, her worries about what the others were up to: none of that mattered right now. Right now, it was just her and her opponent.

Even though the man in front of her could barely use his other leg, he managed to move forward at a quick pace and started slashing in the air toward Nola.

She grunted as she slipped the first slash and brought her baton up to meet the second one. Kicking out with an inverted hook kick, she caught him on the inside of his bad knee.

He grunted and twirled the sword around his head. Nola barely managed to shift to the side as the blade sliced down right where her neck had just been.

She slammed her baton into the man's side and then up his chin.

He brought the blade back, catching her on the shoulder with a glancing blow that cut through the sleeve of her jacket.

Enough of this. Nola slammed the edge of her baton into

the hand holding the sword before crashing the end of it into his ribs. With the force she put into the hit, she knew he'd broken at least a few ribs.

Without missing a beat, she swung the baton up, catching him under the chin again. On instinct, he brought his arm down, wrapping it around the baton. But that was all right; Nola didn't need it anymore. She released her hold and grabbed the man's sword arm. Twisting his arm, she pushed against his shoulder as she held his wrist up and forced him down to the ground.

Stomping on the back of his shoulder the way she had done for his partner, she yanked his arm back, dislocating it. Then she twisted the sword from his hand and held the blade to his neck.

"Submit."

The man growled, and Nola pressed the blade in heavier.

Blood pooled underneath it. "Submit," she ordered again.

With a grunt, the man tapped on the mat twice.

The older man clapped his hands. "Well done, Nola James. You have succeeded. Now you are allowed to fight Jonas Wagner. And I will escort you there."

Nola took a step back from the man sprawled on the mat. The pain that she had been pushing aside rolled through her.

Blood rolled down her arm and off her fingertips to the mat below. More blood was caked into her side from the first hit of the throwing star. And there was even more on her thigh.

She was a disaster. She needed a minute. But there wasn't a minute to take. "Where is Jonas?"

"I will escort you," he repeated.

Yeah, that wasn't going to happen. Nola didn't want him near her. The man was obviously well trained. She could see that from his students. And in her current state, she didn't want anyone else to be around her. She shook her head. "No. You're not going with me."

The man raised an eyebrow. "I assure you, you have nothing to worry about from me. I am not part of this."

Nola looked at the two men sprawled on the floor. "Oh, I'd say you're part of this. Now where is he?"

The man opened his mouth and then shut it as if contemplating, before he finally nodded. "Very well. Go to the end of the hall and make a right. Take that hallway all the way to the end and then make a left. Jonas is waiting for you by the indoor swimming pool."

Nola nodded, keeping her shoulders straight. "Do I have to worry about you coming after me?" She raised the sword. "Because if I do, I will handle that right now."

The man inclined his head. "I repeat: You have nothing to worry about from me, Nola James. My blood debt is now repaid. I will be leaving Mr. Wagner's home now."

Nola studied the man and found that she believed him. Slowly, she lowered the sword. "Very well. Then go."

The man wasted no time and headed for the door, leaving his two students sprawled on the ground.

Nola looked around the room and saw the camera in the corner. She walked closer to it and stared up into the lens. "I'm coming for you."

Chapter Eighty-Six

JONAS

Nola James's eyes were fierce as she stared up at the camera.

Jonas smiled in response. She was truly a worthy adversary. She would make this a fight to remember. He watched as she walked out of the room her back straight.

He turned to Brett. "You'll come with me. Make sure no one interrupts her on the way to the pool. The next fight is mine."

"Sure thing, boss." Brett picked up his radio and conveyed the message.

Walking over to his wardrobe, Jonas removed his sweatshirt and pants and pulled on his gi. He ran a hand down its smooth black façade. He always felt stronger in his uniform.

He slipped his feet into his black slippers and then headed down the hall toward the indoor pool. For a moment, he pictured Bishop. Soon they would be together, just as he imagined. He called his security in the basement as he walked. "Any problems?"

"No, the captive is, uh, still here in the control room."

Jonas frowned. "What about Ivan?"

"He left a while ago with his security."

Jonas's steps faltered. "He left? Why?"

"Um, I think he was kind of getting nervous."

His grip tightening on the phone, Jonas narrowed his eyes. "Nervous?"

The voice on the other side of the phone hurried to speak. "But I'm not. You've got this."

Jonas glared down at the phone before disconnecting the call. Ivan had left. He didn't trust him to win this fight.

Ivan had been with the family for decades. And he usually was pretty good at reading which way the wind was blowing.

Which caused Jonas to pause for just a moment, but then he shook his head. No, this was his destiny. He was meant to face down Nola James. He was meant to finally have Bishop for just himself. Nola James wouldn't be able to keep them apart.

After today, Nola James wouldn't be able to do anything at all.

Chapter Eighty-Seven

BISHOP

Bishop's eyes were locked on the screen. Nola was bruised and battered. Bishop could see the blood even with the lousy camera image. More than anything, Bishop wanted to find a way to stop this, but she didn't know how.

The phone next to her vibrated, and she quickly pulled it out. The movement was too quick.

The man over at the computer desk looked over at her with a frown. Bishop was careful to keep her body language nonthreatening and the phone hidden next to her.

Once he looked away, she glanced at the screen. *They're heading in. They'll be at you in five.*

Bishop felt herself tense. Her gaze locked on the screen where Nola was stepping into the swimming room. *Just a little longer, Nola. Just hold out a little longer.*

Chapter Eighty-Eight

RAFE

The doors to the backyard were wide open.

Rafe glanced around the backyard, not seeing any movement. It was pitch black out here. They hadn't put any lights on in the estate. Stepping outside, he glanced up at the two windows that overlooked the yard, just above where he was.

Although he couldn't see him, he imagined that Avad nodded at him. He glanced down the way to where Jack was positioned. The two of them would cover Rafe, Chandra and Rascal until they were in the house, and then Avad would come in with Jack covering him. They were situated with sniper rifles with silencers, which hopefully wouldn't make any noise that anyone would notice.

Once they were inside, Stan would follow them on the cameras. Bishop had texted him that they were watching everything, which meant that there were cameras everywhere in the house, allowing Stan access to them.

Now they were just waiting to make sure that Stan was in before they went. They'd secure Bishop first and then back up Nola.

"Everybody ready?" Stan asked through the earpiece.

"Good to go," Rascal said.

Chandra nodded, and Rafe gave a thumbs-up.

Ileana, who stood behind Stan, placed a hand on his shoulder. "Go."

Stan's hands flew over the keyboard, his focus intense. After two minutes of silence, he looked up. "I'm in. Go."

Rafe, Rascal, and Chandra sprinted across the backyard.

They climbed up the ladders that they had placed against the fence earlier and were over the side as a small burst of air sounded. As Rafe crested the top of the brick wall, he saw one of the guards grab his neck and then drop to the ground.

The other two guards followed in quick succession.

Rafe was over the wall quickly. He hit the ground, rolled to his feet, and started sprinting for the deck along the back of the house. He skirted around the massive swimming pool and headed for the door to the left.

It led to a wine cellar that was adjacent to where they believed Bishop was being held. He reached the door and saw the keypad next to it was red.

"Need a code here," he said into his mic.

"Hang on," Stan said.

The light turned green as Rascal and Chandra hurried down the steps to join him.

Rafe opened the door quickly, sweeping his weapon inside. There was no one nearby. "Where's the nearest guards?"

Ileana's voice answered him. "There are two outside the wine room door."

Rafe clicked his mic to indicate that he understood. He nodded at Chandra and Rascal, put up two fingers, and pointed at the door.

Both of them nodded back at him.

Silently, the three of them made their way through the racks of wine. Chandra reached the door first. There was no lock on this side.

She grasped the handle and looked at the other two. Rafe and Rascal flattened themselves against the side of the door with Rafe closest to the entryway. He nodded at Chandra.

She pulled the door open a little bit, and Rafe peeked through. There was a guard ten feet down the hall to his left. He couldn't see if there was a guard on the other side, but there was no time to waste.

He leveled his tranq gun and took the shot. It caught the man in the neck, and he dropped instantly.

Chandra pulled the door wide, and Rafe was out in the hall as the guard at the other end turned, a surprised look on his face. Rascal and Rafe both fired their tranq guns into the man's neck and chest. He dropped to his knees and then fell face first.

The three of them went still, listening, but there was no sound of running feet.

Rafe jogged down the hall and grabbed the guard and pulled him into the wine room while Rascal and Chandra grabbed the other one and did the same.

Then they closed the door and hurried down the hall.

Ileana's voice once again sounded through their earpiece. "Go through the door at the end of the hall and turn left. You're going to go down to the end of that hall and make another left. You'll see the doorway there to the bunker."

Rafe nodded and continued at a fast clip forward, trusting Ileana to warn him if anyone was coming. He could hear the sound of Rascal and Chandra's breathing and the muffled drum of their footsteps. His own breathing sounded as if it was echoing. He reached the end of the hall and then looked to the left. A man was just stepping out of the blast door. He walked down the hall toward them, unconcerned, and even pulled out his phone, scrolling through as he walked.

Rafe put up one finger and nodded.

Rascal and Chandra flattened themselves against the hall. As soon as the man reached the corner, Rascal reached out and grabbed him. Chandra shot him in the neck with the tranq gun. His eyes closed, and he dropped to the ground.

Chandra had insisted on the less-lethal rounds. All of this was highly illegal, but going in and executing everyone they came across was not a line most of them were willing to cross. The tranqs would keep all of them out for two hours at least. And they all had Glock backups.

"You won't have any cover from here until you're in the panic room," Ileana said. "You're going to need to go in fast. There are no guards in the doorway, but there are three situated in a room just in the door to your left. After that, there's two more in the control room with Bishop."

Rafe tensed and put up three fingers. He counted down to one, and then the three of them burst straight for the panic room.

But it wasn't a panic room. It was more of a panic suite. There were four doors the first one on their right.

Just as they reached the opening of the suite, the door to their right opened.

A man looked up, his eyes going wide with shock. Chandra burst forward, slamming her boot into the man's chest. He flew back into the room. She led the way, her gun out as she shot each of the individuals before they could move.

Rascal leaned his head in the doorway and nodded. "I guess she didn't really need us."

Chandra grinned at him over her shoulder. "You can take the next room."

"Don't mind if I do," Rascal said.

Rafe tapped his mic. "Which room is Bishop in?"

"The second one on the left. It's a theater room," Stan said.

Rafe nodded up toward the room Stan had indicated. "Bishop's in there."

With a nod, Rascal hurried down the hall and stopped at the first door on the right and flicked the door open. It was a small kitchen and completely empty of people.

"Any sign they know we're here?" Rafe asked as he closed the door.

"No. Everything's quiet," Ileana responded.

Rascal led the way down the hall and paused outside the theater room.

"Bishop's in the back-left corner. Stan told her you're coming. She's going to stay down. The two guards are in the front by the door. They're sitting in chairs watching what's happening on screen."

Rafe wanted to ask what was happening on screen, but he knew it would only distract him from what was going on right now. "Tell Bishop we're coming in in three."

Chapter Eighty-Nine

Nola walked slowly down the hallway. She didn't see anyone, but she had no doubt that there were cameras trained on her. Up ahead was a small alcove with a window overlooking the lawn. Nola slipped into it, hoping that she was hidden from the camera's view.

She reached down and pulled up her shirt carefully. The wound in her side was still bleeding pretty ferociously, but the ribs underneath weren't broken, so she supposed that was something.

Pulling off her jacket, she tugged on the sleeve of her shirt. It took two tries before she heard the tear. Ripping the sleeve off, she did the same to the other one. Taking a deep breath, she wrapped one around the wound on her thigh, wincing at the burst of pain. Then she quickly did the same for the wound on her arm, using her teeth to make the knot.

But those were the easy injuries. The wound at her waist would be much more difficult to bind. The alcove had a windowseat with decorative pillows. She grabbed the seat cushion and using her knife, cut along the seam. Then she ripped the stuffing out from it. She wrapped it into quarters. Pausing for a moment, she steeled herself and then held it against the wound at her waist with a hiss of breath.

The cut was deep. The throwing star had jagged edges, so when she pulled it out, she had done even more damage than when it had first gone in. It needed stitches but she had neither the time nor the supplies for that. She was just going to have to hope the makeshift bandage slowed at least some of the bleeding.

Leaning her head back against the wall, she took stock. As much as she wanted to say she had the fight ahead in the bag, her wounds were making her more than a little worried. She wiped the blood from her hands on her jeans. *Come on, Nola. One more fight. You've got this.*

But her body didn't want to comply.

She reached a hand into the pocket of her jeans and pulled out the small pill, slipping it into her mouth and swallowing it quickly. The painkiller would give her a bit of a boost for maybe twenty minutes, which hopefully was all she would need. The side effect was it would also make her bleed quicker.

She pulled the belt from her jeans and wrapped it around the makeshift bandage at her waist and then pulled tight. It took everything in her not to cry out as pain roared through her side at the move.

Instead, she took short, shallow breaths, reminding her of when she had given birth to Molly. She closed her eyes as the world wavered for a moment.

Then she threw her eyelids open. Bishop was counting on her. She pushed herself off the wall and continued down the hall.

Chapter Ninety

RAFE

Outside the control room, Rafe counted down to three and threw open the door. Rascal went in first. He slammed his elbow into the man who was standing right next to the door while he shot at the other one, who'd been sitting in the front row.

By the time Rafe burst through the door, both men were down.

Then a light in the room began to flash red.

Bolting from her spot in the back corner, Bishop sprinted across the back of the room, slamming her fist into the face of a man that Rafe hadn't noticed until just now. Bishop's hit sent him flying. Chandra bolted up the steps and shot a tranq into his chest.

Bishop looked at the monitor on the desk, and then her terrified gaze caught Rafe's. "The blast door!"

Rascal darted out into the hall with Rafe right behind

them. They sprinted for the blast door, nearly colliding with Avad.

Without a word, Avad joined them. They sprinted down the hall, watching as the door slid closed inch by inch. Rascal just reached it as the door slammed shut.

He stopped dead, staring up in it. And looked back at Rafe. Rafe stared at the door, his heart in his throat. "Nola."

Chapter Ninety-One

NOLA

The chlorine from the pool extended down the hall, letting Nola know that she was getting close. She slowed her steps as she approached, listening, but she heard no sounds of any threat outside the pool room.

The meds had kicked in, and she was feeling a little bit of energy, although not a lot. She could still feel the blood rolling down her stomach and her arm, the bandages not as tight as they needed to be.

I am a mess, she thought again as she approached.

But none of that mattered. Getting Bishop safe, that was what mattered. Hopefully, the rest of the team were already on the grounds and getting Bishop out. Nola just needed to hope that if she lost this fight, that she kept Jonas busy enough to allow them the time to save her.

Just give them time, she thought before pulling on one of the frosted glass doors that led to the pool room.

A man stood on the other side of the pool, a gun aimed at her.

Nola stopped still. "A gun? I thought that was against the rules."

"It is, it is, at least for combatants," Jonas said as he stepped out from behind a screen on the other side of the pool area. "But I just wanted to make sure that you were following the rules."

If she'd had the extra energy, she would have rolled her eyes. "You should know. You've had cameras following me the whole time I've been in the house."

Jonas smiled. "That I have. But this is just a reminder in case you had any ideas of not engaging in a fair fight."

"Oh, yeah, I can see you're really into a fair fight." Nola looked down at her bloodied and bruised body.

Jonas narrowed his eyes. "This is how it has to be. Now let us begin." He gestured to the pool.

Nola stepped forward and realized that the pool was now empty. There were stairs on one end, and it stretched out to a full Olympic-sized pool. It looked like it went to about ten feet at the deep end.

Jonas walked down the pool steps, carrying a long bo staff. It had a knife at one end.

She rolled her eyes. A fair fight indeed. "I don't suppose I get a staff?"

"You were allowed to bring whatever weapon you wanted, save a firearm. You have everything you need." With a smile, Jonas continued walking until he was in the deep end and then turned, waiting for Nola to join him.

A quick glance at Jonas's security showed the man watching her impassively. Then she headed toward the stairs, her side screaming with pain with every step.

But she shut it out. She shut everything out except for

what she needed to do right now. Jonas's staff was about six feet long, which would give him extra reach. But if she could get the fight closer to the sides of the pool, then it would restrict his movements. It could actually work against him.

A strategy forming in her mind, she walked down the last few steps and then down the incline toward him.

Jonas stepped back, bracing on his left foot, the staff held comfortably in his hands and extended in front of him.

Nola eyed it, knowing she was going to get hit by that thing. There was no way she was going to be able to avoid that.

She would just have to take the hit, but what she did after the hit was what was going to count. The key was to take the hits at the middle of the stick so she avoided the sharpness at its end.

Of course, that meant she'd have to dive and dodge quickly, which she wasn't entirely convinced she could do right now.

But there was no other option. This man held Bishop, and this was the only way that she was going to be able to get her out safely.

Nola pulled out the bamboo batons that she'd grabbed from the wall in the dojo and twirled them in her hands, feeling the familiar comfort of them in her grip. They weren't metal, but they could do the trick.

Jonas nodded at her. She nodded back. Jonas moved immediately. He darted forward, swinging the staff toward her head.

It was an obvious move, and Nola used the batons to deflect the staff and bring it up and over her head.

Then she shot toward him. But Jonas shifted, thrusting the end of the staff toward her.

Nola barely managed to dodge back. But she had shifted toward the side of the pool. Jonas wouldn't be able to get a full swing of the staff toward her.

As Jonas thrust the end at her again, she darted forward. The staff crashed against the side of the pool without touching her. His eyes widened as she moved toward him.

Nola slammed her foot toward his groin, but he jumped back and brought the staff around enough that the middle slammed into her side, catching her wound. She hissed in pain as blood dripped onto the white pool floor.

Jonas smiled as he darted back and then brought the staff up, sliding it at her.

Nola jumped back, but she wasn't able to move fast enough and a new slice erupted along the other side of her ribs.

Backpedaling quickly, Nola stumbled, her legs feeling heavy.

Jonas smiled as he moved forward.

Nola blinked hard, gripping the batons as she watched Jonas's smiling face. He thought he had this, and Nola wasn't entirely sure he didn't. *Come on, Nola. Just a little longer.*

He was too confident at this distance. If he kept her out, then yeah, he would have the fight, which meant she needed to make him shorten the distance.

She tensed, waiting, and Jonas swept toward her mid region.

Nola rolled to the floor, pulled one of the throwing knives from the strap around her thigh, and flung it, catching him in the thigh.

He let out a cry.

Leaping to her feet, Nola bolted forward.

Jonas's attention, diverted by the knife sticking out of his thigh, tried to bring the staff around, but he was too slow.

He dropped it and ripped the knife from his thigh, swinging it wildly at Nola. She backed up, avoiding the swing, and then stepped in before he could bring his arm back.

She speared his arm and then elbowed him in the face. Kneeing him in the chest, she wrapped her arm around the back of his head and twisted his head below the arm that she held, forcing him to the ground.

Slamming her knee into his side, she dropped down and then stripped the knife from his hand. She slipped another knife from her thigh, Chandra's lucky knife, and held it to his throat. "I win. Now give me Bishop."

She sensed rather than saw the guard moving to the edge of the swimming pool. She ducked behind Jonas, holding him up as his shield as the sound of bullets rang out. But she didn't move fast enough, and one grazed her thigh.

She gritted her teeth against the pain. "What happened to no guns?" she demanded.

Jonas laughed. "Yeah, unless I'm losing." He reared his head back and caught Nola in the nose.

Surprised by the move, she stumbled. Jonas managed to wrench himself out of her grasp. He turned around and aimed a front kick at her chest.

Nola shoved the kick to the side and brought her own side kick forward, slamming it into the side of Jonas's knee. He cried out as he dropped, his knee dislocated.

Another gunshot rang out, catching her in the arm. She cried out and dove behind Jonas again and held him up. She held the knife to his throat. "Tell your man to drop his gun."

She pressed the knife into his throat.

Jonas laughed. "Kill me, and you kill Bishop."

Chapter Ninety-Two

BISHOP

Up on the screen, Nola was entering the empty swimming pool. Jonas held some sort of long pole with a sharp knife attached to the end.

Bishop stared at Nola as she made her way toward him.

Even from here, she could see the dots of blood that trailed behind her.

Rafe, Avad, and Rascal returned to the room. Bishop looked up at them, but they shook their heads.

Chandra had already incapacitated the guy who'd sat behind the computers, and Bishop was now working her way in through the system to try and open the blast door. "I need a headset and a mic."

Chandra immediately ripped hers off, placing the earbud in Bishop's ear and the mic around her throat. "Stan?"

"Bishop. Thank God. You okay?" Stan asked.

"I am, but they closed the blast door. We need to work together to get this thing open."

"Oh my god," Rascal said.

Bishop's gaze shot to the screen.

Blood dripped from a new wound along Nola's other side. Her face looked pale and haggard. More blood was clearly visible against the white pool surface.

Bishop's hands shook as she focused on the code on the screen. "Stan, I need your help. There's too many firewalls. We need to get through this."

Chandra placed a hand on Bishop's shoulder and gave her a squeeze. "Hurry, Bishop, hurry."

Chapter Ninety-Three

NOLA

Jonas's man stood up at the edge of the pool, his gun trained down on Jonas and Nola.

Nola kept Jonas in front of her, but she could feel the blood rolling down her leg, her arm, and her side. She was leaving a trail of blood as she walked.

Worse, she kept blinking hard as if it would keep the spots that were dancing along the edges of her vision away. She grabbed Jonas roughly by the back of his jacket and hissed into his ear. "What is this?"

Jonas laughed. "You don't think I'm actually going to let you get her, do you? The only way to save Bishop is for you to die."

"That was not the deal."

"It doesn't matter!" Jonas screeched. "You can't have her again. She's mine. She belongs to me."

"She doesn't belong to anyone."

Jonas took a deep breath, seeming to pull some of the

rage back. "She will stay with me. And if I die, she dies. That's what my men have been ordered to do. So, the only way for Bishop to walk out of this is for you to step out from behind me and let me kill you."

Nola stared past Jonas to the gunman up at the edge of the pool. He was focused solely on them, his intention clear. Somewhere down deep she'd known it would come to this. Somewhere down deep, she'd known that Jonas couldn't be trusted, despite all his talk of honor.

But she'd thought that maybe, just maybe, she would figure out a way to make this work. But apparently that was not going to be.

She looked around the pool but saw no sign of Molly.

And that was good. Maybe Molly wouldn't be hurt by seeing what was about to happen, but Nola didn't want to take the chance. The idea of Molly being with Bishop, even if Bishop couldn't see her, filled her with a sense of rightness.

Take care of her, Molly, she thought silently.

Then she reached up and shoved Jonas forward, providing the gunman with a perfect shot at her.

Chapter Ninety-Four

RAFE

Together, the group of them sprinted down the hallway. It had taken Stan and Bishop working together to get the blast door open. As soon as it was, the four of them bolted down the hall and through the doorway.

Stan was keeping the cameras locked so that the rest of the guards didn't know that they were even on the property. But they still encountered four guards on their way there. Rafe wasn't sure who took out each of the men.

His heart was pounding so hard and he was so focused on getting to Nola that he barely even registered the guards getting in the way and dropping to the ground. But vaguely he registered that the tranq guns were a thing of the past. They needed whoever they hit to drop immediately.

He was being reckless, he knew it. But he could not get himself to slow down. The image of a bloodied Nola in that pool was the only thing that he could focus on. And that only made him want to move faster, not slower.

While Rafe's heart raced as he sprinted, he had no doubt that Bishop's was pounding even harder. She was right beside him, her face a mask of fear and worry. She'd watched everything that Nola had gone through. She knew the state that Nola was in. It was bad enough seeing the end result of what she had been through. He couldn't imagine having to watch how she had gotten those injuries.

And there was so much blood. Too much.

This couldn't be how it ended. It wasn't possible that this was going to be the end of Nola James.

But the pounding of his heart and the silence amongst the others as they sprinted toward the pool room made it clear that all of them held the same worry.

The scent of chlorine hit him, and the smell spurred him on.

He sprinted forward and through the pool room door without even stopping to take a look at what was happening inside. It didn't matter. Nola needed him. Nola needed all of them.

A man stood on the edge of the pool, his gun trained on Nola, who stood exposed, her hands up in the air.

Chapter Ninety-Five

NOLA

With the help of Nola's shove, Jonas stumbled away from her. "Shoot her!" he yelled.

Nola tensed, closing her eyes. *I'm sorry, Bishop. Please don't blame yourself for this. This is my failure. Not yours.*

Nola heard the report of a gun, but no new pain joined the chorus of agony that was currently playing in her body.

She opened her eyes to see the gunman had fallen. Footsteps rang out, and she turned slowly as Rafe bolted into the room, followed by Bishop, Rascal, Chandra, and Avad. Rafe and Bishop tore down the stairs of the pool toward her.

Nola looked over at them with a smile. "You found her," she said as she sank to her knees, her legs finally giving out.

Rafe caught her before her head could hit the floor of the swimming pool.

"Nola!" Bishop cried. Her eyes filled with tears as she fell down to her knees at Nola's side and grabbed her hand.

"You're all right?" Nola asked.

Bishop nodded. "Yes. I'm fine. They got to me in time."

"That's good," Nola said as she watched her blood trickle down the swimming pool.

Rascal stood pacing along the back of the pool, a phone to his ear, as Chandra sprinted toward them with a first-aid kit in her hands.

Avad stood up above, watching.

And then there was a cry from the other side of the pool.

Nola turned her head to see Jonas rise up, a gun in his hand. He let out a yell, and Nola could do nothing but watch. She didn't even have the strength to stand up.

Gunshots rang out, and blood burst from half a dozens of spots on Jonas's body.

Nola looked around. Everyone on her team had fired.

Rascal, his gun still trained on Jonas, moved forward and kicked the gun out of Jonas's hand. He glared down at him, looking more angry than Nola had ever seen Rascal look.

Molly appeared next to her, sliding her hand into Nola's. And Nola looked over at her. "You did good, mommy," Molly whispered.

Chapter Ninety-Six

BISHOP

Bishop's heart was in her throat.

There was so much blood. She didn't know how Nola was still alive. There was a pool of it underneath her, and they had followed a trail of it down the hallway here.

She wasn't even sure if Rafe had noticed it, but Bishop certainly had.

Now Nola lay with a calm smile on her face as she talked to the air. But from the corner of her eye, for just a moment, Bishop could have sworn that she saw Molly. Her heart raced, and she turned, but there was nothing there but emptiness.

Chandra had broken out the first-aid kit, and Bishop held a bandage to Nola's ribs while Chandra did the same to the other side.

"She's lost a lot of blood," Chandra said, her gaze meeting Rafe's.

Rafe nodded. "Yeah, but she can do this. We just need to get her to the hospital."

"Rascal called for an ambulance. They're five minutes out," Chandra said.

Bishop stared down at Nola and held her hand tight. "Nola, please. You've got to stay with us, ," she begged as Nola's eyes closed.

Anger burned through Bishop as she looked over at Jonas and wished that she could shoot him again. He had caused all of this. He had created some crazy fantasy in his head and forced Bishop into a role that she never wanted to play.

Which had forced Nola into the role she was born to play: protector.

Bishop held Nola's hand tightly. Her eyes were closed, but her chest was still moving up and down, and there was still some pressure in Nola's grip. She looked over at Rafe. "She'll make it, won't she?"

Rafe nodded. "Of course she will."

But the look on Chandra's face said she wasn't so sure. And then Nola's hand went slack.

Bishop gasped. "Nola? Nola!"

Chapter Ninety-Seven

NOLA

Quiet. That was the first thing that Nola noticed. That and she felt like she was sleeping on a cloud. She opened her eyes slowly and recognized her bedroom on the estate.

Warmth was pressed against her side. She reached out a hand and gently rubbed Cora's head.

The dog looked up, wagging her tail before bouncing off the bed. She headed over to where Molly sat reading a book in a chair by the fire. In the chair opposite her, Bishop sat with a blanket over her, her eyes closed.

Molly looked up with a smile. "You're awake."

Nola nodded, keeping her voice low as her daughter walked over to her and climbed onto the bed. "How long have I been out?"

"You were in the hospital for a day, and then Ileana managed to get you flown home. Dr. Ahmad's been looking after you. It's been about four days now."

Four days. She had lost four days. "Jonas?"

"He's dead, Mommy."

"Is he where you are?"

Molly shook her head. "Not yet. But maybe one day."

Nola didn't ask for any more information. She wasn't sure she wanted to know what happened to tortured souls. "How's Bishop?"

"She never leaves your side. Ileana had to force her to take a shower yesterday because she refused to leave. She's really worried about you. She feels guilty for what you went through."

"There's nothing for her to feel guilty about. It wasn't her fault."

Molly snuggled in next to Nola. "That's what I tell her when she's sleeping. But I don't think she can hear me yet."

"Well, keep trying. Because she needs to understand that."

"I will, Mommy." Molly lay next to her, comfortably snuggled in Nola's arms.

And the two of them sat there for a few moments, neither saying a word before Molly lifted her head. "I need to go now, Mommy."

Nola nodded her head. "I know," she said, pushing back the hair from her daughter's face. And for the first time, she could actually feel the hair, the same way she could feel her next to her. She'd known for a while that her daughter would be visiting less and less often. She'd become more and more transparent these last few times that she had seen her. And now she was practically invisible.

"Will you be all right?" Nola asked.

"I've always been all right, Mommy. You're the one who needed help. But you're okay now."

"I don't know about that," Nola said.

Molly smiled. "I mean your heart. It's not as broken

now. You have people in your life again. And you're ready to let them in. You don't need me anymore."

"I will always need you," Nola said, her heart feeling like it was going to break.

"I know that. But you don't need me visiting you like this. You'll see me again one day. We'll both be here, and it will be good, Mama, I promise."

Nola didn't know what to say. In her heart, she knew that it was long past time for Molly to find peace. But her heart still broke at the idea of not seeing her again.

"I'll miss you, Mommy."

"I'll miss you forever, baby girl," Nola said, tears cresting in her eyes.

"I'll always be with you, Mommy, even if you can't see me," Molly said as she slowly drifted away.

Tears rolled down Nola's cheeks as she reached for the spot where her daughter had just been. But her hand passed right through the empty air. *I love you, Molly.*

"You're awake." Across the room, Bishop struggled to get out of her blanket as she blinked hard and tried to get to Nola. She finally disentangled herself from the blanket and threw it to the floor, hurrying over to the bed as she wiped at her eyes. "How are you? How are you feeling?"

Wiping at the tears on her cheeks, Nola nodded. "I'm okay."

Bishop sat on the edge of the bed carefully. "Nola, I'm so sorry. I mean, I should have known that that guy was at my apartment. I should have known that he was there, and I should have been paying attention. And I should have—"

Nola gripped her hand and squeezed it. "Hey, none of that. None of this is your fault, you know."

Bishop shook her head. "Nola, it is. I mean, if I'd just

realized he was there, that Fitzpatrick guy, none of this would have happened."

Nola sighed. "Don't do that to yourself, Bishop. Don't think about what you should have or could have done or any of that. That's not a game you can win. What happened, happened. But now you're home, and you're safe, and that's all that matters."

"How can you say that? I mean, Nola, we nearly lost you."

"But you didn't. I'm right here. And this is where I'm going to stay."

Bishop's eyes widened. "You mean you're stopping the missions?"

Nola shook her head. "No. I don't think I'm ever going to stop those. But I think, no, I *want* to be home more often. I want to be with you more often."

Tears crested in Bishop's eyes, and she flung herself at Nola. Nola grunted as pain lanced through her side, but she wrapped her arms around Bishop and held her tight. And realized that while she had lost one daughter, she still had one here.

"What happened after I passed out?" she asked as Bishop sat back.

Bishop blew out a breath. "A lot. The ambulance showed up, along with a federal task force. They locked up all of Wagner's guys. Apparently they've been building a case for a while."

"How's that going?"

"Pretty good, actually. Stan was able to get into some of their older video files and sent them to the FBI. They've got them on everything from racketeering to human trafficking to simple assault. No one's getting a get-out-of-jail-free card on this one, including the lawyer."

"The lawyer?" Nola asked.

"Oh, right, you didn't know about that. Rafe and the others kidnapped the lawyer after he left the estate. It's how they knew where I was inside. He gave them the layout. They had him trussed up in the Santarro estate and handed him over to the feds as well.

"With all the data Stan and I gathered from their computer systems, they even managed to arrest a bunch of bigwigs from other crime families."

"What about those two crooked FBI agents?"

"They were arrested at the FBI field office in New York. Chandra flew down to watch them get hauled away. She said they were trading info on everyone to get a deal. It's helped build a case against the Chicago crime families. Honestly, things are pretty crazy in Chicago with all the arrests right now."

"I'm glad I missed it. But what about the rest of us? Are any of us in trouble?"

"Well, there was some trouble with the local cops because of the Wagner estate and the safe house. But once they realized you didn't kill anybody at the Wagner estate and that we only killed Wagner and his bodyguard, they weren't exactly upset. Plus, Stan recorded everything. I think you have a whole new legion of fans in law enforcement."

Nola groaned. "Great."

"Hey, it could be worse. We could all be locked up." Bishop's smile dimmed. "How are you feeling? You're okay, right?"

"I've got a little pain, but nothing that won't heal."

"Are you hungry?"

Nola nodded. "Actually, I could eat."

"Okay. Stay there. I'll go get you something from the

kitchen." Bishop hurried across the room and then paused in the doorway. "You know, this whole situation has made me realize that you really need to say the things that are in your heart because you might not get a chance later. So thank you, Nola, for taking me in and giving me this life, this family. I love you."

Then Bishop disappeared out the door before Nola had a chance to respond. Nola watched the empty doorway, picturing Bishop's face. *I love you too, Bishop.*

Nola fell back asleep before Bishop returned, and it was another two hours before she woke up. But now she was awake again and feeling hungry.

This time, Bishop wasn't taking the chance of her falling back asleep while she went to go get food. So she simply went to the door and yelled, "She's hungry!"

She headed back to the bed and shrugged at Nola's raised eyebrows. "They've all been waiting for you to wake up."

And apparently, they had. Rascal, Rafe, Sofia, Enzo, Avad, Ileana, and Bishop were all scattered around her room ten minutes later, having a small feast.

Chandra and Jack had headed back home, but both wanted Nola to call her as soon as she was feeling up to it. Now Nola sat on the bed, eating Rafe's famous enchiladas with Sofia and Enzo curled up at the end of the bed and *Hotel Transylvania* on the TV across from her.

Bishop sat curled up on one side of her, and Ileana sat next to Avad in the two chairs on the other side. Rascal pulled up a chair next to the bed. He was staying in town for a few more days.

Rafe walked around all of them to her side. The bed dipped as he sat next to Nola, his hip resting against hers. He glanced down at her with concern in his eyes. "Is this okay? You're not too tired."

Nola reached out and took his hand. "This is exactly as I want it."

More by R.D. Brady

www.vinci-books.com/belialstone

A discovery in Montana. An ancient mystery. A race to save humanity's future.

Follow Delaney and Jake as they unravel a millennia-old plot that threatens mankind's existence.

Turn the page for a free preview…

The Belial Stone: Prologue

HAVRE, MONTANA

Two Years Ago

The dirt drive was doing a number on the Mercedes. It dipped and dived with the bumps. Watching it approach, Kenny Coleman's stomach felt like it was doing the same. The last time he'd been this nervous, it was proposing to his Mary.

"It's just a professor. No big deal," he muttered to himself. The butterflies in his stomach, however, ignored him, continuing their maniacal flying.

The Mercedes rolled to a stop in a cloud of dust in front of his porch. Lifting his head, his old Australian shepherd emitted a low growl.

Surprised, Kenny reached down from his rocking chair and patted him on the head. "Hush now, Blue."

The dog quieted. But as the car door opened, he growled again. Kenny could feel the dog's body tense as he got to his feet. Pushing himself from the rocker, Kenny grabbed hold of Blue's collar. When the driver stepped into view, Blue emitted a feral snarl and lunged for the steps, nearly yanking Kenny's arm off.

Kenny struggled to hold him back. "No, Blue, no!"

While Kenny might be pushing sixty-five, his life as a cattleman had given him muscle. He wrapped his beefy arms around the dog's torso, carrying him back to the house, ignoring the sting as claws raked his forearms.

Kicking open the front door, he half-shoved, half-threw the dog across the threshold, slamming the door shut behind him.

Stepping back, he gaped at the door as Blue slammed his body into it, again and again.

What in the world? Kenny stared down at his forearms. Angry red welts crisscrossed the skin. They were from an animal who'd let his grandkids flop on him while they watched cartoons. In the twelve years he'd had him, he'd barely heard him growl.

Blue was getting up there, just like Kenny was. He didn't want to think that maybe the final trip to the vet was coming sooner rather than later.

With a deep breath, he pushed his concerns for his dog's uncharacteristic behavior to the back of his mind. He felt the professor's eyes on his back and felt the flush creep up his neck. *Damn.* This was not the first impression he wanted to make.

Rolling down his green flannel sleeves, he walked down the stairs and across the expanse in front of his farmhouse.

"I'm sorry, Professor Gideon," Kenny stammered out. "He's never like that. I don't know what got into him."

"No harm done, Mr. Coleman. I appreciate you taking the time to show me your find." A polite smile graced the blond professor's angular face, but that politeness didn't quite reach his cool blue eyes.

Back in the day, Kenny knew he was considered a handsome man—strong and tall with thick, dark hair. The girls had loved to run their hands through it. And in spite of his full head of now white hair, he was vain enough to think he still was.

But he knew this professor was what currently stood for handsome: slim, with pale blue eyes perched above a patrician nose and sharp cheekbones. Dressed in expensive slacks, a brown suede jacket, and shiny loafers, he was one of those "metrosexuals" his daughter talked about.

Kenny couldn't say he ever really understood the appeal of a man who was pretty, but hell, he never did understand much about what was cool.

Extending his calloused hand, Kenny spoke a little louder than usual, trying to block out Blue's unending barks. "I'd really like to know what I've found. I just can't figure out what something like that is doing on my ranch."

The professor's hand was soft, the shake just shy of limp. "Well, let's take a look. How did you come across it?"

"It was the strangest thing. I was looking for a stray calf one day, and I literally stumbled over the tip of it."

"How much was showing at first?"

Kenny shrugged. "Not much. Maybe four, five inches. It was just such a strange-looking rock, all black with those brown and green veins running through it. I'd never seen one like that anywhere around these parts. So, I marked the spot and went back later to dig it out. I couldn't believe it when I saw it. I took some pictures and posted them online to see if anyone could tell me anything about it. Less than an hour later, I got the call from you."

"Have you spoken with anyone else about it?"

He avoided the professor's eyes, less he read the desperation there. The last few years had been lean and if this strange rock was worth something, well Kenny could definitely use the money. "No. I wasn't sure it was anything important."

"And no one else has called?" Gideon's gaze was intent.

"No, no. You're the only one. I thought for sure I'd get a couple more people interested. But my pictures disappeared from the site I posted them on and I couldn't repost them. I'm not real good with the computer."

Realizing he might need to sell this professor on the object, he spoke quickly. "It really is an amazing sight, though. You won't be disappointed."

"Well, let's have a look, shall we?" Gideon gestured for him to lead the way.

Behind him, Blue's growls had turned to desperate howls. A chill crawled up his spine as he flicked a glance back at the door, unsure. Blue just didn't act like this. Maybe this was a bad idea.

But he knew the medical bills for his grandson were piling up. This strange rock might be his only chance of making some extra money. He sighed. There really was no choice. And besides, he was just a professor.

With a nod, he led the professor to a trail created by wild horses and buffalo generations ago. And they walked, Kenny tried making conversation. He talked about the Sioux and the Crow that used to summer in the area and pointed out where he'd hunted for arrowheads as a kid. The professor only grunted in response.

Small talk about the weather and questions about the professor's research resulted in equally unenthusiastic responses. Soon, Kenny just lapsed into silence.

For the first time Kenny could recall, he felt the isolation of his ranch press down on him. He knew there was no one around for miles. Montana was the size of New England, with only the population of Rhode Island. Generally, the isolation of his ranch was the reason he loved it. But walking next to the professor, he couldn't help but feel uneasy.

It wasn't just Blue's reaction, which, to be honest, scared the hell out of him. It was like the dog had seen the devil himself. It was also that this man looked nothing like a professor. He was too young, too good-looking, and too well dressed.

And there was something about him that just felt off. The man had barely spared a glance at the snow-topped mountains that were a backdrop to Kenny's property. He'd never had anyone come to the ranch that hadn't commented on that incredible view.

Walking next to him, Kenny was reminded of the time when, as a kid, he'd been stalked by a mountain lion. He'd had a vague sense of uneasiness that day. But until the cat screeched as it leapt out at him, he hadn't realized the true danger he was in. That day, his dad had cut the lion in half with a shotgun. Kenny gave the professor another surreptitious glance and couldn't help wishing he'd brought his shotgun along today.

"Are we getting close?" Gideon asked.

Startled, Kenny stumbled. Shaking his head at his clumsiness, he pointed to an arrangement of three small boulders twenty yards away that stood out in the flat, almost treeless ground. "Just beyond those boulders is where I started digging. I still haven't been able to get to the bottom of the rock."

Gideon nodded and picked up his pace. As he passed the boulders, he came to an abrupt stop and stared at the small excavation.

The monolith stood five feet tall, although it was

obvious there was still more buried beneath the earth. At first glance, the obelisk appeared smooth. Kenny's first thought had been that it looked like one of those fancy granite countertops. On closer inspection, though, the niches carefully carved into the black stone depicting figures and what resembled Egyptian hieroglyphs became clear.

Seconds stretched into minutes as the professor simply stared at the rock in silence. Kenny's nervousness increased. "Uh, Professor Gideon, are you all right?"

Gideon's eyes snapped to Kenny. The anger and longing in those eyes sent Kenny a step back, his heart pounding.

But when Gideon spoke, his voice was calm. "It's an amazing sight, isn't it? Would it be all right if I went closer?"

The professor's words reduced Kenny's fears, making him feel foolish. *What the hell is wrong with me today? He's just a professor interested in my find.*

"Sure, sure. After all, you're the expert." Kenny watched the professor eschew the ladder he'd placed in the hole and gracefully leap down.

Gideon reverently touched the stone, tracing some of the carvings with his index finger. "Finally," he murmured.

After a few moments of internal debate, Kenny's curiosity won out over his uneasiness. He clambered down to stand next to the man. "So, any idea where it came from? It kind of looks like something you'd expect to find in Egypt or down in Central America or some other ancient place."

Gideon looked over at Kenny. "Actually, this site predates those other sites by quite a significant margin."

"Really?" Kenny asked, astonished. "Even older than the pyramids?"

"Yes. Even older than that." He pointed to a spot on the

artifact about three quarters of the way up. "Do you see this mark here?"

Kenny squinted at the etching. "That little circle?"

"Yes. That little circle is something I've been trying to find for an incredibly long time."

Kenny's eyes shifted to the professor. The man couldn't be any older than twenty-nine. This younger generation seemed to have a different view of time than his generation.

"Hmm," he murmured. "What is it?"

"Why, it's the end of the world," Gideon said with a slow smile.

"What?" Kenny glanced over at Gideon, thinking he must have misunderstood him.

Gideon turned to face him. His smile looked almost lethal and what Kenny had thought were pale blue eyes seemed to have darkened. "You've been very helpful, Mr. Coleman."

The words were polite, but the tone sent the fears Kenny had been pushing down right back to the surface. The professor pulled a gun from under his suit jacket. Kenny didn't hesitate. He shoved the professor and scrambled out of the hole.

Looking back over his shoulder, Kenny expected to feel a bullet between his shoulder blades at any minute. Instead, he saw Gideon still in the hole, smiling at him. He was even nodding. Kenny didn't understand the man's reaction and he had no interest in figuring it out.

Kenny panted as he sprinted for the house. He didn't hear the professor behind him. He hoped it stayed that way until he reached one of his guns. He had a shot if he could just get to his truck or the barn. He kept rifles in both of them. That hope kept pushing him forward as his legs turned to jelly, and his breathing to sharp, painful gasps.

The farmhouse came into view and the sound of Blue still barking urged him on.

Footfalls echoed through the empty space behind him. Panic charged through Kenny's chest. He knew he should keep running, looking behind would only slow him down, but he couldn't help himself.

A hundred yards back, the professor sprinted towards him, his legs moving like train pistons. He didn't even look winded. How had he caught up with him so fast?

Kenny dug down deep for a last reserve of energy, but his body wouldn't comply. He was slowing. Dark spots were beginning to form around the edges of his vision, causing him to stumble and weave.

The professor had no such affliction. Kenny could feel his attention focused on him. The pounding of his feet maintained their steady cadence. He kept coming, like a missile locked on its target, covering the distance to him in seconds. As he caught up with him, he didn't pull him to stop.

To Kenny's astonishment, the professor started to run next to him. He glanced over at the man in terror. Gideon just smiled in response.

Then in a blur of motion, Gideon sprinted a few feet ahead. He came to a dead stop and whirled to face Kenny.

Kenny tried to dodge around him, but he was too exhausted and too slow. Gideon's hand snaked out and easily grabbed him by the shoulder. He turned Kenny around and pulled him close.

Kenny struggled and managed to throw a feeble right hook at Gideon's ribs.

Gideon smoothly blocked the punch and trapped both of Kenny's arms with one of his own. He leaned down into

Kenny's terrified face and smiled, pressing the gun to his chest.

"Good for you, Mr. Coleman. Everyone should have such a sense of self-preservation. You'd be amazed at how few people actually do. And you've given a good effort, especially for a man of your age. You should be proud of yourself."

Kenny wanted to rail at the man. He wanted to scream at him for doing this to him and plead with him to spare his life, if only for the sake of his daughter and grandchildren. But all he managed to rasp out was a single question. "Why?"

Gideon's voice was almost a caress when he answered. His eyes looked strangely bright, as if covered in a sheen of tears. "It's the only way for my misery to end. You have brought my search to its conclusion, Mr. Coleman. I will always appreciate that." And with a beatific smile, he pulled the trigger three times.

Pain slashed through Kenny, and then, blessed numbness. He felt himself being lifted as the echoes of the gunshots retreated. He thought of his daughter and his heart already beating unsteadily, felt even heavier. *I'm sorry, sweetheart.*

Blue's frantic barking changed to mournful howls as they approached the farmhouse. *Run, Blue, run,* Kenny shouted in his mind. But the only words that were heard weren't his.

"Don't worry, Blue," Gideon murmured. "I haven't forgotten about you."

The Belial Stone: Chapter One

DEWITT, NEW YORK

Professor Delaney McPhearson glanced at the clock above the white kitchen cabinets. She was barely a quarter of the way through the tall stack of undergrad criminology papers in front of her.

"Crap, crap, crap," she muttered. She needed to move if she was going to make her self-defense class.

"Crap, crap, crap," Max Simmons, her roommate Kati's three-year-old son, repeated from his spot on the floor.

Wincing, Laney gave Kati an apologetic smile. "Sorry. Forgot he was there."

Jotting down two more quick remarks, she whisked the papers off the table and placed them next to the larger stack of still-to-be graded ones on the kitchen island.

She knelt down to Max and ruffled his sun-kissed brown hair. "That's a bad word, Max. I shouldn't have said it."

Max nodded at her. His bright blue eyes, which matched the Sesame Street t-shirt he wore, were solemn. "Crap bad."

Laney restrained the urge to smile. "Yes, bad."

Over Max's head, Kati gave her an exasperated look even as she struggled not to smile herself. Mother and son shared the same soft, brown hair, slim build, and button nose. Kati's hair, now in a short pixie cut, only accentuated the similarities between them. The only difference was their eye color: Kati's were a deep brown.

"You better move if you're going to make your class," Kati warned as she nodded toward the clock.

"I'm going. I'm going." With a quick kiss to the top of Max's head, Laney jogged to the stairs.

Taking them two at a time, she ducked into her room, and rummaged through her dresser for her workout clothes.

Pulling off her pajamas, she struggled into the sports bra and yanked on a deep purple t-shirt. Pulling her long, wavy, red hair into a ponytail, she had just slid into the black pants when her phone rang.

I have no time for whoever this is, she thought, even as she reached over to her nightstand to check the caller ID. She smiled and flipped the phone open, putting it on speaker. "Drew. Where the hell have you been?"

Drew Master's familiar chuckle made Laney smile even wider. She pictured him sitting at his desk, his mop of curly brown hair falling over his deep blue eyes.

Her uncle had always hoped the two of them would turn their platonic friendship into a romantic one. At least, he'd hoped it up until she explained that the main stumbling block was their identical taste in men.

"Sorry, Lanes. Work's been insane."

"See? You're working too hard. You should have taken that position with my uncle." Laney's uncle, Father Patrick Delaney, was one of the Roman Catholic Church's premier archaeologists. He'd gotten custody of Laney after her parents had died in a car crash when she was eight. As a result, she'd spent almost every summer at one dig site or another since childhood.

Since Laney met Drew freshman year of college, he'd spent every summer with them as well. Even when they went to different doctorate programs, they'd stayed close. When Drew finished his doctorate, her uncle had offered him a position with one of the Vatican's dig sites. Drew turned him down. Instead he'd agreed to work with Dr. Arthur Priddle. Not a good call in Laney's opinion, but also not her decision.

"You know I think the world of your uncle. But Arthur's research is much more in line with my own. And, at the time, I thought it would come with fewer strings."

"Not the case, huh?" Laney asked as she grabbed socks from the drawer and started to pull them on.

Drew snorted. "Hardly. He's been running me ragged. I don't think he understands that we're colleagues and I'm not his grad student. And he's been even more security conscious than usual. The man has taken paranoia to a whole new extreme."

Laney caught her reflection in the mirror, her dark green eyes reflecting her concern. This wasn't like Drew. He wasn't a complainer. He'd spent one summer in Egypt covered in bug bites, in the sweltering heat, with an unknown rash that caused his feet to swell to the point that he'd had to hobble around in sandals two sizes too big. He'd barely mumbled a complaint.

Seeming to sense her worry, he added some bounce into his next words. "I mean, it's intense, but good. Priddle really has a way of looking at things from a new angle and developing an innovative approach."

Laney opened her closet, looking for her gym shoes, and

grimaced. "Right. Innovative and without any social skills or conscience."

At Drew's silence, she sighed, realizing she wasn't helping. "Sorry. Ignore that. I just don't like you being so far away. So tell me, how are you doing? Really doing? And no placating."

Drew let out another laugh, this one less good-natured and more nervous. "Okay, maybe things are a little stressful right now. But you know Priddle, perfection is his goal."

Although his tone was light, Laney heard a heavier emotion under the words. "Drew, is everything okay?"

He hesitated before answering. "I don't know. Like I said, he's been even more intense than usual lately. We've got this new project we're working on, and he won't let me talk about it with anyone. And I mean anyone."

Leaning down to tie her sneakers, Laney tried to think of a way to give her thoughts an optimistic spin. "Well, he's not exactly known for his openness. And besides, his research is so esoteric and off the map, it's often dismissed before anyone really gives it a chance. Maybe he's just trying to make sure word doesn't leak out before he can present his entire argument." She paused. "Are you regretting your choice to go work with him?"

"No. I mean, I really think ancient civilizations hold the answers to who we are and where we're going. There's so much out there we can't explain—who built the sphinx, why the older pyramids are more technologically advanced than the newer ones, the maps of Antarctica that predate our history. And those are only a few. There are thousands of examples of unexplainable history. Pre-historic civilizations are the only possible answer. And he's the archaeologist doing the most innovative research. So, I don't regret it. I just wish . . . "

"He was a normal human being?" Laney deadpanned.

Drew barked out a laugh. "Exactly."

Laney didn't disagree with Drew's interest. Before she'd turned to criminology, she'd thought hard about archaeology, for many of the same reasons that Drew had mentioned. According to mainstream archeology, the dawn of civilization began around 3,000 BC. Yet, there were more and more archaeological sites and discoveries of great skill that were being uncovered that predated that arbitrary timeline—the Piri Reis map, the research of Steen-McIntyre, Puma Punku.

None of which could be explained by the traditional timeline. So she knew why Drew was so passionate about the topic. She just really wished the academic who was top in the field wasn't also such an ass.

Grabbing her exercise bag off the bed, Laney headed down the stairs. "Well, at least I got you to laugh. And I hate to do this to you, but can I call you later? I'm heading to my self-defense class."

"You still teaching that?"

"Yup. Every Saturday, me and Rocky have a group of anywhere between five and twenty women we take through the paces." Rocky, a.k.a. Detective Rochelle Martinez, was a pint-sized powerhouse. Six months ago, she and Laney had started offering a free women's self-defense class Saturday mornings at the Y.

"Maybe that's what I need—some martial arts. I liked those classes you took me to in undergrad."

Laney smiled. She'd been studying martial arts since she'd been a kid. And she always loved introducing people to the discipline. But Drew, while a gym enthusiast, was not exactly the most coordinated student she'd ever taught. "Well, I think exercise is always good," she said diplomatically, as she cut back through the kitchen, waved goodbye to Kati, and headed outside.

Walking down the porch stairs, she crossed the lawn to her silver Pathfinder. "I really do need to go, though. Can I call you later?"

"Um, yeah. Actually, though, I do have a favor to ask."

"Anything.," she said as she unlocked her truck and opened the driver's door.

"Any chance you could read over a paper I've been working on?"

"I thought you weren't allowed to share any of that work," she teased as she threw her bag into the passenger seat.

"I'm not. But I thought maybe if I showed him something that we could send out, it would kind of pave the way for some of the bigger findings we're going to be revealing down the road. Before I give it to him, though, it has to be perfect. I want to make sure there are no glaring errors in the logic, or God forbid, a typo. But I really need you to keep this on the down low."

Settling behind the steering wheel, Laney started the truck before she placed the phone in the dashboard holder. "Not a problem. I have some papers to grade tonight. I can look at it tomorrow, though, and get some comments back to you by around lunch. Will that work?"

She could practically feel Drew's relief pour through the phone. "That would be incredible."

She started to back out of the drive. "What's the paper on, anyway?"

Drew was silent.

Laney waited for a slow-moving Honda to pass and maneuvered out onto the street. "Drew?"

The sigh was barely audible, but she caught it. "Promise me you'll be open-minded?"

"Of course."

"It's on an ancient technologically-advanced society that existed prior to written history."

Laney slammed on the brakes and stared at her phone, knowing exactly what Drew was trying to avoid saying. "Drew, are you talking about what I think you're talking about?"

"Yes. It's about Atlantis."

Grab your copy…
www.vinci-books.com/belialstone

About the Author

Author, Criminologist, Terrorism Expert, Jeet Kune Do Black Sash, Runner, Dog Lover.

Amazon best-selling author R.D. Brady writes supernatural and science fiction thrillers. Her thrillers include ancient mysteries, unusual facts, non-stop action, and fierce women with heart.

Prior to beginning her writing career, R.D. Brady was a criminologist who specialized in life-course criminology and international terrorism. She's lectured and written numerous academic articles on the genetic influence on criminal behavior, factors that influence terrorist ideology, and delinquent behavior formation.

After visiting counter-terrorism units in Israel, R.D. returned home with a sabbatical in front of her and decided to write that book she'd been thinking about. Four years later she left academia with the publication of her first book, *The Belial Stone*, and hasn't looked back.